I0675067

# THE EMPTY HOURGLASS

## A DEAL WITH A DEVIL

# CORNELIA
# GREY

ANGLERFISH
PRESS

Anglerfish Press
PO Box 1537
Burnsville, NC 28714
www.AnglerFishPress.com
Anglerfish Press is an imprint of Riptide Publishing.
www.RiptidePublishing.com

The Empty Hourglass
Copyright © 2016 by Cornelia Grey

Cover art: Jay Aheer, jayscoversbydesign.com
Editor: Danielle Poiesz
Layout: L.C. Chase, lcchase.com/design.htm

ISBN: 978-1-62649-394-0

First edition
April, 2016

Also available in ebook:
ISBN: 978-1-62649-393-3

# THE EMPTY HOURGLASS

## A DEAL WITH A DEVIL

# CORNELIA GREY

ANGLERFISH PRESS

*To Adam Benson-Davies,*
*my most beloved friend*
*who guided my first steps in the Big Smoke*
*and once again held my hand*
*as I figured out a new life.*

# TABLE OF
# CONTENTS

# CHAPTER 1

T homas Escott jolted awake, almost tumbling out of his seat as the train's brakes screeched. He rubbed his left hand over his mouth. He was sweating under his threadbare brown jacket—he'd been having that nightmare again.

It was always the same, always left him out of breath and soaked with perspiration. He reached over to his right arm, placing his hand over the stump, the searing pain further branding in his mind the memory of what had happened. The explosion. The spilled oil. His toy shop burning to the ground.

A tinny sound swept into the compartment, getting louder by the second. Thomas craned his neck to see the wooden box slowly huffing along the corridor, its ancient wheels clunking and creaking as it squeezed between the seats. It had a red enamel gramophone bolted to the top, and it puffed out small, quick clouds of steam as it announced, in a scratchy voice: "Montrale! Montrale station next!"

The train crept up to a dark platform, only lit dimly by round glass gaslights bolted to the walls. Thomas grabbed his meager luggage, containing the few clothes he'd managed to salvage from the fire, and made his way through the narrow passage to the door. Two bronze steps tried to unfold to lead him to the platform, but they clacked and banged and resolutely remained half-straightened. Like the wings of the little clockwork owl he'd been trying to fix when his sleeve had caught fire . . .

With a sigh, Thomas jumped over the steps and landed on the station's stone platform. It was utterly deserted. Nobody else got off the train, and it started huffing again and rolled away before he even had time to turn around and watch. He'd known this village would be different from the capital of Lunaris, but it was only just past dinnertime.

*Perhaps there is something going on in town tonight,* he reasoned. *This is the hometown of the esteemed Jethro Hastings, after all.*

Showing up on the inventor's doorstep hadn't been an ideal plan, especially when he needed to ask such a big favor. He didn't even know what Hastings was like, if he'd kick Thomas out, annoyed at being disturbed, or welcome him in, seeing Thomas as another opportunity to show off his state-of-the-art prosthetic limbs.

Thomas looked around the station. An old clock hung from the iron rafters, marking three o'clock—it was quite obviously broken—and there was a dim light coming from a little dilapidated station building to his left. He tugged on his right sleeve to hide his stump and headed toward it.

When he stepped inside, his breath caught. A ragtag crowd of men were gathered there, and they turned to stare at him. Some seemed surprised, but most were decidedly hostile. He eyed them for a moment. They were not similar in the slightest to the assortment of thieves and beggars he was used to encountering on the streets of Lunaris. He was accustomed to the drunken, the mad, and a cunning, thieving, murderous lot, loud and always smoking and drinking and constantly moving, just like the capital itself. But these men stood or sat stiffly, wrapped in thick dark cloaks that all looked the same, with dark gloves and dark hats and well-trimmed mustaches.

And they were staring at him. Each and every one of them.

Thomas swallowed. He had seldom felt so out of place. He was painfully aware of his too-light, too-modern clothes that moderately smelled like smoke, despite his best attempts to get the stench out of them, and of the blond hair that he kept long, as was popular in the capital at the moment. But mostly, he could feel their gazes almost piercing the right side of his head, where the hair had been scorched off in the fire and was now replaced by tender, gnarled skin, thin scars running from his mangled ear to his cheek and spreading down his neck before disappearing under his collar.

At least they couldn't see his arm . . .

The men were still looking at him, slowly advancing, forming a semicircle that barred his way to the exit. He flexed his hand, feeling

A stocky dwarf was standing in the doorway, a storm of anger darkening his face. But it wasn't his weatherworn, wrinkled face that attracted Thomas's attention, nor his thick black beard or frayed stovepipe hat. It was the mechanical arm emerging from the cut sleeve of his coat—a heavy-looking contraption of tarnished brass reaching all the way to his elbow, the joint shielded by a black leather sheath, masking the point where it connected to the man's dark skin.

Thomas's lips parted. He'd never seen anything of the sort in the capital. Judging from it, maybe this Hastings character was exactly the person he needed after all.

"Mind your own business, Herman. We're just having a little fun," Gray Mustache tried, but he didn't sound so confident anymore.

The dwarf snorted. "Fun is over. Put him down. Now." He strode forward and forced his way through the gaggle of men, effortlessly shoving them out of the way with his mechanical arm. Then the hands holding Thomas let go almost at once, and he landed on the stone floor with an undignified *ooph*.

"Fuck," he muttered. Instinctively, he made to brace his right palm on the floor to push himself up, and stopped himself in time, remembering to lean on his elbow instead of his stump. A pair of boots moved into his line of sight, stepping right beside him while everyone else backed off and, when Thomas glanced up, he saw that the dwarf's eyes were fixed on Thomas's right wrist. He fought the urge to jerk his arm back and hide it from sight, his face heating up. But the man's eyes were filled with neither disgust nor sympathy, not even the morbid and disturbing curiosity he encountered all too often since the accident.

"You here to see Hastings, boy?" the dwarf asked.

Thomas swallowed and nodded. "I . . . Yes, sir. I am."

The dwarf watched him for a few more seconds, then turned to the others and sharply raised his hand. "Back off and let us leave."

"Come on, Herman, we were just playing around . . ." one of the men commented.

"I said back off *now*, before I tell Hastings you're harassing one of his *very* rich customers, whose money and commissions could feed this village for months," Herman growled, dramatically pointing at Thomas. He raised his chin, doing his best to look important and aristocratic, even though he was barely more than a bundle of rags on the floor. "Is that what you want? For Jethro to stop selling prosthetics, to go bankrupt and leave, so if your son's arm stops working, Franz, there will be nobody to fix it? And if you, Evan, get silicosis in the mines you will *die* instead of getting your lungs fixed? Eh? Is *that* what you want?"

The men's mouths clamped shut. They exchanged glances, shuffling from foot to foot, then reluctantly stepped back and waited in silence, their heads hung low. Except Gray Mustache, of course, who continued to shoot dark, mistrustful glances at Thomas.

Herman stared at Thomas and nodded sharply toward the door. "Come, boy. Let's sort you out."

Thomas pushed the screwdriver back in his sleeve and scrambled to his feet and followed him back into the building, picking up his luggage on the way. He cast a last glance toward the cloaked men. He was mostly relieved, but he was also tempted to throw a quip behind him. He thought better of it, though. They could still change their mind and tie him to the tracks.

Herman held the door open for him, and they both stepped out onto the street. "Thank you, sir," Thomas said. "So you . . . you know Jethro Hastings?"

"Of course I do. Who doesn't, around here?" The dwarf grunted, heading toward a handful of dark, rickety hansom cabs waiting by the other side of the station. They were old models and still had horses, not steam-powered like the ones Thomas was used to. His eyebrows rose. Considering this was where Jethro Hastings lived, well, he was expecting something more advanced.

But then again, maybe the man just focused on his miraculous prosthetics. Why on earth would he waste his talent on common toys like hansom carriages? *Let the others handle things like that.*

Curiosity was whirring in Thomas's head. The inventor inside him was dying to take a closer look at Herman's arm, to get an idea of what might be waiting for him in Hastings's laboratory. Maybe it was his chance to get some more information, prepare himself a little better before he got there. "Excuse me, sir, if I may be so bold . . . I was just wondering, is that one of Jethro Hastings's prosthet—"

The dwarf banged on the side of a carriage, resolutely ignoring and interrupting him at the same time. A grunt and a curse answered him, and a rumpled mass of brown hair appeared from the driver's seat. "What?" the man slurred.

"You wouldn't happen to be drinking again on the job, I hope," Herman chastised the man in a stern voice.

The driver hurried to sit up, rummaging around to shove a mangled cap on his head. "No, sir. Most certainly not."

*Sure. And I'm prince regent,* Thomas thought. He could smell the whiskey all the way from where he stood, as if the man had recently bathed in it.

"Take this young man to Hastings's house," Herman directed. "Now."

For the first time, the driver craned his head to take a look at Thomas. He seemed very much unconvinced, much like the men inside the station. "But sir . . ."

"Now, Jens. Thank you."

"Of course, sir. Right away, sir."

And with that, he clicked his tongue and barked something to the horse. Herman nodded and turned to leave, without so much as a second glance at Thomas.

"Sir! I wanted to— I might be getting a mechanical hand too, and if I could just take a—"

The dwarf stopped and looked over his shoulder at Thomas. "Listen, boy, I said what I had to so they'd back off, but don't get your hopes up. It's true that people in this town don't like strangers, and Hastings is no exception."

Thomas opened and closed his mouth.

"Good luck." The dwarf walked off, his mechanical arm gleaming under the few streetlights.

Thomas watched him go. *Good Lord. What a welcome.*

He sighed and put down his luggage in order to open the door, then laboriously maneuvered into the cab and dragged the luggage after him, not holding on to anything but keeping his head low to avoid hitting it on the ceiling. He'd barely shut the door behind him when the carriage started moving, the horse's hooves clopping steadily on the cobblestones.

He let himself fall onto the seat, closing his eyes, repressing a sigh of relief at having gotten over that first hurdle.

*What a strange place this is, indeed.*

When he opened his eyes, he was startled so abruptly he almost banged his head against the low roof.

A giant pink plume vibrated with the movement of the carriage. It sat atop an impressively large pea-green hat, and under the hat sat what was quite possibly the strangest man Thomas had ever seen, and considering the fellows he routinely came across in Lunaris, that was quite a feat. He pressed back against the seat and looked at the man, silent for a moment. The man was a bundle of pea-green and pale-yellow rags covered in medals, pendants, and faded cockades, sporting that extravagant plumed hat and a scruffy blond beard. And he was staring right at Thomas with a vaguely sinister grin on his face.

"God. I . . . I'm sorry, sir. I didn't see you there." But how the *hell* had he missed him? He might have been tired and it might have been dark, but . . . Hell, he wasn't *that* tired.

"Never mind. I do tend to go unnoticed most of the time," the man said, scratching his beard. His sleeves were rolled up, and in the light seeping in from the windows, Thomas could see a smudged tattoo of a large black spider on his forearm.

*Yeah, I'll bet . . .*

In such a small village, the guy had to stick out like a peacock among blackbirds.

"If I may . . . What are you doing here, exactly?" Thomas asked. As odd as the guy was, somehow he felt more at ease with him than the fellows at the station. It made him feel like he'd found a little bit of Lunaris even in this remote place.

"Why, I was waiting for you, of course."

Thomas gaped but, before he could manage to speak, a grin slowly spread on the man's lips. "I'm kidding. I just sneaked in to have a nap. Better than spending the night on the street, don't you think?"

Thomas had spent his fair share of nights huddled on the floor of some alley, so he supposed it was a valid explanation. But there was something about the man's grin, something cold and wolflike, that made him feel a different kind of discomfort.

"I see. We should, um, we should stop and let you off." He was about to turn to bellow for the driver, but the guy raised his hand, which was covered in big, mismatched silver rings.

"And then what? I'm left stranded on the street in the cold? No thanks," he said. "The driver will go back to the station anyway. I might as well enjoy the ride on these comfortable seats. And in your company, of course, sir."

Thomas opened his mouth to reply, but he couldn't think of a convincing reason to say no. Once again, though, while the stranger's words sounded perfectly reasonable, his smile and his piercing aqua-green eyes were making Thomas's nape prickle. He discreetly flexed his wrist, still holding the man's gaze, feeling for the reassuring pressure of his hidden weapon.

He cast a quick glance out the window. It looked as though they had left the town and were now taking a narrow, winding path up a steep mountain. Even though he didn't really relish the idea of having company right now—his every instinct was telling him to be wary of the guy—he couldn't bring himself to leave the odd stranger in the middle of nowhere.

"So you're going to see Jethro Hastings, are you?"

Thomas jumped again and looked down at his arm, mindful of his stump resting in plain sight on his knees. There probably weren't many other reasons that would bring a stranger all the way to Montrale. "Yes. As a matter of fact, I am."

The guy leaned back against the seat, crossing his legs. "You're not the first one to require his services. Although, to be honest, his . . . *customers* are mostly local. How did you find out about him?"

Instinctively, Thomas reached into his pocket and brushed the paper again. The slip of paper that had started it all, that had led him all the way here to chase after one last ray of hope that might turn out to be nothing but a mirage. The strange note that had been delivered on his doorstep one week ago, in the middle of the night without a return address or any clue to identify who had sent it. He didn't need to read it again; by now he knew it by heart.

*Dear Thomas,*

*Sorry to hear about your unfortunate accident. It has come to my attention that the esteemed Jethro Hastings, from the town of Montrale, is leading groundbreaking experiments involving mechanical prosthetics. I strongly encourage you to head there at once, for he is the only man on this Earth who might be able to help you.*

*Regards,*

*F.*

Thomas had done his research, of course. He'd heard mention of that name before, so he'd consulted all his contacts in the scientific circle. They had confirmed that Mr. Hastings was an authority in the field—a skilled, if somewhat odd, inventor who lived holed up in a godforsaken village in the mountains. Rumor had it he was indeed an authority on prosthetic limbs, revolutionary implants that were far superior to the prosthetics commonly found in the capital. Hastings seemed to have isolated himself lately, however, and hadn't been at a single conference in months. In fact, nobody Thomas had spoken to could remember the last time they'd seen him. He wouldn't answer any correspondence, either. But still, it was a glimmer of hope, and Thomas was desperate. A train ticket was a small price to pay.

"He was . . . recommended to me," Thomas said carefully.

The guy seemed to be eager to chat, even though that sinister smile still hadn't faded from his lips. "Really? I wasn't aware his prosthetics were known outside of Montrale. He seems to be quite keen on keeping it secret, at least for the moment." The man rubbed his fingers over the tattoo on his forearm, drawing Thomas's gaze to it. He blinked. It must have been the pale, trembling evening light, but it looked like the spider was wriggling its legs. "Whoever recommended him must be very knowledgeable."

Thomas cleared his throat, fighting the urge to reach into his pocket and rub the note between his fingers. He wondered again who this *F* was that had sent him the letter. A few of his associates shared that initial but had denied any involvement. They had agreed, however, that the suggestion had been a wise one. And they certainly *had* known of Hastings. Clearly this man was uninformed. Regardless, Thomas wasn't about to admit that he'd come all the way here because of an anonymous message. He felt foolish enough admitting it to himself, thank you very much.

"Yes, indeed," was all Thomas said in response.

The stranger shrugged. "Anyway, you might have come all the way here for nothing. Mr. Hastings is very busy right now. I doubt he will have the time to help you."

Cold spread through Thomas's body, freezing him in place. "I— What do you mean?"

"Well . . ." The guy leaned forward, conspiratorially cupping his hand around the side of his mouth. "He's working on some big project, you know. He hasn't wanted it out, but he's got a big event planned. Some kind of soiree ten days from now. He's been inviting all sorts of fancy inventors from all over the country. He wants to reveal some revolutionary invention or other, and I hear he's way, way behind on it."

"Oh . . ." Thomas didn't quite know how to reply. Of course, it stood to reason that Jethro Hastings would be a very busy man. Why would he have time to drop everything and help a stranger who came knocking on his door asking for one of his inventions? Thomas had chosen to ignore that line of thought. No, he'd stubbornly and determinedly ignored it as he'd rushed to buy his ticket and jumped on the first train before he had time to think it through fully and was forced to admit the many reasons why it had been a stupid, stupid idea. Once he was there, he would figure something out.

Or so he'd hoped . . .

"You seem disappointed. You in a hurry?"

"Well, yes. Pretty much." Thomas was planning to leave it at that, but the guy's piercing eyes were fixed on him, waiting for him to continue. So he sighed and let his head thump back against the seat. "I need to make a living, you know? I'm a toymaker. I need two hands to do that."

"A toymaker? How delightful." The man's tone sounded anything but delighted. His voice reminded Thomas of a snake's hissing. "So you make marionettes, wooden toys, and such, yes? There's quite an industry here—"

Thomas groaned, stopping the man midsentence. Thomas had played out this conversation more times than he could count. "Not those kind of toys. Clockwork, mostly."

"Oh?" The man's eyebrows rose. "Well, I'm afraid you won't have much luck here with that."

"Well, neither would I in the capital, really." Thomas snorted. At the man's interrogative gaze, he raised his right wrist and shrugged. "I haven't got a workshop anymore, and nobody wants to hire a toymaker with only one hand. So I'm afraid that until I get fixed, I am out of a job."

Granted, there were other things he *could* have done. If all else failed, he could always join the crowd of crosswalk sweepers, mud larks, and petty thieves that inhabited Lunaris's underbelly. But he had dedicated his entire life to his little clockwork machines. It was the only thing he'd ever wanted to do. It had taken him years to work up from assembling scrap metal on the streets and selling his little toys at the market to finally being able to open his own little workshop. And it had all disappeared in an instant.

He *would* get his hand back, and he *would* get back to work. It was the only option. There was nothing else for him.

"Well, I understand Hastings's current work will be his priority now," Thomas continued, swallowing the knot in his throat. "But I *suppose* he could have some time afterward . . ."

"I don't think he'll be able to do that, either. I hear he'll be leaving the village." The stranger's smile was beginning to get on Thomas's nerves now. As if he was making fun of Thomas, enjoying stringing him along, playing with his meager hopes. If the man kept smiling like that, some of those jingling silver bells attached to his clothes might end up lodged in his throat, instead.

"Surely after his invention is unveiled," the man said, "he'll be whisked away to present it all over the world. I don't see how he would still have time to tinker with such trivial toys."

*Trivial toys?* Heat flared through Thomas's body. The prosthetic limb would change his life. It was nothing short of a miracle, and this guy was dismissing it? What the hell did he know about it, anyway?

*Keep talking, fellow, and you'll have to hike your way back to town.*

"Why, you seem awfully well-informed. What are you, Mr. Hastings's assistant?" Thomas asked, not quite able to keep the snark out of his voice. "So pray tell, what is this amazing invention he's working on?"

"Oh, I wouldn't know about that. I don't understand technology stuff. I'm just a poor beggar." The guy tilted his head, looking at Thomas with those infuriatingly cold, blue-green eyes. "But you and Jethro are colleagues of sorts. Maybe that will make him more inclined to help . . . After all, maybe you can return the favor, somehow. Help him with his work, stuff like that."

That dampened Thomas's rising temper a little. At least it seemed that the guy had gotten the hint that he had better back down.

"Or maybe you can just make him feel sorry for you by telling him your sad tale. I hear he's quite sensitive. What happened to your hand?"

Then again, maybe not.

Thomas gritted his teeth at the stranger's invasive question. And those eyes . . . those snake eyes of his were telling him it wasn't an innocent question at all. He was trying to push Thomas's buttons, wasn't he?

For a moment, he considered punching him. Even with just one hand, he'd had enough experience fending for himself on the streets. He was fairly sure he could take the man. But the inside of a cramped carriage as it barreled along on the edge of a steep cliff didn't seem like the best place to start a brawl, and he didn't want to show up at Hastings's place with a black eye or a bleeding lip, not to mention a passed-out beggar to explain. His chances with Hastings were slim enough as it was.

"I don't think that's any of your business," he said at last. He crossed his arms over his chest, glaring right back at the stranger, determined to hold his gaze. *Let* him *back down*. And back down he did, although he did so while shaking his head and chuckling in a way that made the impulse to deck him almost irresistible.

If nothing else, it would be a good distraction from the memories that the man's question had brought rushing to the forefront of his brain. He had no intention of thinking about that. He relived it often enough in his dreams and every time he looked at himself in the mirror. He didn't want to remember what it had felt like rolling on the floor, screaming as the flames enveloped his right sleeve and the fire bit into his flesh, devouring his skin and . . .

He shook his head as his stomach twisted. *No*. He'd said he didn't want to think about that. He had to focus on his impending meeting with Hastings. Now he needed the stranger to kindly keep quiet for the rest of the ride, as he seemed intentioned to do since he'd pulled his hat over his eyes and peacefully folded his hands over his stomach. Thomas took the opportunity to surreptitiously slip his hand in his pocket to rub the letter between his fingertips. He'd all but worn the paper thin. But it was all he had, his last hope of going back to who he was *before*.

He would do anything it took to persuade Jethro Hastings to help him. He'd sold everything he had left, which wasn't much after his laboratory and equipment had been mostly destroyed. Even so, the cash he was hiding in his inner pocket was a pitifully small amount. He wasn't sure how much one of the prosthetics might cost, but he was fairly sure it would be way beyond his means. But he could work for Hastings, doing . . . something. That had already been the plan, even before the stranger had mentioned it. Unless the beggar was right about Hastings being whisked away to tour the world, of course. So much for his hopes and dreams then.

The hansom cab shuddered to a stop. "We're here," the driver bellowed.

"Thank you, sir," Thomas said, his voice wavering a bit as his nerves really started to set in. He had to get that under control before he met Hastings.

After a quick look at the stranger, who didn't even budge, except for the pink plume on his hat gently moving up and down as he breathed, Thomas opened the door and glanced out. They were near the top of the mountain, nothing around but rocky cliffs and dark evergreen trees. They had stopped right in front of a large mansion with stained glass windows, the facade almost entirely covered in ivy. It was completely dark and silent, more than a little ominous. He repressed a shiver. It seemed abandoned, and even though it was barely past dinnertime, the darkness all around made him wish he'd waited until morning to go knock on Hastings's door.

A second hansom was parked nearby, refined and apparently extremely expensive. It was a steam-powered one, with the driver seated in front with his eyes closed. Someone must be home.

*Here we go, Thomas. Time to get this show on the road.*

With a deep breath, he turned to collect his luggage and nearly fell backward out of the carriage. The stranger had apparently awoken, then moved quietly as a cat because he was now mere inches from Thomas, staring straight at him, that somewhat mocking expression on his face again. Thomas choked down a curse and very nearly head-butted him in the face to send him back.

The beggar's lips curled up in the coldest smile Thomas had ever seen. "Good luck, toymaker. I'll see you soon."

*Yeah. And next time you'll walk away with a black eye.*

Thomas backed out of the hansom cab, his eyes never leaving the stranger, ready to drop his luggage and whip out the screwdriver should he make any more sudden movements. Thomas had barely set foot on the ground when the beggar slammed the door shut behind him.

*And here I thought I'd met enough strange people in Lunaris . . .*

With a last suspicious glance at the door, Thomas paid the driver, then turned to look at the house, trying to clear his head from that strange encounter, and focus on not botching the upcoming conversation. His whole future depended on it.

# CHAPTER 2

Thomas stood on the doorstep, trying to gather the courage to ring the bell. He looked up at the large, dark mansion. He couldn't see any lights on, and the facade, which must have been beautiful at some point, was all but crumbling to pieces close up. He wondered whether the hansom driver had played a trick on him and just dropped him at an abandoned house in the middle of nowhere. Or maybe Hastings was already asleep, though that would have been a little absurd at the current hour. Anyway, Thomas was there now, and he certainly couldn't spend the night camping in Jethro Hastings's garden.

He tucked his hand in his pocket, nervously brushing the letter between his fingertips as if it were a magic amulet, trying to draw some strength from it. Just one more hurdle and he would get a new hand.

He could do this.

Thomas raised his unsteady hand, reaching for the doorbell rope . . .

And the door exploded in his face, flying off its hinges. It shattered into a spray of splinters as Thomas dived to the side, landing heavily on his elbow, rolling onto his back in time to see a blurred, metallic shape careen out the doorway, tearing away the frame, leaving a jagged hole where the massive wooden door used to be.

Screams were coming from behind it, the sound of running footsteps as a woman shrieked and a man's deep voice yelled from inside the house. "Come back! By Jove, somebody stop that thing!"

Thomas's eyes went wide. It was a machine, an agglomeration of mechanical arms and pipes surrounding a rounded, steaming container, the vapors hissing furiously as it sprayed a jet of boiling hot liquid all around. Tea, judging by the scent. He scrabbled to his feet as the thing stopped, spinning around as if seeking a target for its fury. Then it seemed to focus on the elegant hansom parked nearby. It started toward it, and Thomas had a split second to take in the driver's frightened eyes, the way the carriage was so close to the edge of the cliff, the size and impetus of the tea machine . . .

Without even thinking, Thomas sprang forward. With a flick of his wrist, the thick, sharp screwdriver snapped out of his sleeve, and he brandished it like a weapon, his brain spinning frantically as he assessed the tea maker. The brass boiler, the junctures, the coils of wire, mechanical limbs cutting the air, and right there, at the center of it was a steaming and shrieking valve, barely able to contain the pressure.

*Right there. If I knock that valve off and let the steam out . . .*

The tea maker raised up on its legs, aiming its boiling-hot jet at the carriage, and Thomas dove under it. He rolled, coming up below its belly, and he slammed his hand forward, the tip of the screwdriver hitting the base of the valve, knocking it off with surgical precision.

The effect was instantaneous. The machine stopped moving, the wheezing and hissing dissipating as it deflated. A spray of boiling steam erupted from the broken valve and missed Thomas by an inch, singing his eyebrows. He covered his head to protect himself should the machine fall on him, but the thing just slumped, folding in on itself and remaining still and silent, a last trickle of tea spilling all over Thomas's clothes.

There was a moment of silence, then the shrieking resumed, coming from the plump, middle-aged woman who was running out of the shattered doorway in a flurry of green velvet. "This is *outrageous*! We will never buy such a devilish creature! We would never allow a thing like that in our home. You are nothing but a madman!"

A short man tottered after her, adjusting his monocle with pudgy hands, an expression of fascination on his face. He studied the slumped machine, completely ignoring Thomas underneath it. "But come on, Poopsy Doodles, darling, maybe we could—"

"*Not another word*! Get in this carriage right now, Hector, or God help me I'm leaving you here!" the woman yelled, wriggling to climb through the too-narrow door. Casting a dejected, apologetic look behind him, the husband followed suit, and within moments, the hansom came to life.

An olive-skinned man hurried out the door after them, adjusting his round, golden glasses on his thin nose, not even sparing a glance at the broken tea maker. Or to Thomas, who was still on the ground beneath it.

"Mr. and Mrs. Hildebrand," the man called to the couple, "please don't make any rash decisions, this was just a . . . a minor malfunction that I can assure you will never—"

The door was slammed in his face, and the woman shrieked something through the window—something that sounded like, "Over my *dead body* that thing will come in my house, you rascal!"—and the hansom took off at full steam, leaving the man standing there in his rumpled pinstripe trousers and vest. He scratched his head, then sighed and took off his crooked glasses. He wiped them with the hem of his button-down shirt, muttering a disconsolate, "What the hell."

Meanwhile, Thomas had rolled out from under the machine, clothes soaked and tea dripping down his neck, and he'd been torn between examining the thing, and watching the scene that unfolded right before his eyes. Here he was with his dusty shoes, tea-soaked clothes, and his meager luggage resting small and lonely at his feet, anxiety and trepidation fluttering wildly in his stomach. When had this become his life?

The man noticed him then and turned toward him, wide-eyed. "Who the hell are you?"

For a moment, Thomas forgot he was supposed to ingratiate himself to this man and was about to snap back in kind, because his shirt was soaked and ruined and his hip hurt where he'd landed on the ground and, what the hell, a little gratitude, man. *Why, there's no need to thank me or anything* . . . But he caught himself and took a deep breath . . . and a good look at the man while he was at it. He was young, probably just a few years older than Thomas. For all his ragged appearance, with those untidy clothes and messy black hair, he was a handsome man, tall and slender with olive skin and green eyes shimmering behind his glasses. If that was Hastings . . . well, he was a far cry from the old man Thomas had been expecting.

"My . . . my name is Thomas Escott, and you're most welcome. Mr. Hastings, is it?"

The man opened his mouth, apparently intentioned to reply unkindly, finger already lifted midair. Then he deflated, turning meek much as his tea maker had done. He ruffled his curls with his hand, seeming suddenly very tired and fed up, something apologetic in his eyes. "I . . . You're right. Thank you, Mr. Escott." There was a moment of silence as he looked at Thomas, really looked at him for the first time. Instinctively, Thomas tried to hide his stump, suddenly painfully aware of his own ruined clothes and generally bedraggled appearance. "And I guess, um, if you'd like to come in and have a seat for a moment . . ."

Thomas glanced down at himself. He was soaked in tea, growing steadily cold in the night air, the sweet scent mixing with the smell of smoke he might never be able to wash out of the fabric now. "Why, that would be great. Lead the way."

"So, Thomas . . . Is that right?" Jethro asked, taking a seat in front of him. He kept running his fingers through his unruly curls, pushing them away from his forehead. "Your presence here was providential. I really can't thank you enough."

They had dragged the broken machine inside and were now sitting in a small parlor, crammed with furniture covered in dusty blankets. Judging from the additional layer of dust and the spiders running around on the small table in front of him, Thomas was fairly sure that the room had not been used in years. Thomas was sitting somewhat uncomfortably on one of the stiff velvet armchairs, shivering in his soaked clothes.

"Well, I'm glad I could be of help," he said, trying to keep his teeth from chattering in the cold room. He eyed the big marble fireplace, dark and empty along the wall, desperately wishing there was a nice, roaring fire he could warm up beside. His gaze fell on the slumped tea maker, awkwardly folded by the door. "Pretty dangerous contraption you've got there, Mr. Hastings."

"Jethro, please. And really, it's not supposed to be." He shook his head, shooting a frustrated look at the thing. "My machines are not supposed to hurt people. This was just a . . . minor accident. A little malfunction, nothing more."

*Little malfunction? If you say so . . .*

"Of course. I-I understand," Thomas replied, and this time he couldn't prevent himself from stammering when a shudder ran down his spine.

Jethro's gaze snapped to his. The inventor pushed his glasses up his nose. "I'm sorry, would you like to change out of that sodden shirt? I'm sure I could find you something to wear."

"Oh, I do have a few changes with me." Thomas pointed at the luggage resting at his feet.

Jethro nodded. "Please do feel free. I would offer you some tea, but . . ."

Thomas snickered, getting up to unbutton his jacket, shrugging it off before dropping it on the armchair's back. "Thank you, but I think I've had enough for tonight. Or we could always squeeze some out from my shirt."

Jethro laughed at that, a rough, deep chuckle that sent a different kind of shiver up Thomas's spine. He turned around and quickly undid the buttons of his shirt, hating the way the cold, wet fabric clung to his skin, the way it peeled away, and as he was pulling it off his right shoulder, he froze. He didn't know whether Jethro was looking, but he suddenly felt a knot in his stomach at the thought of revealing the ruined skin of his shoulder and arm. In his haste to get out of his wet clothes, he'd forgotten about it for a moment.

He closed his eyes, hoping his hesitation wasn't long enough to be noticeable, and inhaled deeply through his nose. After all, he would have to show Jethro, to let himself be examined, if he wanted to have a prosthetic implanted. Might as well let him see now. He supposed it was the best summary he could give of his reason for being there in the first place. And besides, Jethro must have seen plenty of people in similar conditions, Thomas tried to reassure himself. The inventor wouldn't be horrified and disgusted by what he saw.

Even so, the thought of revealing his scars to the handsome man sitting at the table was unnerving. Thomas swallowed. He shouldn't care about that. He was there with a precise goal, and he needed to stay focused on it.

The silence was heavy in the room, only the wet sounds of the shirt suctioning to his body as he pulled at the fabric. The air was cool on Thomas's damp skin as he used his teeth to ease the sleeve past his hand, then folded the fabric over his arm and placed it on top of his jacket. He bent to retrieve another shirt from his luggage—this one a bit darkened on the sleeve—feeling exposed like he never had in his life. He could practically feel Jethro's gaze on him now, and he closed his eyes, glad that the inventor couldn't see his face as he laboriously slipped his fresh shirt on and buttoned it one-handed. Just another skill he'd mastered in the past five months.

"So," Jethro said, his tone serious. "I get the feeling you were not accidentally passing by."

Thomas straightened his collar and turned around, forcing a smile to his lips, even though it felt foreign and twisted. "Yeah, well, although I'm sure it's a lovely sightseeing spot, you're right." He sat back down in the armchair, his cheeks heating up as he met Jethro's penetrating gaze once more. "As you can see, I find myself in need of your help."

The inventor adjusted his glasses again. "So I do see."

Thomas swallowed hard. He was clutching his stump to his chest, and even though it was securely covered by the fabric now, the scar beneath was prickling. He could feel every inch of burned tissue on his arm sizzling, but he held his ground. "There was . . . an accident. My laboratory was destroyed, and I lost my hand. I need one of your prosthetics if I'm to work again."

"Your laboratory?" Jethro asked, tilting his head to the side. "Who . . . who are you, exactly?"

Thomas took a deep breath. "I am a toymaker from Lunaris. My grandmother raised me when I was a child, but after she passed away . . ." He shrugged. "I lived on the streets for a while. Somehow I survived, and I started assembling little mechanical toys with the scraps I could find in the mud by the river and the few broken, defective parts some shop owners would give me for free. Just to entertain myself, at first, but then I realized I could make some money off them. The rich kids liked them, and their parents could pay. Eventually, I was able to open a little workshop of my own. Barely enough to have a roof over my head and food every day, but still."

It was strange to talk about it. As if he were telling the story of somebody else's life. Someone he knew intimately, maybe a close friend, but not himself. "But that's . . . who I *was*. Who I am now, after it happened, I'm not quite sure. I guess I haven't quite figured it out yet."

Jethro hummed quietly. "A toymaker? Do you mean . . .?"

Thomas interrupted him. "And no, I don't mean an artisan. I suppose an inventor might be a better description, as I mostly focus on clockwork toys, little animated ones. Marching soldiers, flying birds, trains, ballerinas. I was just working on a series of miniature animated insects, from scarabs to butterflies, which—" He caught himself as he was getting more excited and snapped his mouth shut. Jethro's expression was unreadable, but he doubted an inventor with his reputation would be very impressed listening to Thomas ramble about the details of the mechanism for his butterflies' wings. "I've worked with bigger machines, of course. And during the war, I was rounded up like everyone with mechanical skills and put to work in the weapons factories. I hated it, every last minute of it, and . . ."

Thomas shuddered at the memory. Having to go from building his toys to building things that would kill and maim and bring nothing but pain. When the war had finally ended and he'd been free to go back to his workshop, the relief had been greater than anything he'd ever felt in his life. He'd sworn he would never again work on something he didn't believe in, that he would spend the rest of his life building things that would make people smile, even if just for a moment. And now . . . now, he couldn't do anything anymore.

"It doesn't matter. Anyway, miniatures and clockwork creatures are what I do best. What I prefer."

Jethro tilted his head. "You . . . prefer toys?"

"Yes. I much prefer detailed precision work, and toys allow so much more creativity and flexibility than clocks and weapons." Thomas shrugged. He was used to people being surprised by that. A tough-looking street guy like him wasn't exactly what they pictured when they thought of a toymaker, not even in the capital, and people were not inclined to take his inventions seriously, either. Hell, just because their purpose was entertainment and might not be as practical as, say, pendulum clocks or murderous tea makers, it didn't mean they were any less complicated.

"Well, so we are colleagues, then." Jethro's features relaxed into a smile, and something tight and tense in Thomas's chest snapped loose. He took a deep, relieved breath. At least Jethro wasn't laughing at him. But Jethro's next words squashed that relief right back down. "And then you . . . You mentioned an accident?"

"There isn't much to say, really," Thomas replied. "I was working in my laboratory. It was late, I was in a hurry. I spilled some oil on the table, soaked my sleeve. And then I'm not exactly sure how it happened . . . There was a spark, and then everything was on fire."

He swallowed, a knot forming in his throat. His hand was shaking now, even though he was doing his best to stop it. He didn't know whether that memory would ever stop sending him into an involuntary, uncontrolled panic.

"Somebody managed to drag me out before the entire workshop was destroyed, put out my burning clothes. But it was too late to save my hand. The chirurgeon . . ." He swallowed heavily again, his mouth dry. He didn't want to say any more. "Well, you get the gist."

Jethro slowly rubbed at his chin. "I'm . . . I'm so sorry to hear about that. I feel for you and your accident, I truly do; however, I'm . . . I'm extremely busy at the moment, and I'm afraid . . . I'm afraid I don't have the time to help."

"Listen, Mr. Has—I mean, Jethro. I don't expect any charity. If money's a problem, I can pay." Thomas cringed at the thought of how little money he had hidden in his inner pocket.

"No, that's not it. I don't need the money." Jethro shifted uncomfortably in his seat, seemingly uneasy. "As I said, I'm sorry, but I just can't help."

Thomas swallowed, trying to collect himself. Conflict made him anxious, as did begging and cajoling, but he was good at persuading people to do things they didn't want to do. But right then his instincts were telling him to back off, to apologize for the bother, and go back to where he'd come from. Then he felt his stump burn and pull and itch, the echo of the intense pain that had shot through his body when his hand had been taken from him. He gritted his teeth, trying to seize the determination, stemming from the sheer desperation, roaring inside him. He needed this to happen. And goddamn it, he wouldn't take no for an answer. Maybe he would never have done this in his previous life, but everything was different now. He had nothing left to lose.

"Then I could work for you. Be an assistant of sorts, for however long you desire or need, to help with your workload." Thomas tugged at his collar. The stench of smoke from his shirt was growing suffocating, seeming to fill the entire room, and he wondered how Jethro could possibly not smell it. "I mean, I don't know exactly how long it would take for me to learn how to properly control the prosthetic, but I could, I don't know, find a place to stay down at the village for however long it took—" *And pay for it with what money?* his brain tried to interject, but Thomas shut that little voice down "—and then get started right away."

Jethro puffed out his cheeks, distractedly pulling at his curls. "That wouldn't be a problem. There are dozens of unused rooms here, and my prosthetics are, so to speak, quite unique. You would be able to achieve full functionality in a matter of days."

Thomas couldn't prevent himself from gaping. "Days? But that's imposs—" He cut himself off. He didn't want to contradict Jethro, of course. They were *his* inventions, so he obviously knew what he was talking about. But still . . . "I met a few people down in the capital, wearing very basic prosthetics—nothing mechanical, of course—and they told me it took them months to learn to maneuver them properly. I thought that surely, with something more complex . . ."

Jethro smiled, a mysterious grin, as he lowered his eyes for a moment to the dusty table. "My prosthetics, as you can imagine, are quite different from anything you've seen before. They are permanent, implanted directly into your body, connected to muscles and nerves. That, among other things, is why it takes the body such a short time to adapt to it. It would respond to your commands just like your real hand used to."

Thomas tried to restrain his heart from jumping out of his chest. Holy mother of God, this sounded entirely too good to be true. A sheer miracle. There was no other way to describe it. Why wasn't Jethro world famous already, swimming in mounds of gold and shipping his prosthetics all over the continent?

"That is . . ." He swallowed. He was still so amazed he was having trouble untangling his tongue and finding the right words. "That's simply *amazing*. How is it possible? How did you manage it? It's just . . ."

Jethro's smile was small but so, so bright it was lighting up his whole face. It looked good on him. "You'll forgive me if I don't divulge the specifics. You are, after all, a colleague . . . and a competitor."

Thomas settled back into the armchair, still thrumming with energy but obediently backing down. In his excited blabbering, he had asked too much. It wasn't like he was really expecting Jethro to reveal his secrets. "Of course. I'm sorry, it's just . . . Wow. I'm simply astonished. I don't think there's anyone in the world who has ever achieved anything of the like. You, Mr. Hastings—Jethro—are truly a genius."

"Um, well." Was that a blush on Jethro's cheeks? "Of course, this also means a little more attention is necessary. Since the prosthetics cannot be removed, one has to be careful when doing activities that might somehow damage them."

"Of course. Of course." Thomas nodded, his brain whirring. He had to get one of those prosthetics. He *had* to. "Well, that would be even more convenient. I would be able to start helping you right away, even in time for . . ." He paused, an idea sparking in his mind, considering for a moment whether he should try to see if there had been any truth at all to what the strange beggar had been saying. Choosing his words carefully, he said, "I've heard that you might have a special event coming up?"

Jethro actually looked gobsmacked for a moment, eyes wide and lips parted, and a wave of triumph swept through Thomas's chest.

*Bull's-eye.*

He carried on, trying to look confident. "Should that be the case, you'll need some help to organize things. After all, you'll have a much harder time focusing if you have to spend all your time chasing after inventions running amok. You can let me do that while you work on what's actually important."

"How do you—" Jethro cut himself off. Obviously he didn't want to admit he was surprised, or that Thomas had hit the target, but it was too late. Thomas had seen it on his face, clear as day. So he swallowed down the knot in his throat and straightened his shoulders, tackling Jethro head-on.

"That's not important. What matters is that I can help. Give me a new hand, and I will be at your disposal night and day. I'm good at what I do, and I can help you ensure everything is ready in time for your big event."

He saw Jethro open his mouth to reply, maybe to rebuke him, but then something changed in the inventor's expression. He was actually considering it now. Thomas could see the cogs turning, calculating the time Jethro would lose implanting the hand versus the time he would save with an assistant. Yes, Thomas was on the right path. He had to insist, to strike while the iron was hot.

"Think about it," he pressed on. "You will have twice the skill to take care of things in the lab. I can handle the inventions running wild, the smaller stuff, deal with customers, hell, even cook and clean. Anything that distracts you from your big project, I can take on. And once you've seen how good I am, maybe you can let me help with that too. The time I can save you is much greater than the little time you will spend implanting the prosthetic."

Good God, he was blushing furiously, his heart hammering in his chest. He was going out on a limb, and he knew it. He would never dream of saying something so arrogant under normal circumstances, but . . .

*Nothing to lose. Go for it with everything you've got, because if you don't get this right . . .*

Nothing was scarier than that thought.

Jethro opened his mouth to reply, then paused. Thomas saw him glance furtively at the tea maker, still slumped where they had dragged it. Finally, he said, cautiously, "Do you know your way around a real laboratory? I can't have someone in there who doesn't know what the hell they're doing. Miniature work is the very core of my prosthetics, but I'm not sure if your . . . skills would be suitable for my kind of work. After all, these are complex pieces of machinery, not . . . I mean . . ."

*They're not toys.*

Of course someone like Jethro Hastings wouldn't take Thomas's work seriously. Why should he?

Thomas weighed it for a second and decided that a little more bluntness wouldn't hurt at this point.

"May I remind you who just stopped your rogue tea machine from making an even bigger mess than it already did?" Thomas said, squaring his shoulders and trying to ignore the heat flaring on his cheeks. "If that isn't a good enough guarantee, then I don't know what is."

Jethro was silent, mulling it over. Thomas considered pushing harder but decided it was best to let him think about it for a minute. Thomas had played his cards. Now he had to give Jethro a moment to let everything fall into place.

Thomas held his breath as the moment seemed to stretch into hours.

"All right. I guess maybe you have a point," Jethro conceded. "I've only got ten days left, and I suppose I could use some help. And after all, I do owe you. If the tea maker had tossed that hansom and its driver off the cliff . . . God, I don't even want to think about it." He drummed his fingers on the table for a moment. "Suppose . . . suppose I did consider this. How . . . I don't mean to be mistrustful, but I've got to ask: how do I know you're not just going to take the prosthetic and bolt as soon as it's functioning?"

"And give up the chance to work with an inventor such as yourself?" Thomas shook his head, flashing his most charming smile. A little flattery? That he knew how to do. "I'd have to be crazy. I'm pretty sure there are plenty of inventors out there who would gladly give up a limb to have such an opportunity."

That actually startled a laugh out of Jethro, who finally seemed to relax a little and leaned to rest his elbows on the table. "All right, fine. I suppose we could work something out." He pointed at the slumped tea maker. "You can start by helping me drag that thing to the laboratory so I can chop it into tiny little pieces. Then we'll find a room where you can rest for the night, and tomorrow we shall see about finding you the right prosthetic."

Something jumped in Thomas's throat, but he managed to keep it in check. "Thank you, Jethro. I promise you won't regret it." He stood up and shook Jethro's hand. His skin was dry and warm, his grip strong and steady, and the contact sent a subtle shiver through Thomas's body, making his knees just a little weak.

As he followed Jethro to the machine, Thomas did his absolute best to hide the triumph and excitement that were somersaulting in his chest like an overwound clockwork toy. He was almost sure he succeeded, too.

# CHAPTER 3

Thomas woke up the following morning, and for a moment, he couldn't remember where he was. He opened his eyes, brain still tangled in the sticky spiderwebs of his confused dreams, and the grayish light seeping in from the window lit up a room he didn't recognize. One of the many empty rooms in the servants' quarters in Jethro Hastings's house, he remembered then, a thrill running through his body. He blinked as he took in the faded wallpaper, the scraped dresser he'd dropped his luggage next to the night before, the musty, scratchy covers on the bed, but there was something he was forgetting, something dark and heavy lodged in the pit of his stomach, something urgent that he couldn't seem to—

His hand.

He managed not to flinch when the memory suddenly sprang to the forefront of his mind, as it did every single time he woke up. He swallowed down the bitterness as he sat up on the bed in the chilly room, his eyes darting down to confirm that yes, indeed, his hand was still missing. He hated that, hated being slammed with that reality every time he opened his eyes after being asleep. At least it was better now than it had been before. In the early days, that torturous morning routine of having to remember, having to realize it *once again*, had more than once reduced him to tears.

But it would be all fixed soon, he reassured himself, squashing down the anxiety like a bothersome moth. Soon he would have to get used to waking up with his brand-new prosthetic hand attached. Why, was he ever looking forward to that!

He sighed as he swung his legs off the side of the bed, resting his feet on the thick, dusty carpet covering part of the dark hardwood floor. Everything else seeped in more slowly, simple memories bubbling up from the thick waters of his sleep—the letter, his reckless trip, the events of the previous day. He could hardly believe he'd done it, catapulted himself so far from his home, his life, and managed to convince Jethro Hastings to take him in. But then again, he could hardly believe the turn his life had taken ever since the accident.

He walked to the cracked ceramic basin in the corner and splashed his face with cold water. It was almost over. Soon he would have his hand, and he would go back to his life, and everything would go back to normal. Return to exactly how it had been before. And the sooner he was done with this whole endeavor, the sooner that day would come. Jethro wasn't the only one in a hurry. He quickly slipped on his brown trousers and a baggy long-sleeved shirt, pausing to make sure the cuff was hiding his stump, shrugged on a waistcoat, and headed out of the room.

He made his way along the creaking stairwell, brushing the cold iron of the banister with his left hand. The light came in from the cracked, dirty windows, illuminating the dust motes fluttering sleepily in the air. His footsteps were impossibly loud in the vast, echoing hall. He wanted to call out for Jethro, but it seemed inappropriate in the silence of the house, which felt more abandoned than it had looked the night before. Ivy crawled in from every nook and cranny, and spiders built their kingdoms undisturbed in every corner. It seemed impossible that anyone lived there.

But traces of a lived-in house became clearer as he wandered around the ground floor—a path worn in the dusty carpets from someone pacing, gas lamps kept impeccably clean, new and shiny pipes running along the walls. He must be getting closer to the wing of the house where Jethro lived or worked, so he followed those signs in the hopes of finding the kitchen. His stomach was grumbling for a meal.

As he wandered, he tried not to get lost in the dark corridors, sending mice scurrying back into their nests and occasionally stepping over a wrench or a pile of pipes abandoned in the middle of the passage. It was stuffy too, the smell of mold and dust almost suffocating, and Thomas was beginning to feel trapped like a little animal in that too-big, too-empty house. So he was more than happy when he spotted a door whose ample glass panes were letting in the sunshine from outside.

Forgetting his quest for breakfast, he stepped through the door, just to catch a breath of fresh air for a moment. But once Thomas was on the other side, he stopped in his tracks, looking up. The entire garden was encased in a giant glass house of sorts, with thin black lead bars climbing up and curving into a graceful dome that captured the sun's rays and amplified them, giving the still air an eerily comforting warmth. The glass panels, dirty and cracked and shattered in places, bathed him in sunlight. It was so quiet and cozy and beautiful, in an unlikely kind of way. An intricate pattern of ivy and trees had climbed as high as they could on the glass cage, and a couple of trapped crows were tapping softly against the unbroken panes, trying to find a way back out.

"Who are you?"

The sudden intrusion in the silence almost made Thomas jump out of his skin. Especially since it most definitely wasn't Jethro's voice. In fact, it sounded like a woman. But not even. A little girl, maybe?

He looked around the space. Maybe Jethro had a daughter. He didn't look like a family man, but who was Thomas to judge. It just went to show how little research he'd done before throwing himself headlong into his adventure. But he couldn't find anyone, merely thick, dark cypress trees crowding in the narrow space and a large oak tree that seemed entirely too large to—

Thomas did a double take.

A girl was perched among the branches of the oak tree that nearly filled the space under the glass canopy with a cascade of leaves. She must have been twelve years old or so, her hair tied in a long braid, and she was sitting way too high on branches way too thin to hold her weight. But that wasn't even what perplexed him. The girl's dress was a faint gray and so were her face and hair, and . . .

And he was pretty sure he could see the tree's leaves right through her.

Thomas rubbed at his eyes, blinked, then looked again.

*What the . . . ?*

"What's your name?" she asked, but his tongue was a little tied at the moment. He gaped at her, not quite knowing what to say. His brain was refusing to process what he was seeing, the cogs stuck in molasses and refusing to move. All he could think was that he probably should have done at least a *little* bit of research before coming here.

He pulled himself together and somehow managed to croak out a reply. "Uh, Thomas. My name is Thomas Escott. And you are?" He rubbed his eyes again.

"My name is Mina." She dangled her legs from the branch. "What are you doing here?"

"I-I'm just . . ." Thomas shook his head. He'd like to focus on what to say, but his brain was otherwise occupied trying to make sense of what he was seeing. "Maybe . . . maybe you could come down?"

As soon as he said it, he was no longer sure it was such a good idea. Too late, though. There was a gust of wind, and within moments, the girl was standing right before him. She had a sweet, round face, almond-shaped eyes, and a curious yet kind expression on her face. An old-fashioned ruffled collar hid her neck from sight.

And, yes, she was definitely transparent.

"Hi," she said, shooting him a bright, expectant smile.

Thomas stared. He knew it was kind of rude, but he couldn't think of anything else to do. Eventually he replied: "Hi. So . . ." Good Lord, he was really speaking to a transparent girl, was he not? He kind of wanted to pinch himself.

*I really wish I'd had that breakfast.*

"So who— I mean, are you . . . a relative of Jethro's, or . . . or a friend, or . . .?"

"No, nothing like that! Don't be silly. I've been here for much longer than Mr. Hastings has." It seemed to be something she was proud of.

Thomas nodded along, still stunned. "Oh, I see. Of course." He swallowed, looked around as if the crows fluttering above were the thoughts circling around and around in his head without finding a trajectory to follow. He turned back to her.

Yes, he could still definitely see through her. *There's the tree and the patch of violets, and there's a robin hopping on the ground . . .*

He brought his gaze back to her face, trying to look her in the eyes, which seemed a little more solid than the rest of her, but it was so distracting to stare at her and see what was behind her. His eyes didn't quite know where to focus. It was like she was made of glass, except she was talking and moving and smiling a very much human smile at him.

"Listen, I . . . I hate to bring this up, but . . . but you're kind of, you know. I can *see through you*," he finally blurted out, feeling pretty stupid. "Why . . . I mean, what . . ."

"Oh. Well, yes, of course you can," she said, shrugging, like it was the most obvious thing in the world. "I am a ghost, after all."

Thomas plopped down on an elegant wrought iron bench, half-colonized by moss and ivy, and the ghost girl sat by his side, resting her chin in her hands and swinging her feet above a mound of fallen leaves. He couldn't stop staring at her, mildly transfixed.

*A ghost, eh? Good Lord.*

He ran his hand through his hair, puffing out his cheeks. That was . . . well, unexpected. He'd heard of their existence before, of course. His grandmother, God bless her soul, used to tell him about the conversations she sometimes had with spirits, or ghosts, or whatever you wanted to call them. They had some interesting stories to tell, apparently. She'd told him about long hours spent in her little tearoom, chatting with them about times long gone.

But, well, they were things of another time. They had been gone for a while, or so he'd thought. He'd always figured they didn't like modernity or some such. There was simply no longer space for them, for ghosts and legends to exist in a modern city like Lunaris. These were times of science and inventions, no longer times of mystery and superstition. Even his grandmother had said she hadn't seen or heard from her otherworldly friends in a long time—years, decades, even.

And he was a man of technology, for heaven's sake. His mind was occupied with other things like building machines and progress. *These* things, these outdated things, he had just kind of forgotten about them.

He supposed if there were any ghosts left, it stood to reason they would be in a place like this, an isolated village crouching in the mountains, in a forgotten garden of an abandoned house. It was probably one of the last places where they *could* still exist. A safe haven of sorts, perhaps. But, God . . .

He ruffled his hair again, a nervous yet excited laugh escaping his lips. To find one right there in the backyard of the most brilliant inventor of their time? If only his grandmother was still around. She would be ecstatic. She had missed them. She had never been too keen on modern contraptions, as she called them. In fact, she'd been quite perplexed when her only grandson had dived headlong into the technology she so mistrusted.

"So what are you doing here, Thomas?" Mina asked, shaking him out of his reverie. She was staring at him with endless fascination, as if *he* were the odd sight.

Thomas's tongue untangled enough for him to reply in a somewhat coherent way. "I'm . . . I'm here to help out Jethro. Um, Mr. Hastings, I mean. With his work."

"Really?" The girl tilted her head to the side. "He never invites anyone here. He doesn't really like to have people around," she added in a somewhat confidential tone.

"He didn't exactly invite me." He swallowed. It sounded sort of rude when he put it that way, but then again, it was exactly what he'd done. "I just invited myself, I guess. But . . . but who are you? D-do you live here?"

"I'm Mina," she repeated patiently. "And of course I live here. Ever since I can remember. I was asleep for a while, but then I was awake again. I've been dead for a pretty long time, you know."

"Oh. I . . . I'm sorry." Thomas guessed that was the right thing to say, but he was way out of his depth. It was seldom that he was so completely off his game in a conversation. It flashed through his mind that maybe he should ask what happened, but he figured that was a very inappropriate question to ask a ghost. Although he wasn't quite sure if anyone had ever bothered to write down the etiquette for such encounters. "Here . . . in the garden?"

"Of course." She scrunched up her button nose at him. "Where else would I be?"

*I most certainly have no idea.*

"It's all right, though," she went on. "I like it here. It's my home." She got up and took a dance step or two. "It gets a little boring sometimes, though. There is never anything to do. And no fun company. Mr. Hastings never comes to see me, you know." She turned and smiled brightly at Thomas. "But now you're here. You're going to come play with me sometimes, aren't you?"

"Why, um, sure. I will," he replied returning a slightly uncertain smile, but he was surprised to find he actually meant it.

"It would be more fun if I had a body. I could go to the market, then, and buy a new ribbon for my hair."

"Can't you do that already?" Thomas asked.

Mina shook her head, huffing. "No. I can't get out of here."

Thomas scratched his chin. He couldn't remember his grandmother mentioning anything about where ghosts were or were not allowed to go. He really wished he'd asked her more questions. "Why can't you get out of the garden?"

Mina shrugged. "I don't know. I just can't." She looked at him, something anxious in her eyes. "You *will* come visit me, won't you? He never does . . ."

He wondered how the inventor dealt with having a ghost living literally in his backyard. "Does he know you're here?"

"Of course he knows. He doesn't care. I don't think he really cares about anything except all his machines." She clapped her hands, frightening a bird, which flew off in a flurry of black feathers. "He's *so* dull."

"Oh. I see." Thomas wondered if he should ask Jethro about Mina. He definitely had questions, but maybe it was too soon to start prying. But he figured he would have time . . . at least some. "Well I'll be happy to come talk with you. It's really lovely out here."

Mina pursed her lips and slowly nodded her head, her long braid dangling on her back. "I guess . . . Boring, though."

Thomas could sympathize with her boredom. As lovely as the garden was, being stuck there with nothing to do for years would be tiresome for anyone. Maybe he could make something for her. He was a toymaker, after all. *Or you were*, a little cruel voice whispered in his head. He'd take a look in the laboratory, Thomas continued with his train of thought, determined not to let his traitorous mind drag him down. Maybe there was some scrap metal he could use to build a little something for Mina, who was now busy chasing after a crow that could obviously see her and was flying about, utterly terrified.

Thomas was dimly aware that he should probably go get breakfast and then make himself useful or Jethro might have his butt on a plate on the very first day, but he couldn't quite stop watching Mina.

"Thomas? Are you out here?"

Thomas startled at the sound of Jethro's voice. He turned around to see the inventor's head peeking out of the door, his dark hair even messier than the previous night, if that was even possible. "Um, yes. I'm sorry. I was talking to . . ."

But Mina was nowhere to be seen, vanished into thin air just the way she'd appeared.

"Come, let me show you around the laboratory. We don't have much time. You'll have to take a tour of the grounds in your spare time."

Jethro turned on his heel and disappeared back into the house. With a last look around the strange garden inside the glass, Thomas followed him in, excitement already welling in his chest, making him restless. He had more important things to think about than ghosts.

*Like my new hand*, he thought with a smile.

# CHAPTER 4

J ethro's laboratory was impressive. It was a vast hall that could have fit Thomas's own modest workshop several times over. Sunlight seeped in from several skylights, and small gas lamps were mounted all along the walls and on each of the numerous worktables. And he had *so many* instruments. Thomas's gaze skimmed every which way, unable to even identify most of them. He could never have afforded anything like that, not even in his wildest dreams.

Tables were covered in instruments and mechanical parts, and pulleys hung from the ceiling, as well as chains and hooks to lift bigger pieces of machinery. In a corner, he recognized the half-dismantled tea maker from the previous night. A knitting contraption of spinning gears and running cables steamed away softly, hiccupping now and again, making a lumpy scarf.

And in the center of the room, placed in the middle of an empty desk, was a large hourglass about two feet tall, mounted in a heavy-looking, carved mahogany frame with a richly carved base and four twisting pillars holding up the top. The rounded bottom half was almost filled with the strangest sand Thomas had ever seen. It was black and yet shimmered in a way, silver sparks dancing in front of Thomas's eyes as he watched. The dark grains kept steadily trickling down, glowing with a cold light as they fell. They whispered softly as they passed through the neck of the hourglass and fell onto the growing mound beneath, and yet there was something wrong about that sound, something that made his nape prickle and his skin break out in goose bumps, as if the grains of sand were nails scraping on the glass, screeching as they tried to cling on, tried not to fall.

Thomas shook his head, trying to bring his attention back to the laboratory, where it should be, and away from that strange hourglass.

Yet he found his gaze continually drawn to it. He got the odd impression that the mound of sand in the bottom half was moving, swirling, the silver spinning as if it was trying to draw him in, right into its belly.

Thomas frowned. What a strange item to find in such a high-tech laboratory, especially given the grand pendulum clock against the wall. It almost reached the ceiling, miniature reproductions of the moon and stars rotating slowly above the face of the clock. An astronomical clock, maybe?

"Did you build that too?" he asked Jethro, pointing at it and trying to sound conversational. "You know, I've been working as a clockmaker for several years too, but I've never—"

"Don't touch that," Jethro snapped. His vehemence startled Thomas for a moment. He sounded very different from the affable, if a little distant, man he'd been speaking with so far. "I mean . . . don't *ever* touch that. Or anything I don't explicitly allow you to. It's . . . it's very delicate. That's all."

Thomas hummed. Well, he guessed it wasn't anything too odd. Jethro certainly wasn't the first inventor to be possessive of his work space. Thomas himself wasn't sure he could ever have allowed anyone to work with him, to poke around his inventions, touch his instruments . . . He shuddered at the mere thought. They would just make a mess, break stuff, and put things where they weren't supposed to be.

"Of course. Don't worry about a thing," he said, giving Jethro a reassuring smile. "I won't touch a thing without your permission."

*Although God knows that's exactly what I would like to do for the rest of the day.*

There was so much stuff packed into the lab that he didn't even know where to look. He turned around, spotting a cluster of wires and pipes, which, with some creativity, might have looked like a bowel system, resting on a table. But why would anyone ever build something like that? He chuckled to himself. Must have been part of some complicated engine Thomas couldn't even begin to understand. God, what he wouldn't give to have the time to dawdle around that workshop, examining all Jethro's projects. But with some luck, he would have time to do it in the following . . . Oh. Now that he thought about it . . .

"So, this big event of yours . . . It's in nine days now, correct?"

Jethro paused, turning to look at him for a second, his head tilted to the side. "Yes, it is. But I still don't understand how you knew about it . . . I mean, I did send some invitations already, but none to scientists from Lunaris."

Thomas considered just telling him, but somehow he felt stupid admitting he'd been getting his intel from a bizarre half lunatic he'd met in a hansom cab. "I've got my sources," he said instead, winking and casually tucking his hand in his pocket. "But what I don't know is what it is you'll be presenting. Does it have something to do with the prosthetics, or . . .?"

Jethro shot him a small smile. "That, I'm afraid, will have to remain a secret for a little while longer. After all, I wouldn't want to spoil the surprise."

*Ah.* Thomas was still capable of recognizing when someone was blatantly evading his questions, but he figured it was fair enough. He'd have to keep his eyes open in the upcoming days, after he started working in the laboratory. Surely he'd be able to figure something out.

"And now, let's have a look at the prosthetics, shall we?" Jethro asked. "We need to choose a suitable one for you."

That completely captivated Thomas's attention. Forget about the big event or whatever it was that Jethro was going to dazzle the world with. "Oh. Yeah, sure. Show me what you got," he said, trying to be flippant despite the nervous excitement brewing in his stomach.

Jethro steered him toward the back of the large room, where various prosthetics were piled up on tables, hanging from the walls, and tucked in boxes. Thomas's eyes widened, amazed. He felt as if he'd stepped inside a place of worship. He'd never seen anything like it in any of the laboratories he'd visited, never mind his own, and he was almost afraid to breathe near them.

God, there must have been dozens of them. How long had it taken Jethro to build such an astonishing collection?

There were many prosthetic legs lying on the table, and among them was one made of porcelain and leather, wood and brass, finely crafted—the right size to fit a petite lady with the refined look to go with it. It actually appeared similar to some prosthetics he'd seen before, but it lacked the straps necessary to fasten it to the body. Instead, it sported an intricate web of pipes and wires. The thigh and the calf were layered in porcelain, encasing God knew what wonderful mechanisms. Thomas's fingers itched to unscrew those miniature bolts and open the cases to see what wonders were hiding inside, what kind of miraculous engines put it in motion.

He didn't even know where to look among the sea of ceramic, wood, delicately welded plates, cogs, and junctures lying before his eyes. He almost reached out to touch a whole mechanical arm, all the way to the shoulder, much bigger and stronger than the other prosthetics. It was obviously intended for a hardworking man with its heavy structure of brass, solid junctures, and thick wires. Just like the others, the machine seemed impossibly refined, polished and tidy, not an extra loop of wires or bolt anywhere.

"This is amazing," he whispered. He was stunned by the thought of having one of these works of art attached to his body permanently. And maybe a little intimidated, too.

When his eyes fell on a selection of mechanical hands, he was even more amazed. What a variety! There were so many different kinds it made his head spin. Silver ones, elegant and etched in classical motifs, fit for a lord or a nobleman. Delicate ones where every digit, and even the back of the hand, was covered with a thin ceramic plate painted with flowers and lace, like an expensive glove for a lady. Then there were very complex elaborate ones. Thomas marveled at the precision, a far cry from the hooks and pincers he'd seen elsewhere. Some were definitely too decorative for him—he really couldn't see himself with something that fancy—but they were astounding, nonetheless.

"So take a look. Think about it for a while. See if there's anything that strikes your fancy." Jethro was standing nearby, hands in his pockets, letting Thomas take his time inspecting the selection of hands.

Thomas turned around suddenly, finding that Jethro wasn't even looking at the prosthetics. He was staring straight at Thomas, his lips parted. He seemed almost . . . Was that a blush on his cheeks? No, surely it couldn't be. There was no reason . . .

"Everything all right?" Thomas asked.

Jethro's eyebrows jumped, and he quickly averted his eyes. "Yes. Yes, of course. It's just . . . You seem so . . . ." He fell silent, somewhat awkwardly, and yes, there was definitely a blush darkening his cheeks now. "Never mind. Keep looking."

So Thomas tried to stop acting like an awestruck child and focused on the technicalities. He needed something with more precision than strength, as that was essential for his work, so he should pick one of the smaller, more detailed ones. And he didn't want anything fancy; he needed it to be strictly functional, without any frills. It should be practical, easy to clean. And he wanted something as discreet as possible.

He was scratching his head, comparing two gleaming silver models, when he spotted one that immediately attracted his attention. It was almost hidden in a corner and seemed to be exactly what he needed. Understated, functional, nothing flashy. It was made of brushed brass and had a brown leather wrist cover. He shot Jethro a quick look, silently asking for permission to pick it up, and the inventor nodded. It wasn't shiny, but it was very detailed—a clean and simple, yet solid, mechanism, refined without any too-fragile parts that might wear out and break too quickly.

Out of the entire lot, except for the massive, heavy ones built for miners or woodcutters, it seemed the one most likely to function properly for the longest time. That was just fine by him. He didn't need it as an extravagant accessory to show off out on the town with some toffers or at a theater soiree; he needed to work with it every day. Of course, he supposed he would be able to do some repairs himself if need be. At least, he hoped so. The whole mechanism must have been hidden under the brass covering because, apart from some wires and connections, he couldn't see anything to indicate how the thing worked, or even how on earth it could be attached to his body. He would really like to open it and see for himself. He simply *had* to know.

He cradled it in his left hand, turning it over to examine the fingers, the palm, the knuckles . . . It seemed perfectly oiled and in order. The weight seemed right too. It felt *familiar* in his hand. He had a gut feeling that this was the one.

"That's a good choice," Jethro said, startling him. He'd been so caught up in his thoughts, he'd momentarily forgotten that he wasn't alone. "Practical, no-nonsense, just purely functional. It's got an extra set of joints in the palm, and as you can see, the brass is unpolished to guarantee a stronger grip. Full range of movement of all junctures, too. It will take some time to get used to the finer movements, but with some practice and time, you should be able to gain full functionality."

Thomas nodded, rubbing his thumb along the rough fingertips of the mechanical hand. Precisely what he needed to handle small screws and wires. "Yes . . . yes, that sounds good. How is it powered? Is there, I don't know, a key to wind it up or something?"

Jethro shook his head. "There's no need for anything of the sort. I told you, it will work on its own, just as your own hand did, with signals from your brain."

That answer might be enough for someone unskilled in mechanics, but for Thomas, it just increased his curiosity tenfold. Surely it had to require some kind of power source. He couldn't possibly imagine how it would work otherwise.

"I see," he said, even though he didn't. "And how are you going to attach it? I've never seen this kind of implant, and I don't understand . . . What kind of maintenance will it require? Maybe I could take a look inside, see how it works." Then he quickly added, "For purely practical purposes, you understand. I might need to do some maintenance work myself."

Jethro was once again blatantly evasive. "Um . . . maybe later. It's a very complex piece of machinery, you see. Opening it would require a long time to put it back together again. You'll have all the time to investigate once it's attached. Besides, don't worry, it won't give you any trouble."

"Right. Sure." Thomas tactfully avoided mentioning the rogue tea machine he'd so recently disarmed. He was more than a little disappointed, but, even if reluctantly, he understood Jethro's motives. Obviously he wouldn't want to share his secrets with strangers. Especially since this was the kind of stuff that could earn Jethro worldwide recognition. Jethro had nothing to worry about, though. Thomas would never dream of passing off someone else's inventions as his own, which Jethro obviously couldn't possibly know about him. Besides, Thomas was honest enough about his capabilities to know there would be no way he could copy something like that. He wouldn't even know where to start. Even if he opened it up bolt by bolt, most likely the only result would be that he would be unable to put it back together. Hell, he was a toymaker, not some sort of magician like Jethro appeared to be.

"So if everything's settled, I'll get the prosthetic ready for implantation. Meanwhile, I was actually planning to go down to the village today. The weekly market is in town, and I need to pick up some technical supplies I ordered. I trust you'll be able to take care of that for me?"

"Certainly. I can do that," Thomas replied.

Jethro nodded and bent to rummage under a desk. "Let me just send Frida to call a hansom cab. I'm afraid mine broke down a while ago, and I haven't quite gotten around to fixing it yet." He pulled out a small object made of copper. It was a pigeon, Thomas realized as the little mechanical bird flapped its wings in Jethro's hands, one of the clockwork messengers that were so common in Lunaris too. The sound of their metallic wings flapping and their shrill artificial call was a common sound as they crisscrossed around the streets.

"I suppose I should warn you of something, though," Jethro began. "The people of Montrale can be—how should I put this?—less than enthusiastic when it comes to strangers."

"Oh, I noticed that. As a matter of fact, I was greeted by a bit of an *unwelcoming* committee when I arrived at the station yesterday."

Jethro momentarily gave up trying to restrain the flapping pigeon and almost got a wing to the face for his distraction. "You did? What happened?"

Thomas shrugged, casually slipping his hand in his pocket. "Just a bunch of fellows in dark coats who didn't seem so happy to see me. But one fellow showed up and rescued me, sent me on my way to your house. He had a prosthetic arm . . . A guy named Herman."

"Ah, yes, Herman. Gave him that arm a few years ago after he lost his own to gangrene. A good man, and he's actually the one you'll have to look for at the market." Jethro nodded almost to himself as he tucked the pigeon under his elbow and tried to scribble on a scrap of paper at the same time. "What about the others? I'll bet Franz must have been among them, maybe even Darren."

"I, uh, wouldn't know. I think I heard the name Franz, but they didn't exactly introduce themselves. But I'll be damn sure to steer clear of them if I see them anywhere today," Thomas said.

"Ah, don't trouble yourself too much. They're just old grouches." Jethro finished scribbling. He rolled up one small piece of paper and placed it in the capsule attached to the mechanical pigeon's leg, then released it, and "Frida" flapped her wings enthusiastically, flew in a clumsy spiral around the large hourglass—for a moment Thomas was afraid she would fly right *through* it—and shot out one of the open skylights.

Completely ignoring her, Jethro was now scribbling furiously on another piece of paper. "Here's a list of the pieces and supplies I need. Go to Herman's stall. It's the one right below the clock tower. Believe me, you won't miss it. He's the only one selling this kind of stuff."

He muttered to himself as he kept writing, and Thomas took the chance to look at him, feeling a small smile creep unbidden onto his lips. It was strangely endearing to see the inventor like this, biting the end of his pen and distractedly mussing up his hair as he seemed to often do when he was thinking. "I'll be preparing the prosthetic for the implant while you're out. Grab a bite to eat, if you wish, and be back sometime after lunch, and we'll proceed with the operation."

Thomas froze then, distracted from his idle musings about the way Jethro's lips were parting around the nub of the pen, how his white teeth flashed as he nibbled on it. Something tightened inside his chest, his emotions suddenly torn between thrumming excitement and something else, something like fear sinking its long nails into his stomach. "Today? We're doing the operation today, already?"

Jethro looked at him intently, head cocked to the side. "Yes. There's no reason to delay, is there? We don't have much time. And you're in a hurry too, aren't you? Unless . . . unless there's a problem?"

Under Jethro's piercing eyes, Thomas felt too exposed and uncharacteristically nervous. He stammered an answer. "No. No, of course. No problem at all. I was just . . . surprised. I didn't think it would be ready so soon."

That was all, of course. It was what he wanted. The only thing he wanted, more than anything in the world. The reason he was here. It was . . . In a way, he was hoping he would have more time to prepare himself. Everything had happened so fast. He had more or less resigned himself to spending the rest of his life without a hand when that letter had come, then here he was, and now it was already happening. It had been a whirlwind. Maybe he needed a little more time to wrap his mind around it. Maybe the fresh air would help, he hoped.

Jethro stepped forward, placed his hand on Thomas's left arm, and squeezed gently. The warmth of his touch seeped through the worn fabric of Thomas's shirt. It was surprisingly soothing, calming his nerves instantly. He'd be damned if he understood why Jethro had such an effect on him, but he took a deep breath. He knew better than to turn down the comfort.

Jethro offered him a small smile, looking a little shy. "Don't worry, all right? I've done this kind of operation dozens of times. You have nothing to be concerned about."

Thomas cleared his throat. "I . . . Yes, of course. Thank you for, uh, sorting this out so quickly. I can't wait."

He smiled, hoping he looked and sounded way more confident than he felt.

# CHAPTER 5

The mechanical pigeon must have flown fast, as there was soon a hansom cab out front, the driver bellowing for their attention. Thomas walked out, straightening his clothes with his good hand, and hopped in, the list in his pocket, leaving Jethro to fiddle with the mechanical hand. Just a few more hours and it would be his. Thomas couldn't quite wrap his mind around that.

He sat looking out the window as the driver headed down the poorly kept road, jostling them this way and that. Thomas hadn't been able to observe the landscape when he'd arrived in the dark, and truth be told, he would feel a lot better if he couldn't see it now, either. The road, little more than a trail, wound down the mountain like an endless snake, and on more than one occasion, it coasted steep cliffs, nothing but a long, dark drop to the ground on their side. And the driver, goddamn him, was skimming so dangerously close to the edge that Thomas could see the stones and gravel sprayed up by the wheels as they disappeared down over the mountain toward the dark pine forest nestled all the way at the bottom.

That would be a long, long way down, and he wondered uneasily if he would plummet to his death before he even had the chance to receive the implant. He sure as heck felt a lot safer on the flat streets of Lunaris.

His legs were still a little shaky once they mercifully stopped by the station where Thomas had arrived the night before. Thomas thanked him, silently swearing that he'd rather walk all the way back up than entrust his survival to that driver again, and paid him with money from the pouch Jethro had given him. It held way more money than he'd ever had in his pocket.

The streets were bustling with villagers—men carrying piles of pots and pans on their heads; plump ladies holding trays laden with freshly baked pastries; a lone drunkard trying to climb a statue, bellowing about the end of times. It was obviously market day. Thomas remembered the beggar he'd seen the day before, keeping an eye out for the telltale plume of his hat. He puffed out his cheeks and looked up for the clock tower, a redbrick affair poking out from between the dark tiled roofs. He wove his way between the small houses of the village, with their black wooden beams crisscrossing over off-white plaster, packed close together like a herd of goats resting on a mountain.

It all seemed pretty normal for a small village. He was, however, a little surprised when he spotted a man sporting a prosthetic limb who wasn't Herman. He was a tall, skinny fellow dressed in colorful rags, and he had an entire mechanical leg from the thigh down, the articulation of the knee bending smoothly as he walked. Thomas tried not to stare, yet found himself craning his neck to follow the man until he disappeared around a corner. But before he had walked even ten feet more, he bumped into a stocky bald man who lugged around an absolutely massive artificial hand, large and heavy enough to work in the mines, he figured.

"Sorry, sir," he mumbled, and the man dismissed him with a grunt and carried on, waving him off with that impressive mechanical hand. After that came another, this time a man with a large enamel trumpet affixed to the side of his head where his ear should be.

By that point, Thomas was trying not to openly gape. It was incredible to see so many folks with prosthetics in such a small village. He had seldom seen any in the capital, with the exception of more banal ceramic and wooden artificial legs, or a hook replacing a hand every now and then. They must all be from Jethro's laboratory. And even though they reminded Thomas of his own impending operation, which he'd been doing his best to avoid thinking about too hard, seeing them was also comforting. All their prosthetics seemed to be working just fine.

He was so busy rubbernecking to watch the man with the artificial ear that Thomas walked right into the corner of a stall.

He choked back a curse when he banged his hip against it, causing a pile of colorful fabrics to tumble to the ground.

"Mind your step, young man, will you?" a woman's voice reprimanded.

Thomas started apologizing profusely. "I beg your pardon, madam, I didn't mean—"

His voice died in his throat. A plump old woman was waving her finger at him, blowing smoke in his face from the pipe in the corner of her mouth, but what had astonished him were her eyes. Or the contraption where her eyes were supposed to be, rather. A gleaming pair of silver binoculars were attached to her face, discreet wires curving around her ears and disappearing behind her nape. The filigreed optical devices were neatly nestled inside her eye sockets, two perfectly polished lenses pointing right at Thomas as she scolded him.

"What are you staring at?" she snapped, and Thomas flushed hard, bending to pick up the fallen fabrics as best he could with his one hand and only managing to make more of a mess in his flustered state. Was there any way, any way *at all*, that he could ask about her implant without sounding like a complete ass? Somehow he doubted it, but he couldn't tear his gaze away. In all his life he had never seen— hell, never *imagined*—anything of the like.

*Artificial eyes? Damn!*

If that was Jethro's work, the man must have been some sort of wizard.

"So? Are you daft, young man? Are you going to buy something or not?" she ground out, her voice rough and ruined like an old grumbling engine.

Thomas realized he was still holding a handful of now-crumpled fabrics and ribbons, and he dropped them back on the table.

"I, uh," he stammered, looking around. He figured he had to before she lost her patience and started hitting him with her pipe. Now if he could just stop thinking about her eyes for a moment.

"Uh, I would like . . . that one. Yes. That one is perfect." On a whim, he pointed at a length of pale-green ribbon made of some kind of lace. Yes, that was a good idea. Mina had said she'd like to have a ribbon for her hair, hadn't she? And he still had some of his own money somewhere in his pocket.

But the woman was now staring at his arm, his *other* arm, where his sleeve was carefully tucked around his stump. Her binoculars buzzed and whirred, the lenses shifting slightly. She must have been adjusting the focus.

He paid, tucked the ribbon in his pocket as he walked away, stepping on a woman's shoes and bumping into a boy carrying a basket of vegetables because he kept looking back to catch another glimpse of the woman's binoculars. If he'd had any doubts about Jethro's skills, they would all have been vanquished now. In fact, he was beginning to wonder if the man truly did have supernatural abilities. Why wasn't he living in the capital, making a fortune selling his prosthetics to the noblemen? Why wasn't he the star of the scientific community? They would worship him. *Or be terrified of him*, a little cynical voice added in his head. *Come on, Thomas. It's too much, isn't it?*

But he squashed it down, indulging himself in the elation that was swelling in his chest. This was nothing short of a miracle. Whoever had sent him that note had earned his eternal gratitude. An answer to all his prayers had just been dropped right in his lap. It seemed too good to be true.

His stomach clenched at that thought. Maybe the voice in his head was right and he should think about it a little more, consider that maybe something wasn't quite right here.

A dark shadow at the corner of his eye attracted his attention, his instincts honed by years spent living on the streets. He pretended to be very interested in a selection of cabbages on the nearest stall and glanced in the direction of the shadow. Yes, a man in a dark coat. He had a large gray mustache and was not so discreetly trying to hide behind a stall. He was looking in Thomas's direction.

*Oh, wonderful. One of the fellows from the station . . .*

Thomas dove into the bustling crowd, ducking his head and trying his best to go unnoticed. It didn't take him long to reach the clock tower, and then right there by the redbrick wall, he spotted Herman's stall. It was easy to recognize as Jethro had said. Among the handmade wooden toys, spiced sausages, and roasted chestnuts of other vendors, there it was, a long table laden with piles of mechanical scraps, crates of bolts, coils of wire, cogs, an assortment of clocks all ticking at precisely the same speed, and sheets of metal. It was as well stocked as the mechanical shops Thomas used to visit in the capital. In fact, maybe even better stocked than most of them.

What was a stall like that doing in such a small village? How many customers could he possibly have? There was nobody even there at the moment, not even the owner. Could he possibly only sell to Jethro?

"Fancy seeing you again, boy." Herman, muscular shoulders bulging under the fabric of his jacket, emerged from behind a tall pendulum clock. He stepped forward, carrying a bunch of bronze pipes that looked so heavy Thomas doubted he'd be able to carry it even strapped to his back, let alone in one hand as this man was doing. He was holding it like a simple loaf of bread.

The dwarf stopped before him, not even a drop of sweat on his shaved head, and dropped the pipes on the table. The thick wooden table shook under their weight.

"I . . ." If Thomas had learned anything from his recent meeting with the fabric seller, it was to try not to stare. Not too blatantly, at least. So he contented himself with stealing what were hopefully subtle glances at Herman's powerful mechanical arm while he fumbled with the list. "Jethro sent me. I have a few things I need to—"

"Hastings sent you? I thought he'd send you right back from where you'd come from," the dwarf interrupted, his black eyes widening in surprise. "I haven't seen him in such a long time, anyway, I was beginning to wonder if he'd died up there in that house."

He snatched the list from Thomas, and, with a flick of his mechanical hand, a small magnifying glass snapped out from the tip of his index finger. He held it to his eye, squinting to decipher Jethro's unreadable scrawling.

"Ah. Finally some good business. Was just about time," he muttered to himself. "How am I supposed to make ends meet if that grouch doesn't—" He stopped as if he suddenly remembered something. He looked up at Thomas, who was valiantly trying to keep his eyes away from the prosthetic arm.

"Hang on a second. I thought you were in town just to get a prosthetic. Are you working for Hastings?"

Thomas cast another quick glance behind him. Was that another man in a dark coat trying to keep an eye on Thomas from behind a meat seller's stall? "I . . . Yes. I guess I am. And thank you again for rescuing me the other night."

"Don't mention it. And working for Hastings . . . Fancy that. Didn't think there would be anyone who could stand being around him for more than an hour without trying to bash his skull in. He's become insufferable lately." Herman shook his head and dragged a wooden crate out from under the table, then started packing items into it, mumbling as he worked through the list. "Look, boy, I'm telling you this in confidence because I still like that lunatic: don't go around saying you work for him. It's better for you. Plenty of people might refuse to do business with you at all if they hear. He's not really someone you want to be associated with."

Thomas gaped at him. Surely Jethro must be popular in the village. After all, he was a famous inventor, and all the prosthetics Thomas'd seen around the market must have been made by him. All right, so maybe Jethro was a little odd, he'd give Herman that, but what inventor wasn't?

"Oh. I see. But why?" Thomas asked. "I mean, surely his work must be, well, respected and—"

"Oh, it was. Until a few years ago, at least. But after the rumors started, well . . ." Thomas kept quiet, waiting for Herman to carry on. "People talk, you see. Witchcraft and magic, dabbling with the dark arts—stuff that has no place when it comes to science and technology."

Thomas laughed. Oh, so *those* were the kind of rumors Herman'd meant. Typical village hogwash. And to think that, for a moment, he'd almost taken him seriously. "Oh, come on, now—"

"They speak of a devil," Herman interrupted Thomas to continue. "A charming devil who trades in human souls. He can grant you any wish, and your soul is the price. They say Jethro's soul is lost now, and that's why he suddenly started creating such incredible inventions."

Thomas smiled, a smile he knew was a bit condescending. A lot of people tended to have that reaction to science; however, considering how incredible Jethro's prosthetics were, he could see why they would jump to such a conclusion. "Sure. Thank you. I will bear it in mind. Keep my eyes open for witches and devils and whatnot."

Herman lifted his head from his work filling the crate, frowning. Thomas could have done a better job at hiding the mockery in his tone. "Suit yourself. But then don't say I never warned you."

Thomas had other things to worry about than the rumors about Jethro. He lowered his head, pretending to examine a coil of wire, looking to his left to see a third cloaked man emerging from an alley while Herman dragged out a second crate and started filling that, too. He was definitely going to need some help carrying all that stuff back up the mountain.

"I'm only missing one of the items on his list," Herman said. "I'll have to send someone to round it up from my warehouse. Hope you don't mind waiting for a while . . ."

*Well, actually it might be a problem*, Thomas thought, acutely aware of the dark cloaks moving steadily closer. He'd have to find somewhere to hide until Herman was done.

"Oh, and by the way, you should tell Hastings that some of his magical machines have been acting up lately," Herman grumbled. He raised his hand and carefully flexed the fingers. "My own, and other people's, too. The elbow gets stuck sometimes, can't bend it quite right. I tried to look into it, but I haven't got a clue how it works. Can't even figure out how to open it without doing damage. Ferdinand's leg doesn't bend at the knee anymore, either, and Martha's eyes sometimes don't focus, and Ludwig's jaw . . . Well, quite a bunch. You should tell him to come take a look."

"I thought people didn't want him around," Thomas muttered.

*Well, obviously not the ones who needed his help. Fancy that.*

Thomas was already thinking of how he could convince Jethro to take him along when Jethro visited the village to look at the prosthetics. It was Thomas's job, after all, and two pairs of eyes were better than one. Besides, maybe this would be his chance to understand a little more about how they worked.

Thomas looked around quite nervously, spotting the dark shadows in the long coats again. There were four now, and they seemed to be quickly moving closer. He swallowed and turned to Herman. "I'll make sure to tell him. But, um, about this stuff . . . How are we going to transport it? I mean . . ."

"Once I've wrangled up the last item, I could send for a hansom cab, and they can pick you up wherever. Unless you want to wait here . . . ?"

Thomas cast another glance behind him. Oh yes. They were definitely getting closer . . . He had a feeling he'd better get out of there quickly, unless he wanted to force Herman to have another screaming match on his behalf. If he could avoid that . . . "Uh, how about at the station." *Where the cabs are easily accessible.* "Say in an hour? Would that be enough time?"

"Yeah, should be enough. As for the payment—"

"Here. Take whatever you need." Thomas shoved the purse under the dwarf's nose and waited impatiently, looking around for an escape route, as Herman counted out his fee. There was an alley on his left that seemed clear. "Thank you so much, Herman. It was a pleasure seeing you again."

He was already hurrying away when Herman called after him. "Give Hastings my regards. And tell him about my arm!"

"Will do!" Thomas replied, then turned around and bolted for the alley as quickly as he could. Once he was out of sight, he broke into a run.

When he reckoned he was far enough—after running through the maze of alleys until he could no longer see the clock tower, that was—Thomas slowed down, his heart thumping in his chest. He stood still for a moment, all senses alert to pick up any sign of his pursuers, but he didn't hear a thing. Maybe he'd been wrong and was just too tense. Maybe they hadn't even been after him in the first place.

*Better to be safe than sorry . . .*

He started walking again, slowly. He'd have to orient himself and find his way back to the station by the time the hansom cab was set to pick him up. Then he would get back to Hastings's house, and then . . .

He would receive his implant.

*God.*

He ran a hand through his hair, trying to sort out the confused emotions fluttering in his chest. Part of him wanted to run all the way back to the laboratory and dive onto the operating table, eager to wake up with his new hand. After the marvels he'd seen at the market, that should be his first instinct. But there was still part of him that was wary. It really all had been very fast. He'd had to deal with a lot of changes since his life had turned completely upside down, and since he'd gotten that letter, everything had been a blur of activity.

A sharp, ticking sound attracted his attention. A metallic clicking, fast approaching on the cobblestones, and when he lowered his gaze, he saw— *Damn.* It was a spider with eight long, thin mechanical legs and a graceful rounded body made of what looked like finely painted ceramic, sporting a pattern of violets. Could that be one of Jethro's inventions too?

The spider seemed to be looking up at him—insofar as that thing could be said to be looking at anything—then slowly started tiptoeing toward a nearby alley. It paused, turned toward Thomas, then inched a few feet forward and stopped again.

*What the . . . ?*

He followed the spider until it stopped in front of a large, darkened shop window. A familiar gleam from inside attracted Thomas's gaze— polished metal. There were clockwork machines in there, small toys, moving slowly. He could see a butterfly hanging from the ceiling, slowly flapping its filigree wings, and what looked like a large copper caterpillar inching along a cupboard among small brass ballerinas.

Thomas shielded his eyes with his hand to take a better look, pleased and not a little surprised. So maybe Herman had customers other than Jethro, after all.

He wanted to take a look inside, but it seemed closed. He hesitated at the door. He still enjoyed being around other inventors, even though he couldn't help but feel kind of jealous and resentful. At the same time, being around them was somewhat comforting. It reminded him of when he was actually one of them, and made him feel closer to his old life again.

He tried the door, and it opened with a jingle of bells. "Hello? Is anyone there?"

Thomas stepped in. The shop was a little dark inside, but he could still glimpse the colorful tapestries—warm tones of red, purple, and orange—hanging from the walls. There were pillows scattered across the thick elaborate carpets, furniture painted in colors that must have been bright at some point in the past, but now everything was faded, coated in a thin layer of dust. The place looked almost uninhabited, yet it still had a homey feel to it somehow. The walls were covered in old, framed photographs, most of them portraying a handsome young man with sharp features and captivating slanted eyes. It was the complete opposite of Jethro's laboratory, impersonal and purely functional. Funny how a laboratory was really the best reflection of the inventor, of his attitude and temperament. Really, seeing the inside of someone's laboratory was, if you knew what you were looking at, like opening someone's skull and taking a stroll inside. You could understand everything about him. Everything that mattered, anyway.

As for Thomas's laboratory, it had been something between this and Jethro's, he guessed. A bit of a mess. Not very well decorated, but cozy in its own way. He hadn't had the means to afford a large space like Jethro's, either, never mind all the expensive equipment. Maybe he should have cleaned a little more often . . .

"Hello?" Thomas called again, almost ready to give up and leave. He blinked as his eyes got used to the half darkness, and that was when the movements on the wall attracted his attention. Thomas gasped. Dozens of mechanical spiders, all with those porcelain bodies decorated with colorful flowers, were peacefully weaving shimmering nets that seemed made of delicate silk threads.

"Do you like my spiders?" Thomas could hear the smile in the female voice, and when he turned around, he saw a woman standing at the back door with a shawl wrapped around her shoulders.

"Don't be afraid," she said. "I promise they don't bite."

# CHAPTER 6

Thomas perched on a stool, a cup of lavender tea growing cold by his elbow. He watched, fascinated, as the woman sitting across from him worked on the spider that had led him to the shop. Her hands moved swiftly, her instruments all exactly where she expected them to be, and she picked them up without hesitation. Her fingertips mapped the body and legs of the spider, measuring distances, checking the position of each screw and bolt. She knew that machine by heart, and her fingers moved like the legs of her spiders, precise and exact.

Thomas couldn't help but be amazed, because Dragana—that was her name—was blind.

She had olive skin and long black hair. A colorful scarf was tied around her head, and gold hoops shone in her earlobes. Her clothes matched the decor of the room in hues of red and purple. She wore a long, flowy skirt and a crochet shawl draped around her shoulders.

"You're awfully quiet there, Thomas. Have a problem with spiders?"

"What? No, n-not at all," he stuttered, distracted. He admired the spider's porcelain shell, upon which a lovely violet was painted, the petals following the curve of the toy's body. "It's just, well, it's quite amazing, the work you're doing. I mean, how you can build something like this when you're . . . um . . ."

"When I'm blind?"

Thomas blushed. "Well, yes. I mean—"

"Oh, do relax. You act like nobody's ever mentioned it before." Dragana chuckled, her hands never once stopping their quick work. "Everybody wonders that. Not many ask, to be honest. Most are too afraid to talk about it. I can practically hear them straining to ignore it."

Thomas looked down to where his sleeve was hiding his stump as he rested it on his legs. That sounded familiar. "Yes, I know what you mean."

"Well, to answer your question: it's really quite simple. My eyes might be blind, but my hands can see just fine." She opened a little drawer and, without missing a beat, pulled out a thin pair of pincers and delicately bent a piece of wire. "I suppose I do miss being able to see what I'm decorating. I can distinguish the pigments by their smells, but I can only imagine what the end result looks like. Everyone says they look nice, but then again, how am I supposed to know?"

"You shouldn't worry. They look absolutely fantastic," Thomas assured her. It was God's own truth. "You're an amazing artist. As well as an inventor, of course."

She stopped and raised her head to shoot him a warm smile. "Thank you. You're such a flatterer. A man after my own heart." She hesitated for a second but managed to hide it as she carefully asked, "So you said you're an inventor too?"

"Yes. I mostly build mechanical toys. I was working on some butterflies recently, but I never . . . Well, I never thought children would be very interested in spiders."

"Oh, I don't think they would, either. Neither would most people. These little fellows are just for me." Dragana laughed. "And why are you in town, if I may? Montrale isn't exactly famous in our line of work."

Thomas considered her question for a moment, remembering Herman's advice to hide his connection with Jethro. But the woman was an inventor too. Surely she, of all people, wouldn't be buying into that supernatural nonsense. "I'm actually working for Jethro. Jethro Hastings."

Dragana's hands stilled. It was just a moment, but he noticed. "Working for Hastings? I . . . I can't believe it." She was clearly trying to sound natural, but somehow he could hear that it was a loaded question. Maybe they were competitors? It would stand to reason in such a small village.

"Yes, I am. You people seem to have trouble believing that." He chuckled. "Do you know him well?"

Her expression turned a little darker. *Ah*. There was *definitely* something there. "I . . . used to. I haven't seen him in a long time. Except when I had the accident. Well, I didn't really *see* him, obviously, but he came to visit me when he heard. He wanted to implant one of his optical devices in me. Some kind of mechanical eyes."

"I know what you're talking about. A lady at the market has them." Thomas nodded. He hesitated a moment before asking, a little fearfully, "So what happened? Did the implant fail?"

She tilted her head, a strange smile on her lips. "You think like an inventor, toymaker. No, the implant didn't fail. I said no. I never had it put in."

Now it was Thomas's turn to be surprised. "You said no? But why?"

"Jethro didn't understand, either. You're like him, too much of a scientist." Dragana shrugged, getting back to her work. "I like machines. I've dedicated my life to them. But I draw the line at having a foreign piece of metal attached to my flesh. People are free to do as they please, of course, but I will never agree to something like that. And besides, I don't need it. It took some getting used to, but as you can see, I can work just fine. In fact, I might even focus better than I did before."

"Well, but . . ." Thomas couldn't quite wrap his mind around it. He understood what she was saying in theory, but it made no sense to him. "But if it could fix you, I don't see why you wouldn't."

For the first time since they'd started conversing, her voice turned sharp. "There is nothing about me that needs *fixing*. I am whole and perfectly fine as I am."

Thomas flushed. He didn't know what to say, and his gaze flashed down to his wrist. His silence obviously stretched too long, as her hands stopped and she tilted her head to the side. She was clearly very insightful too. Then she asked, something pointed in her tone, "So why exactly did you go to see Jethro?"

He instinctively covered his stump with his hand. He opened his mouth, then swallowed. "I . . ." *Oh, come on. It's not as if it's a secret.* "I came to ask him for one of his prosthetic hands. I had an accident. In my laboratory."

"Oh." She put down her instruments and sat back, adjusting the shawl around her shoulders. "Then we have more in common than I thought, toymaker. I did too."

He remained silent. Of course, he'd always known that laboratory accidents happened sometimes. It wasn't as though he thought he was the only one it had ever happened to. He just had never met anyone else who had experienced it. Though he'd never given it much thought.

Suddenly a hundred questions were crowding his mind. Why hadn't he ever thought of looking up another inventor in his situation? There was so much he wanted to know, and now that he could see how well Dragana was doing, how she was still working, he already felt reassured.

"Aren't you . . ." he blurted, the most pressing of all those questions pushing abruptly to the front. It was the one hurdle he couldn't seem to get over, and he was afraid not even getting a new hand would fix that. "Aren't you afraid? To keep working, I mean. What if there were another accident?"

Dragana shrugged. She was giving him her full attention now, her work forgotten on the table. "No, I'm not. Actually I'm going to close the shop soon, but it's only because I can't be bothered with playing saleswoman anymore . . . I'd rather focus on my spiders. I'm already blind, aren't I? What else should I be afraid of? I can still work, so . . ."

Thomas didn't reply, mulling her answer over. What else should *he* be afraid of?

"So, I suppose the question is: are *you* afraid to keep working?" Dragana asked carefully. "What are you afraid of? Losing your other hand? Of losing your leg, maybe, or your sight?"

He'd never really thought about it. The panicky, frantic feeling in his stomach as soon as he allowed himself to acknowledge the fear was enough to send his thoughts galloping in the opposite direction. Was he even afraid of anything in particular?

"I-I'm not sure," he replied dejectedly.

"Are you afraid of dying, maybe? But then again, every job carries that risk. Would it be safer to drive trains and risk a horrific accident? What about working in a mine? That's a lot more dangerous, I should think."

"I . . . Yes. You're right." Thomas racked his brain, trying to find an answer. Surely he should have one. So much paralyzing terror froze him in place, and he couldn't even pinpoint why? He should be able to explain, to understand. "I guess maybe I'm afraid of not being able to work anymore?"

*Why am I asking her? I should know, shouldn't I?*

Besides, would another accident really prevent him from working? If he lost his legs or his ability to walk, he would still be able to work. Hell, he had living proof before his very eyes that even if he lost his sight, he might still manage somehow, even though he had no clue how she did it. If that was what he was afraid of, did he really have any reason to be afraid at all?

He was almost glad Dragana couldn't see his face right then. Surely he was revealing way too much of his inner turmoil.

"And are you working, now?" she asked.

Thomas cringed. "Well, no, I'm not. But—"

"So your fear is already a reality. Is that correct?"

He clenched his jaw. Yes, it was. He'd like to think it was just a temporary thing since he was unable to do anything without his hand. But if he was honest with himself, he had to admit that even with a simple prosthetic he still would have been able to handle small repairs, even create small inventions. It would be harder, of course, but it could be done. So why was he making his own greatest fear into reality?

Dragana seemed to take his silence as an admission and picked her instruments back up, resuming her work. "The way I see it, you can get back to work knowing that whatever happens—whatever limb you might happen to lose—you could always still keep working, or you can never set foot into a laboratory again, thinking it will keep you safe, and then . . . Well what's the point then?"

Thomas mulled it over. He was afraid of not being able to work anymore, but he wasn't working anyway, so he might as well run the risk. At least he would be doing what he wanted. No, what he *needed* to be doing. Whatever other accident might happen in the laboratory, he would be able to deal with it.

And if he were to die, it would still be better than spending the rest of his life feeling like that.

"I suppose once Jethro gives me the new hand, I will get back to work then." Was he trying to convince her or himself? "Once everything is back to normal, I'll be just fine."

Dragana huffed. "It's not a magic fix, you know. No fancy prosthetic will make things get back to what they were."

Thomas just sat quietly, eyes down. Yes, he knew that. He knew there was no going back. But he'd been fine *before*. If only he could bring everything back to what it was like—a new laboratory, a new hand—then he could just pretend none of it had ever happened. And yet, what she was saying . . . There was part of him that had been saying it all along too. No matter how much he didn't want to hear it.

"Who you are now is fine. You think you need to go back to who you were to be happy, but that's not true." She reached across the worktable to pat him on the arm. "Just look at me. I did much better focusing on my present rather than obsessing over trying to get back to something that didn't exist anymore. And besides, with what I hear, I wouldn't trust having one of his prosthetics in me . . ."

*With what she . . . Oh.* Thomas realized he knew what she was talking about. "Don't tell me you believe the rumors, too?"

Dragana's lips curled in a small smile. One of her spiders climbed up her arm and perched on her shoulder. She paid it no notice. "Why wouldn't I? Because I'm a scientist? Believing in what I can sense and touch doesn't mean I can't believe that there might be something else out there. One doesn't necessarily preclude the other, you know."

He supposed she had a point. He *had* just recently spent some time conversing with a ghost, so there was indeed something beyond the realm of technology and science. But devils and magical deals? That was simply ridiculous.

"So what do you believe?" he asked. "Do you really think Jethro is dabbling with black magic, summoning devils to trade in human souls or whatnot?"

He hadn't quite been able to hide the sarcasm in his voice. Dragana didn't seem offended, though. She merely pursed her lips, thinking, as a spider settled into her hand. She absently patted it. "If only I could have spoken to him, maybe I would know. But he hasn't been the Jethro I knew in a long time. He wasn't always like this. He was such a lovely boy. Smiling and affectionate and, well, you would never say it if you looked at him now, would you?" Dragana sighed heavily. "The bottom line is, I truly don't know. I wouldn't be surprised to know he sold his soul, however. He was just never the same after Stefan died. Something broke inside him back then, and he turned into . . . into a stranger."

Thomas's ears perked up. Dragana must have really known him quite well, then. Stefan . . . Could he be a brother, maybe? Or perhaps a lover? Thomas hadn't even thought about Jethro's personal life until now. Maybe it was his chance to finally learn something about the man, to get a clearer idea of exactly who he was dealing with.

"Oh . . . I see," he said carefully, trying to sound casual. "So what happened exactly? With this Stefan."

Dragana clammed up instantly, her whole body stiffening. "Maybe that is something you should ask him," she said, even though Thomas suspected she knew perfectly well that he would never do such a thing. It would lead to nothing, anyway.

He didn't quite dare ask her more. Besides, it looked like she wasn't keen on continuing the conversation. And it was probably about time for him to get to the station. He glanced around in search of a clock, but the only one he could see was missing its hands altogether.

Dragana and Thomas parted amicably, with friendly good-byes, and Thomas promised he would come visit her again as soon as he could. He would make sure to do so before he left to return to the capital, once he'd fulfilled his deal with Jethro. Thomas genuinely liked her, and now that they had dropped that particular line of conversation, she was once again smiling kindly at him.

She nodded. "You do that, toymaker. It's nice to have some company. But remember I will be closing the shop soon. So don't wait too long."

He promised he wouldn't.

When he stepped outside, the pale, warm sunlight didn't do much to soothe the uneasy feeling that last part of the conversation had left in his chest. Surely he was just letting the villagers' superstitions influence him. He was a scientist, and he should think like one. Then again, he had a ribbon in his pocket he'd bought for a ghost who inhabited Jethro's garden, so . . . Nothing was quite impossible, it seemed.

He walked toward the station where the hansom cab Herman had said he'd call was hopefully already waiting for him, relieved to see no sign of any men in dark coats lurking in the shadows as he went. He couldn't help but think back to Jethro's odd behavior when it came to his inventions—how shifty he seemed, so concerned with preventing Thomas from examining them too closely.

*Oh, nonsense.*

In Jethro's place, he would probably do the very same thing. Besides, whatever Jethro was up to, it was really none of Thomas's business. It had nothing to do with him whatsoever.

# CHAPTER 7

The hansom cab driver helped him unload crate after crate of items, carrying them inside the main entrance of Jethro's house. She was a stout, muscular lady, barely reaching Thomas's chest, but she had a set of shoulders that would have been the envy of any miner. Thomas was incredibly grateful and more than a little amazed. Even if he'd had two hands, there was no way he would have been able to lift half that load, let alone all of it.

"Thank you, madam. So very much," he said, rummaging in his pockets to give her a tip.

She patted her perfectly coiffed curls, shooting him a bright smile of golden teeth. "Anytime, pumpkin," she replied, taking the tip, then climbed back up on her hansom and sped off.

He watched her go, then turned to stare at the crates waiting for him in the hall.

*Not a chance I can even push those to the laboratory alone.*

So Thomas went looking for Jethro and found the inventor right where he expected: in his laboratory. Jethro was delicately tweaking one of the wires emerging from the wrist of the mechanical hand Thomas had chosen. Everything was silent except for the hissing of the gleaming sand inside that large hourglass. Thomas glanced at it. For some reason, it kept captivating his attention. Maybe it was the strange, almost menacing way the sand glimmered, reminding him of bared teeth and predatory eyes. Maybe . . . He shook his head. He would have to ask about it.

Thomas cleared his throat.

"The, uh, the materials are here. If you would like to bring them in now . . ."

"Thank you. I'll take care of that later. I just need a few more minutes on the prosthetic, and then we can proceed." Jethro didn't even look up. "Everything all right at the market?"

Thomas snorted. "The fellows from the station tried to gang up on me again, but I was able to slink off. So no problems, really."

Jethro shook his head, never raising his gaze from his work. "That Franz doesn't know how to let things go. Don't take it personally, Thomas. He just has a thing against foreigners since Marina, this girl he used to fancy, ran off with a traveling salesman."

"I wonder why. He's such a charming man." Thomas rolled his eyes, and Jethro chuckled. He dragged a stool close and sat down, staring with trepidation at the prosthetic hand lying on the table. "So you know everyone around here, I suppose?"

"Mmm, pretty much. When you grow up somewhere, it's kind of unavoidable." He shrugged. "Isn't it the same where you come from?"

"Not really. Living in Lunaris, you're never alone. You meet hundreds of people every day, but most of them you never see again." Thomas rested his chin on his hand. "Even the ones you meet repeatedly—say, the lady at the jellied oysters stall or the girl selling lavender—one day they're just nowhere to be seen, and you will never know what happened to them. And then you want to ask about them, and that's when you realize you never even knew their names."

Something ached in his chest. He was used to it, he had been all his life, but that didn't make the feeling any more pleasant. "Must be nice to know everyone."

Jethro hummed softly. "I see. I never gave it much thought, really, but I guess you're right." He carefully placed a screwdriver aside and picked up a pair of miniature pliers. "But you have some family, don't you?"

Thomas shook his head, even though Jethro wasn't looking at him. "Nah. Had a grandmother, but she passed away when I was still a kid. I think I mentioned that I lived on the streets after that. At least, until I was able to open my own workshop." He sighed. "I suppose that's where I'll be living in the foreseeable future too, until I can convince someone to hire me or earn enough to open another one."

"Oh. I'm . . . I'm sorry to hear." Jethro shot him a quick glance. "That explains why you're in such a hurry to get this prosthetic, then."

"Yeah . . . My work is kind of all I have. I can't imagine myself doing anything else with my life. And the more I stay away from it, the more afraid I am that I might never . . ." Thomas trailed off. He wasn't sure Jethro would be interested in his sad musings. "But you understand what I mean, don't you? You've dedicated your life to your inventions too. I'm sure you can imagine what it would feel like if you couldn't do it anymore."

Jethro paused, turning to look at Thomas with an unreadable expression on his face. Something like sympathy, maybe, or . . . Was that a hint of fear? "I actually can't even imagine. I'm just glad I can help." Jethro reached out and placed his hand on Thomas's knee somewhat awkwardly, and as soon as he did, he froze. He quickly dropped his gaze and jerked his hand back, leaving nothing but a warm feeling on Thomas's leg.

He gaped at Jethro, taking in Jethro's suddenly shy, green eyes, the way he seemed to be trying to hide under the dark curls spilling over his forehead.

Thomas started to add something, then decided to change the topic instead. "So what about you? Any family in town?"

Jethro's lips tightened, and he shook his head. "No. I . . . used to. Something like that, at least. But now . . ." His brow furrowed, and Thomas could almost feel him shut down, biting off whatever he had been about to say. He turned around, resolutely bending his head over the prosthetic, and when he spoke, his voice was distant and dismissive. "Anyway, I haven't really had time to go down to the village in some time. I've been alone up here for, well, quite a while."

"Yeah, I've heard that. I met this inventor, Dragana, and she mentioned the two of you are friends." He caught himself just in time before saying *were*. "I think she'd like it if you stopped by to say hi. When you have time, of course."

Jethro visibly stiffened at the mention of her name. "I see," he said, his voice carefully flat.

It was clear he had no intention of commenting on the topic further, and for a moment, Thomas was tempted to insist. The conversation he'd had with Dragana was still ringing in his ears, and he was dying to ask more about their history, or even mention Stefan's name to see Jethro's reaction. But shortly he was going to be lying on a table while the inventor implanted the hand; it hardly seemed like the right time to piss the man off.

"By the way, Herman mentioned that he's having some trouble with his prosthetic. And some other people too, he said."

That captivated Jethro's attention at once. He abruptly stopped everything he was doing, narrowing his eyes. "What kind of trouble?"

Thomas straightened up on the stool, surprised. What was so odd about some malfunctions? It was bound to happen now and again. The prosthetics were machines after all.

"He said his elbow juncture was acting up. And some other guy's knee too, and . . . a lady's artificial eyes not focusing properly, and . . ." He rubbed his chin. "He mentioned some others too, and asked if you'd have the time to pop down to the village and check them out. But I told him that you're—"

Jethro's face darkened, and his eyes flashed with something like . . . Was that *anger*? Thomas must have been mistaken because, for a moment, he thought he saw such raw hatred flaring up in Jethro's eyes that he almost wanted to take a step back.

Whatever it was, Jethro recovered quickly. "You have no reason to worry. If this is causing you to have doubts, don't let it. Those were old prosthetics, you understand, still kind of experimental. Some of them have been out there for years. Yours is one of the latest models I developed, and I can assure you, it's not going to give you any problems whatsoever."

"Oh. Yeah, no. Sure. I understand." Thomas hadn't even thought about that. It stood to reason that old mechanisms would start malfunctioning after a while, especially if they weren't properly maintained. But then again, it also made sense Jethro would be concerned: the prosthetics were his inventions and his reputation depended on them. Surely he didn't want anything casting any shadows on his name right before this big event of his.

"At any rate, I don't want there to be any doubts about my prosthetics," Jethro continued. "I will head down to the village tomorrow and make sure to check them all and fix them as needed. You won't have a problem spending the day by yourself, right? I'll make sure you have everything you need." After a moment of hesitation,

Jethro reached out to timidly pat him on the shoulder. "You just have to stay in bed and rest. All right?"

"I . . . Sure. I mean, if *you're* sure." Thomas actually wasn't. Being left alone, right after the operation? The thought made him fairly nervous. But obviously Jethro was confident there wouldn't be any problems. After all, it wasn't as though it was the first implant he'd ever put in. And besides, Thomas was a big boy. He could take care of himself. He'd come to Jethro looking for a scientist, not for a nanny or a nurse.

"But I thought you'd be too busy preparing for your event," Thomas added warily. "I mean, you still haven't explained to me what I should be working on, and you said it's only nine days away."

"Yes. We'll need to discuss that." Jethro shook his head, putting down his instruments and rolling his shoulders. Thomas couldn't help but notice the way his muscles moved under the worn fabric of his shoulder, the line of his tanned throat when he tilted his head back to stretch. "These sources of yours . . . How much did they tell you about the event?"

It was Thomas's turn to lower his gaze, feeling his cheeks heat up. "Well, I . . . Nothing, really. Apart from that fact that it's going to happen, that is."

"I see. Well, soon that won't be a secret anymore. The first thing I will need you to do is finish writing and sending out the invitations." Jethro drummed his fingers on the table. "I have to focus on finishing the main piece I'll present at the soiree. That means you'll have to take care of smaller things—organizing the event itself and working on simpler pieces as soon as you have control of the hand. Time is tight, so we'll have to work hard. I trust that won't be a problem for you."

"Of course it won't," Thomas replied. He'd had his fair share of sleepless nights while trying to fulfill last-minute orders. "But if you haven't sent the invitations yet, why not just postpone, organize everything for a later date? That way you wouldn't have to rush."

Jethro stiffened, his hands stilling on the table. He opened his mouth to speak, then closed it again, taking a deep breath through his nose. "I can't. I already sent *some* of the invitations, and there will not be another occasion. If I want them to remember my name, it has to be now." He paused. "I need you to understand how important this is. It is the one chance I will get to make an impact on the scientific community, and I can't afford any mistakes."

His only chance? But why? He would have plenty of time to present his inventions . . . "I understand. After all, well, you won't be here after the event, right?"

Jethro's head snapped up, and he stared at Thomas with wide eyes, his whole body tensing in apparent alarm. "I . . . How do you know that?"

Thomas tilted his head to the side. What the hell was he missing in this conversation? "Well I supposed you would leave for a tour or something, to present your newest invention to the world."

"Oh. Oh. It . . . it's a possibility," Jethro said hesitantly, deflating right in front of Thomas's eyes. "But back to Herman and his malfunctioning prosthetic. Did he say anything else?"

Thomas sighed, deciding to let Jethro divert the conversation. He seemed so tense and jumpy now. Maybe Thomas could lift his spirits before the operation. He did want the inventor to be in top shape, after all. "Why, as a matter of fact, yes. He told me that I should watch my back because you're working with devil magic."

He gave a chuckle and waited for Jethro to do the same. But the laughter he'd expected didn't come. On the contrary, color drained from Jethro's face, his green eyes growing huge as he breathed in sharply.

"Hey, are you all right?" Thomas instinctively reached out to place his hand on Jethro's arm. The contact sent an unexpected tingling through his nerves—and an even more unexpected warmth to his groin—for the briefest moment before Jethro jumped up, moving away from him.

"I . . . We sh-should get on with the im-implant," he stuttered, gathering the prosthetic up with shaking hands while Thomas looked on, stunned.

"Look, Jethro, it was just a joke. I don't think they really believe that," he hurried to try to reassure him, even though it was quite clear to Thomas that people probably *did* believe it. But Jethro didn't even listen to him, turning his back and setting off toward the corner of the laboratory.

"I'll go set up the table for the operation. Remove your shirt, please, and come join me at the table as soon as you're ready."

Thomas fell silent, watching him walk away. Well so much for his attempt at lifting Jethro's spirits. He didn't think a silly joke would backfire so spectacularly. He still had so many questions—about the soiree, the prosthetics, Dragana—and Stefan's name was still practically burning on his tongue. Who was he? Could he have been part of that family Jethro used to have, or maybe . . .

He shook his head. Now wasn't the time to get distracted. Sure, Jethro was handsome, and just about the smartest man he'd ever met, but Thomas had been on his own for years, apart from some occasional encounters. Down in Lunaris, it wasn't too difficult to find other men who shared his inclinations and would be up for a night of fun. But in such a small village, he supposed it might not be as easy. And the last thing he needed was to get the wrong idea about Jethro and then get himself tossed out on the street, maybe into the hands of Franz and his fellows.

With a deep sigh, he stood up and unbuttoned his shirt. He should stop trying to nose around in Jethro's life and just focus on the prosthetic. That was what he'd come for.

He headed toward the table in a corner of the laboratory, where Jethro was fiddling with the leather fastenings attached to the table. He lay down and breathed deeply as Jethro strapped him in. Thomas was painfully aware of the wooden slab below him—his back, arms, chest, legs, and even his head all pressed hard against it now.

"Are you all right?" Jethro asked, pulling on the extra straps to immobilize his right arm. Thomas tried to move, doing his best to wrench himself free, but the straps held tight. Almost as tight as his stomach felt.

"That's . . . perfect," he rasped, his breath almost too shallow to speak. Panic was mounting in his chest, rising to his head like a frothing wave. He was pretty sure he was shaking. He'd been there before, secured to a wooden table and watching through blurred eyes as the chirurgeon picked up the knife after shoving a rag between his teeth. There had been searing pain, then, coming from the burns on his face and arm, and his hand. When the chirurgeon had lowered his knife, Thomas had started screaming, muffled cries as he bit into the cloth, every thought obliterated by the slicing, cutting, *horrifying* pain. It had been like nothing he'd ever felt before, and all he'd been able to think about was that he wanted to pass out.

Jethro seemed to feel his nervousness. "Don't worry, Thomas. This is going to be nothing like . . . you know." He put down the prosthetic and stepped closer for a moment, placing his hand on Thomas's forehead. Jethro must have seen this kind of reaction many times before. Having a limb chopped off wasn't something you forgot. "It's a work of precision, not the hacking of a chirurgeon."

Thomas tried to nod. "Of . . . of course. Go ahead." He managed to keep his voice steady, or at least he hoped so. His insides were twisting into sickening knots.

"Don't be afraid. You won't feel a thing. This is ether, and it will put you right out," Jethro said, showing Thomas a green glass bottle and a carefully folded cotton cloth. "When you wake up it will all seem like a distant dream."

"Is that necessary?" As scared as Thomas was, his curiosity was getting the best of him. He was a fellow scientist, after all. He'd never seen anyone attach a mechanical prosthetic such as Jethro's to a human being—he was fairly sure nobody had other than Jethro, of course—and the chance of seeing him at work was too good to pass. Although certainly it would be much better if Thomas wasn't the patient. "I would like to . . . I would like to see how you work. How you implant it."

Jethro turned cagey again. It was something about the way his eyes went shifty, darting to the sides, instead of looking straight at Thomas. "Listen, it will be better if you just let me do it this way. It will save us a lot of time, not to mention save you a lot of pain."

While that might be true, Thomas was ready to bet that, once again, Jethro just didn't want him to see his technique. That was disappointing. And fairly annoying, really. It was his arm; he had a right to know. But then again, strapped down as he was, unable to even turn his head, he wouldn't be able to see much anyway. And he was certainly not in the best position to pick an argument.

"Of course," he said. "Whatever you think is best. You're the boss."

He strained his eyes to look around while Jethro busied himself unrolling a leather case full of neatly lined up instruments. He couldn't grasp what they were exactly, but he could see them gleam under the bright gaslights, perfectly clean and polished, just like everything in Jethro's laboratory.

The hand he'd chosen was on the table beside him, an assortment of wires spreading from the wrist. Those would be inserted in his flesh, intricately connected to his muscles and nerves in ways he couldn't even fathom. As that picture floated in his head, the bile in his stomach threatened to climb up to his throat. He fought to keep it down, to calm his pounding heart. He had to think of it as the miracle it was. Soon he would have a brand-new hand. Working. Moving. It seemed impossible, and yet . . .

Jethro stepped toward him again, holding the cotton cloth that now gave off a strong chemical smell. Thomas's eyes began to sting and water. "It's all ready. Don't worry, Thomas. I have done this dozens of times. When you come back around, it will all be done, and you will have a new hand."

Thomas didn't trust himself to speak, so he tried to crank out a thankful smile while Jethro placed the cloth over his mouth and nose.

# CHAPTER 8

When he opened his eyes, Thomas was floating and his head was swimming. Where was he? He couldn't remember. He was lying on something soft—a bed?—and there was a strange taste in his mouth. His tongue felt swollen. His head was pounding, and a dull ache thrummed along his arm. That was a situation he was familiar with. It had been hurting for a long time. He squeezed his eyes shut, groaning. He tried to lift his arm but it felt *so* heavy. That was strange. As if there was a lump of metal—

His eyes flew open as a lightning bolt flashed through the confusion swirling in his brain. He jolted upright, wincing when the movement sent a stab of pain through his head.

There was a flurry of movement, and a mass of curly black hair floated into his line of sight. Thomas blinked, trying to focus, and he saw a man—Jethro, he remembered now, the inventor—groping for his spectacles, his eyes glassy. He was sitting by the bed. It took Thomas's slow brain a few seconds to piece together that he must have been sleeping, and Thomas's abrupt movement must have woken him.

"What . . ." he struggled to say. Talking was difficult, as if his tongue were literally tied, unable to move properly. He swayed, barely able to hold himself upright. "Jethro . . . I . . ."

"Shh. Everything is fine, Thomas. You're just confused because of the ether." Jethro turned to grab something from the nightstand. "Here, have some water. Then lie back down, all right?"

He put a hand behind Thomas's neck to support him, then held a glass to his lips. Thomas gratefully took a long sip of water. For a moment, all he could focus on was the feeling of the cool liquid seeping down his throat.

When Jethro took away the glass, Thomas closed his eyes for a second, trying to stop the room from spinning around him. "Hand?" he blurted.

Jethro smiled at him, that much he could tell, even though he was seeing double. "The operation went perfectly. Here, look." His hand still on Thomas's nape, he gently nudged him to look down.

Thomas obeyed, still confused, his vision blurring as he did. But as soon as his eyes could focus again, he saw it. There it was, beautiful leather and brushed brass, resting above the covers. His new hand.

He was expecting a rush of emotion, he was expecting to feel . . . He didn't even know. He couldn't think. *Good Lord, my hand*, he kept repeating to himself, as if that might somehow make it more real. A hand . . . his hand. His *hand*!

Should he try to move it? His whole body was prickling now, and he wasn't sure why. His heart rate was speeding up, the dizziness was worsening, too many thoughts and feelings rushing through him at once. He tried to straighten up, but he had no strength to do so, and Jethro's hand tightened on his nape.

"Hey. Take it easy," he murmured, gently guiding Thomas to lie back down. Thomas tried to resist, tried weakly to fight it. He wanted to look at his new hand again. He wanted to keep looking at it, marveling at it. He never wanted to stop. But the world wouldn't stop spinning . . .

"Sleep, Thomas. Everything is all right. Tomorrow, you'll have plenty of time to try it."

Thomas blinked, trying to focus on Jethro's face. His vision was even blurrier now, and he realized it was because there were tears in his eyes. Jethro was looking at him with such concern that, if Thomas had been able to gather the strength to move, he would have kissed him.

"You gave me a hand," he croaked, his voice breaking. He hoped Jethro would think it was just from the ether.

"I sure did," Jethro said, his lips curling up into a smile. "Now rest. We'll talk when you wake up. Your hand will still be there tomorrow . . . and every day, for the rest of your life."

Thomas was resting, his back against the pillows. His head was clear, now, even though he was weak and light-headed. But the room had stopped spinning, and bright daylight seeped in through the windows. It must have been around noon, maybe later. But Thomas had eyes for one thing only.

He was staring at the hand resting on the dark bedspread—somewhere between elated and cautious, as if it might jump up and bite him at any moment.

He'd been staring for a while. It was just incredible. He had no other word for it. He'd been looking at the fingers and the knuckles over and over again, examining every single small joint. He hadn't tried to move it, yet. He knew he should ask Jethro first. What if it needed more time to heal? What if he was supposed to keep it still for a certain amount of time and he ended up messing up Jethro's work by trying too early? A feeling of dread settled in his belly. What if it hadn't worked? He wasn't sure he would be able to take it if the operation had failed.

And yet, when he gently poked at the bandage hiding the spot where the prosthetic was connected to his wrist, he felt no pain whatsoever. He had no idea how that could be possible. He was expecting pain. A lot of pain. *Excruciating* pain. In fact, despite Jethro's words, he was expecting to be utterly incapacitated for days. God knew the recovery from the amputation had taken long enough. Still, nothing hurt. Jethro must truly have God-given abilities, or something. Thomas should probably recommend him for sainthood.

He took a deep breath. What was he supposed to do in order to make it move again? With his real hand, he would just have to think of moving his fingers and—

The mechanical fingers closed into a fist.

Thomas's heart jumped up into his throat, a rush of excitement coursing through him. He wanted to scream, to dance around the room, around the entire house. He swallowed the emotion that was beginning to clog his airway and tried again.

The fingers snapped open.

*Oh God. It's working! It's moving!*

He was laughing, now. He was smiling so wide he was afraid his face might split open. The surge of joy inside his chest was so powerful it might just burst out like radiant, brilliant light.

He raised the hand and tried one more time, almost drunk on happiness. He could barely restrain himself from jumping out of bed when his new hand once again obeyed his command as he wiggled the fingers. The movements were a little jerky, imprecise, but who the hell cared. He looked around, searching for something he could try to pick up. There was a glass on the nightstand beside a ceramic water jug, and he eagerly reached for it. His hand closed in a fist, shattering it, shards of glass and water raining all over the floor. He didn't even care. He would learn to control it perfectly, no matter how long it took. Right in that moment, he felt there was nothing he couldn't do, and the relief was so overwhelming he was almost choking on it, his eyes filling up with tears of gratitude.

Jethro walked in, carrying a tray with some bread and salted meat. "Oh. I see you're finally awake. I was beginning to wonder whether you'd be out all day. And . . . I see you're already practicing too."

Thomas shot him a smile, eyes watery, but tried to keep his emotions in check. He didn't want to break down crying in front of him, and he felt dangerously close. "I . . . Yes. It's . . . it's working," was all he could say, yet it sounded utterly amazing, like a revelation.

"Yes, it is. I told you it would. Or did you still have doubts?" Jethro was smiling at him, yet as fascinating as Jethro's smile and his satisfied, shining eyes were, and as inviting as the food on the tray seemed, Thomas couldn't quite tear his eyes away from his new hand.

"Who, me? Absolutely not," he said. He tried to grab the jug, which ended up shattering in his grip too. But even as he muttered an apology, he didn't feel sorry at all. He was fairly sure he didn't even look it. He could feel the smile pulling at his cheeks, and he doubted anyone had ever been so jubilant while apologizing.

Jethro took it in his stride, though. He pushed aside the shards with his foot and placed the tray on the bedside table. "I'll be going down to the village, then. You just rest and take care of yourself. No need to get out of bed today. There is food here and nothing you need to worry about. I'll bring you more water, though. Perhaps in a more solid container." He took Thomas's hand and inspected it closely, flexing it for him and examining every digit. "All in proper order. The implant is taking splendidly. Just . . . maybe use your other hand to have breakfast, yes?"

"Sure. Sure. Thank you, Jethro. Thank you so much," Thomas blurted. He would agree to anything the man said. Hell, he would probably sign his future firstborn over to Jethro if he but asked. Thomas felt yet another urge to grab Jethro and kiss him, elated as he was. It was probably best that he didn't, though, regardless of if Jethro would even welcome it, considering how clumsy Thomas had been so far with his hand. He might accidentally punch him in the face and break his nose instead.

"You go and do what you need to do," he said. "Don't worry about a thing. I'll be right here when you get back . . . and I won't destroy anything, I promise. Or, well, nothing important, at least?"

He grinned, and Jethro laughed—actually laughed. It really looked lovely on him. He patted Thomas's shoulder. "I can live with that. I'll see you later, then. Take care and get some sleep if you can."

And with that, he was gone, closing the door softly behind him. Thomas lay back on the pillows, feeling so content he could burst. He let his body rest, the tiredness in his bones and muscles almost pleasant. All he did was raise his arm and look at the hand. He turned it this way and that, admiring how the sunlight gleamed off the brass, creating a warm glow. It was absolutely flawless—five fingers, all the small joints in the proper place, including on the palm so he could make a fist. Every thin cable and minuscule screw was perfectly polished. He moved it again, tentatively flexing his thumb, then bending the other fingers.

Damn, it was nothing short of incredible. A week ago, before he received that note tipping him off to Jethro's existence, he'd never even imagined something like that might be possible. And now . . . He lowered the hand and delicately, somewhat timorously, placed it against his cheek, feeling the cool metal on his skin. He lowered it to his chest and was fairly sure he could even perceive the echo of his own beating heart through the metal, muffled and dull but unmistakably there. A knot of emotion lodged in Thomas's throat. The hand was cool and alien—it was a lump of metal, after all—and yet, it already felt like part of him.

Following Jethro's instructions, Thomas allowed himself a quiet afternoon, spending most of it in bed. He was a little bored after a while, but the mad rush to prepare everything for the soiree would have to wait until tomorrow, as eager as he was to really start living his life again. Eventually he decided to get up, slipped on some fresh clothes, and suddenly remembering the green ribbon, rummaged through the pockets of yesterday's trousers to retrieve the ribbon he'd purchased at the market.

He wobbled downstairs to the kitchen. He didn't really feel he could stomach meat at the moment, but maybe he would manage a little cheese. He destroyed the block of cheese squeezing it too hard with his right hand, then switched hands and ended up bending the knife and leaving a mark on the table where he chopped straight through the thin cutting board.

"Oh, bollocks," he muttered, mentally adding the cost of the damage to the already significant debt he owed Jethro. By the time he cut the last slice, his strokes were actually somewhat even, and he managed to stop before nicking the table again. He felt so proud he only wished he had someone to share it with. He'd have to tell Jethro as soon as he got back. It was a testament to the superior quality of his creation, too. He wasn't sure how quickly the village folks had learned how to properly control these things, and what degree of accuracy he could expect to reach, but he was pretty sure this was excellent progress.

Pale sunlight seeped in through the dusty kitchen windows, and Thomas unlocked the door that led to the garden, and dragged himself to the wrought iron bench where he'd had his conversation with Mina. He could hear the wind rushing outside, but it was warm and pleasant under the glass canopy. Even walking that small way had utterly drained him, so he gratefully stretched his legs as he munched on the cheese.

He realized that, out of habit, he was still keeping his right arm hanging limply by his side, but now there was a new, comforting weight resting on his leg. He lifted his brand-new mechanical hand, slowly opening and closing the fingers, admiring the way they moved.

He couldn't shake the feeling that he was being observed, and when he managed to tear his eyes away from the hand, he found Mina watching him from behind a tree, her head tilted curiously to the side.

"Hey," he mumbled, his mouth full. He swallowed the cheese and beckoned her to come closer, which she cautiously did, her eyes fixed on his hand.

Her voice sounded amazed when she asked, "Did Mr. Hastings make that?"

"Yes. Yes, he did." Thomas nodded, turning his hand this way and that to let her take a good look. "He put it in yesterday. This is why I came to see him."

"Yes. I know this is what he does. Hands and legs and . . . and other things too. Some time ago, there were a lot of people coming to get them," Mina said. There was something torn in her expression, something like a deep, burning craving. "It seems very nice."

"Yes, it does. Jethro is very good at what he does."

Mina hesitated, shuffling from one foot to the other. She was obviously trying not to stare, but her eyes kept darting to Thomas's hand. "I would like to have one too."

"Oh yeah? A hand?" Thomas munched on his bread.

"Yes. But more kind of like . . . a body, for me." She seemed to light up a bit with a shimmer of nervous hope.

*Oh, sweetheart . . .*

Thomas cringed inwardly. How was he going to explain just how impossible that would be?

"Darling . . . See, the thing is, it's a lot more complicated than a hand, you know?" He smiled as gently as he could. "I'm just not sure Jethro would know how to make something like that."

"Oh." She looked dejected. "But . . . maybe just not yet? Mr. Hastings is a good inventor. Maybe someday he'll build something like that?"

"Oh, yes. He is very good. I wouldn't put it past him." Thomas nodded along, his mind spinning, trying to find a kind way to divert the conversation. Luckily, he remembered he had just the thing. "I have something for you, by the way," he said excitedly. He rummaged in his pocket. "This is a present for you." He pulled out the lace ribbon, and warmth spread in his chest when Mina beamed at him.

"For me? Oh, Thomas, it's wonderful! Thank you so much!"

"You're most welcome." He smiled, very pleased and satisfied with himself. But his satisfaction only lasted until the moment he held it out for her and she tried to grab it. The ribbon fell right through her transparent hand and fluttered to the ground, landing gracefully on the grass. The disappointment in her eyes was almost too heartbreaking to bear, and Thomas wanted to dig a hole and bury himself in it. He wanted to smack himself with the mechanical hand so hopefully he would knock himself out and wake up having forgotten all about his idiocy. He really should have thought it through.

"Oh, I'm so sorry, Mina. I . . ." He scrabbled to pick it up, then remained there, the stupid ribbon hanging from his hand, Mina standing before him like a kicked puppy, eyes cast down, seeming even more miserable than before. This was certainly not the result he'd been hoping to achieve. In fact, it was the complete opposite. "I, uh . . . Maybe we could . . . I apologize. I didn't think. I just saw it and thought of you and hoped you would like it and . . ."

Mina pulled herself together and smiled, although a bit weakly. "Oh, no, I love it. It's so beautiful. Thank you, Thomas, really. Maybe . . . maybe when I have a body I can wear it. That would be really nice, wouldn't it?"

"Yes. Yes, it would be." Thomas's mind was spinning to find some way to fix it, even though he was mostly busy mentally kicking himself. Then an idea grabbed him. "You know what, in the meantime, maybe we could tie it to your favorite tree. So you can look at it whenever you like, and . . . and as soon as you have your body, then you can wear it properly. What do you think?"

She nodded, her smile growing a little more genuine. "Yes! That would be nice. It would look really lovely."

"All right. Let's go do it right now, then, yes?"

Thomas's legs were still unsteady and he was a bit light-headed, but he hobbled after her, following her to the oak tree and letting her choose a nice, low-hanging branch covered in crispy, brown leaves. He tied the ribbon around it with great care, even managing to make a nice, albeit slightly crooked, bow. Mina seemed satisfied, tilting her head to admire it and then, after thanking him one last time, she vanished. Thomas looked around and spotted her legs dangling up high in the tree.

He closed his eyes and thumped his head against the trunk. Man, he was such an idiot. He'd just made it worse, hadn't he? And talking to her about the body she wanted so much when he knew perfectly well it was never going to happen . . . He shouldn't have given her false hope like that. But he just hadn't known what to say.

As he walked slowly back into the house, shoulders hunched and his head hurting, Thomas racked his brain trying to come up with something else to entertain her. Suddenly it came to him. But of course! It was so simple. She was a young girl, ghost or no ghost, and he was a toymaker. And he had his new hand, now, so he could get to work and build her something nice. A little ballerina, maybe. Or a little animal, maybe a small bird, a clockwork toy she wouldn't need to touch, something that would run around and do things on its own. Something that could fly up with her and keep her company while she sat on her tree or on the glass canopy. . . Maybe they could even put the ribbon on it. A robin or a small owl, perhaps.

It would also give him a little fun project to work on, something to get the juices flowing again. A little training for his new hand, to get better control of it before he started touching Jethro's inventions. If he screwed anything up there, the man would surely have his head on a platter.

So it was settled. He would make something for her. He would start drawing a few sketches, poke around in the laboratory for some scrap metal to use, and maybe he'd be able to get started the next day. Yes, he should get to work right away. After all, it wasn't as though he felt nervous about it or anything of the like. There most definitely wasn't an anxious, panicky feeling tightening his gut at the thought of working in a laboratory again.

No, really.

# CHAPTER 9

O nce he got back to his room, Thomas fell into an uneasy sleep. Even such a short walk to the kitchen, garden, and back again had been enough to leave him completely drained. He had jumbled dreams of mechanical hands crawling all over him, devils dancing in the shadows of a burning laboratory, chasing after him. They wanted his hand. They wanted to take it away. They were banging on the tables, and the inventions were spinning out of control, clanking and slamming their metal arms together.

He emerged from his fitful sleep to find his whole body drenched in sweat. He rolled out of bed to grab the pewter mug Jethro had provided before he'd left, and took a long sip of water, his hand shaking. He didn't trust using his right hand just then. And besides, his wrist had grown sore. It was to be expected, he tried to reassure himself, putting the mug back down and wiping his damp forehead. Damn, his shirt was soaked through with his perspiration. His head was pulsing, the metallic banging noises still echoing in his ears, sending painful vibrations through his bones.

Thomas stopped, startled. The banging noises were not coming from his dreams. They were real, coming from somewhere downstairs. He groaned.

*Oh wonderful. Could it be the tea maker going crazy again?*

Was Jethro back already? He was supposed to be, wasn't he? Thomas had been sleeping so deeply he hadn't heard a thing. What if Jethro'd decided to spend the night at the village, and he came back to find his laboratory destroyed? What if he *had* come back and was trying to fend off the rogue machine on his own?

His legs were shaking, and his head was spinning, but he had to get to the lab. He made his way along the corridor, swaying, bare feet shuffling along the worn-out carpet. Something was wrong. The walls were bending around him, looking impossibly dark and distorted. He had to cling to the banister as he stumbled down the stairs, which seemed to keep moving, swimming under his feet. He was shivering too. His feet were freezing cold. His whole body, really, except for his head and his wrist. They were burning, and his stomach was roiling. He felt nauseated, and everything seemed muffled, as if he were floating in a sea of cotton, looking at the world through a thick bubble. Thomas squeezed his eyes shut, pausing to regain his balance at the bottom of the stairwell. He couldn't even tell whether he was awake or had simply closed his eyes and slipped right back into the dream.

The big hallway looked ghostly with the gray moonlight seeping in through the broken stained glass windows. Everything seemed too big, too silent, too . . . unreal as the clanging grew louder with every step he took. It sounded rhythmic, regular, more like a too-loud drumming on metal plates than a machine running amok, destroying everything in its wake. *Clang. Clang. Clang.*

He followed the noise to the laboratory, only to find it deserted just like the rest of the house. Thomas shook his head, trying to clear his mind, to make the world stop whirling. There was nothing moving there, merely the sand inside the hourglass, shimmering a cold silver in the darkness, steadily trickling down. He staggered to the middle of the room, instinctively holding his mechanical hand to his chest, the way he used to do with his stump. Even the metal felt hot.

He looked around the lab. Everything seemed in order—the prosthetics hanging in their proper places, the instruments lined up in wait. Even the tea machine was sitting peacefully in its corner, buzzing quietly as it spun a single cup around and around. He should just go back to bed. It was the middle of the night, he reminded himself, turning to look at the face of the—

The pendulum clock was gone. No, it wasn't gone; it was pushed away from the wall, revealing a gaping hole behind it. It took his muddled brain a few seconds too long to realize that the banging noise was coming from that direction.

He moved closer, too far gone to be stopped by the many reasons why he shouldn't. He was in pain. He was shaking, hard. His legs felt rubbery and unsteady, as if he were walking on jellied oysters. But he pushed on. As soon as he got close enough to peer inside the space, a line of gas lamps fluttered to life on the walls, their strange, bluish light casting cold shadows along a narrow, winding corridor and the frayed tapestries hanging on its walls.

Thomas stepped in. The banging noise was winding down, growing slower and slower. He walked along the corridor to a small wooden door at the end. Three heavy locks were lying on the stone floor, and the door was ajar. He pushed it open, and his breath caught in his throat.

It was another laboratory, much smaller and more crammed than the main lab. But what stunned him was what it contained. He rubbed at his eyes, incredulous. On a nearby worktable lay a pair of mechanical lungs made of thin leather, pipes, and miniature golden bolts. It was so precise and exact it didn't even seem man-made. Then there was a rib cage made of delicately curved brass tubes.

Thomas walked deeper into the room and pinpointed the source of the noise he'd heard, moving toward it, bracing his hand on a second worktable as the floor seemed to roll under his feet. It looked like a heart, hissing and wheezing, pumping colored liquid through glass pipes. The mechanical junctures were contracting and releasing rhythmically, mimicking a human heart, each beat causing a noise loud enough to echo through the entire house. It was impossible . . . It made his head hurt, made him want to press his hands to his ears to shut the noise out.

As soon as he got closer, the noise abruptly stopped. The heart kept beating, quietly now, nothing but soft hisses and jets of steam. As if it had just been waiting for him to arrive to stop sending out its call.

He watched in astonishment. He was sure he was dreaming now—a mad, impossible dream. Not even in his wildest fantasies would he have imagined something like that. It was so carefully built; it was beyond anything he'd ever seen in his life. It made his mechanical hand look like child's play.

How would you even go about implanting those mechanical organs into someone? Thomas's only experience in the medical field came from the pages of a manual of anatomical drawings he'd leafed through years before, impressed and more than a little disgusted by the gory, detailed images. But he guessed, in a way, it made sense.

The system of veins, nerves, muscles, and bones was like a machine—a living, breathing machine made of flesh. He figured *theoretically* it might be somehow replicated with technology, but just like with the prosthetics, integrating it with the human body was the trickiest part. How would you attach it, how would you make it . . . *alive*? He couldn't even begin to fathom it.

He turned his back to the heart, leaning against the table for support, his legs threatening to give out. He was covered in cold sweat, shivering and burning at once, as if feverish. He felt like keeling over.

When he opened his eyes, unable to sort his jumbled thoughts into anything coherent, he saw something even more shocking. His mouth dropped open. It was lying on an operating table, secured in place with leather straps. It was missing an arm. Its chest was ripped open, revealing empty holes where its organs—or something like that—were supposed to be. Cables emerged from inside its abdomen, then carefully coiled around the body. It was made of assembled pipes, plates, and cogs, but it was undoubtedly a person. No, not a person—an automaton. A whole, life-size, mechanical reproduction of a human body.

Thomas's eyes were wide as he stumbled closer to it. His heart pounded in his chest. It was impossible. Nobody had ever done such a thing. He wiped his shaky hand across his clammy face. He was torn. Part of him, the inventor part, was absolutely elated, enthusiastic, and wanted to spend the rest of the night examining that incredible creation. On the other hand, it seemed just *wrong*. It was too much. Inhuman. Nobody was supposed to have that kind of skill, that kind of power to grant life.

The automaton had legs, knees, shoulders, a neck, a head— And there Thomas almost took a step back, because its face was a beautiful mask of painted porcelain. It portrayed a handsome young man, and he actually looked familiar. Thomas could swear he had seen that face before. Those cheekbones, those slanted eyes, that nose . . . The image of a faded, black-and-white framed photograph flashed in his head, with the echo of clicking metallic spider legs.

All of a sudden, Herman's words echoed in his ears, about witchcraft and devils and black magic. And maybe it was just a fever dream, but it all seemed so real right then as he stood alone in that secret room, with the wheezing heart and the lungs and this . . . this *thing* that shouldn't exist. His rational brain was shot, and he was actually afraid. What if those painted eyes were to blink, what if those limbs were to move, what if that metal jaw were to open and the delicate pipes in the automaton's neck were to hiss and vibrate and produce a voice calling his name?

"Quite impressive, isn't it?" someone said behind him, and Thomas almost leaped out of his skin, frantically trying to come up with a way to justify himself to Jethro, even though that hadn't sounded like him at all.

Thomas whipped around, and now he was certain it must be a dream. Because there was the strangest fellow he had ever seen hanging upside down from the ceiling, legs hooked over the rafters. He was holding a ridiculously large green hat in place with one hand, its pink plume pointing straight down, and was peering at him with piercing eyes the color of seawater.

Thomas stared at the apparition, stunned, and didn't even mutter, *And who are you supposed to be?*, betrayed by his too-slow, too-muddled brain.

*This has to be a dream. It's the only explanation.*

The odd man hopped down in a jingling of silver bells, straightened his ragged clothes laden with medals and pendants, and secured his hat on his head, the pink plume swishing the air. As he did so, Thomas could clearly see the large tattoo of a black spider on his forearm.

"I know you," he blurted, even though he should know better. What was the point of talking to this dream, or hallucination, or whatever it might be? "You're the beggar from the station."

"Bull's-eye," the man commented, barely even looking at Thomas. Perfectly at ease, he sprawled on the nearest chair and propped his feet on the nearby table, knocking over a handful of tiny screwdrivers. Then he scratched his ear. "Though I'm afraid I might have misled you a little when I introduced myself back then. I'm Farfarello, devil from the Malebolge, in the eighth circle of Hell, at your service."

Thomas just gaped at him. *A devil?* This dream was taking a really strange turn.

The man stared at him peacefully, looking for all the world like the master of the house just waiting for a glass of liquor to chat the night away with a guest. "I was glad to see you decided to take my advice, Thomas."

"What advice?" he replied automatically, before his brain could even catch up and wonder how the man could possibly know his name. But then again, he figured there was no point in trying to find much logic in this.

"The letter. I mean, I was sure it was going to pique your interest, but I didn't expect you to rush here in such a hurry. Just fine by me, really. Time is tight as it is."

He couldn't possibly be talking about that anonymous note. But then again, what else could he be talking about? Thomas hugged himself, fighting back a shiver that ran through his whole body. He was cold. And so, so tired. His brain was struggling to keep up, as though he'd been handed a bunch of mechanical pieces that he couldn't quite fit together. His wrist was burning.

"What . . . what are you doing here?" He shook his head, trying to clear some of the confusion wrapping around his brain. Of all the things he should have been asking . . . He blamed the fever. This strange creature, crawling out of his dreams.

The beggar—the devil—*Farfarello* leaned forward to stare at him and, ignoring his question, went on: "Tell me, Thomas. Would you ever have made a deal with the devil, selling your soul to have your hand restored to you?"

Thomas was taken aback. What was he talking about? He rubbed at his eyes. This curious character, the strange light filling the room, this absurd conversation . . .

"Uh, of course not. That's nonsense. Even if this kind of thing existed—"

"You don't believe? You, the one who spends his time in the garden with a ghost?"

Thomas scoffed. Ghosts were one thing; those did exist, or had existed once upon a time, at any rate. But devils strolling among men, making deals, bargaining in souls? That was the stuff old priests used to frighten gullible villagers.

"I never cared much for fables of religion," Thomas said.

"Devils have been around much longer than religion and its *fables*, toymaker. And as a man of science, I expect you to be a little more open-minded when it comes to what might be at large in the world. You, of all people, should know that just because it hasn't been discovered yet doesn't mean it's not *there*." Farfarello tutted, a somewhat reproachful smile on his lips. "Regardless, you haven't answered my question. Indulge me, will you?"

Thomas shrugged, slightly intrigued by the man's comments, although he was determined not to show it. "In the off chance you're right and this kind of thing indeed exists, in case the priests were right and I did possess an immortal soul, it would be foolish indeed to trade it away."

Farfarello smiled. He actually seemed kind of proud, as if Thomas had given the right answer in some sort of test. "If everyone were as sensible as you, my dear Thomas, I would be out of a job. Anyway, this disposition of yours is precisely why I never came to pay you a visit and make such an offer. Luckily, however, not everyone is so sensible and rational when it comes to these matters."

Thomas wasn't sure what to make of that. He was struggling to pay attention to the surreal conversation, feverish as he was. Besides, dream or not, he was too intrigued by the machine on the table so, as much as he was trying to keep an eye on the weirdo sprawled on the chair, he kept glancing at the automaton.

*If only the apparition would just vanish . . .*

Farfarello waited patiently, a patronizing smile on his lips, like he was looking at an endearing puppy who was a bit too slow. "I see your attention lies elsewhere. What do you think about that thing over there, hmm? Quite impressive, isn't it?" He carelessly flipped up the floppy rim of his hat, which had been dangling in front of his forehead. "I bet you never imagined that Jethro's abilities might reach this far."

"I . . . uh, no, I didn't. I . . . It's quite . . ." Thomas was torn. Part of him wanted to say it was amazing, the other part leaned toward horrifying, and he was too confused to decide which was the right answer. If any of this was real at all.

Farfarello grinned. "Well, I'm afraid they don't. Even he isn't that good. Maybe he needed a little help. As he did with the prosthetics." Farfarello's eyes were gleaming, as captivating as gemstones. "You know how you can't open them to see what's inside? Why do you think that is?"

Thomas cleared his throat. "Oh, that's, well, because he doesn't want anyone to know how they work. Perfectly understandable."

"Oh, Thomas, come on. You are a scientist too. You know mechanics. You *know* this kind of machinery is impossible. Not this small, not this functional." Farfarello shook his head, pendants and trinkets jangling as he did so. "You didn't want to think about it too hard because it was the answer to all your prayers. Because it seemed too good to be true, and you thought if you looked too close, it might melt away right before your eyes. Isn't that right?"

Thomas lowered his eyes. This was kind of what he'd been trying to avoid thinking about. Not too hard, at least. He looked at his prosthetic, the hand that felt almost alight again right now where it was attached to his wrist. Yes, it was too good to be true. But it *was* true . . . It was there; it was functioning. So what if he didn't quite understand how it worked? He was just a toymaker. This was way out of his league. He was not so arrogant to think he possessed the height of knowledge in mechanics.

A proud little voice protested in the depths of his brain. *Come on, have some respect for your own abilities. You are good enough. You should understand more.*

He guessed he *should* at least be able to understand a little about it.

Farfarello looked triumphant, head tilted to the side and a cocky grin blossoming on his face, as if he'd won something. Like planting— or better yet, unearthing—that seed of doubt might have been exactly what he wanted. It was true the seed had been there all along. Thomas wasn't stupid. It was the source of that slightly uneasy feeling he'd been having all along but had chosen to ignore, to cover up and hide in the shadows. Well, Farfarello had brought it into the sunlight and was watering it, allowing it to grow, to spread roots in the crevices of Thomas's mind. All he'd needed was a little push, nothing more.

"Well, if it's too good to be true, Thomas, that's usually the case. You know that."

Thomas shuffled. Once again, couldn't prevent his eyes from darting to the humanoid shape lying on the table. "So what are you saying?"

Farfarello shrugged theatrically. "I'm just saying that maybe our Jethro is a little too ambitious for his own good. Maybe you should take a closer look at the things he's working on in that laboratory of his. Why don't you try to figure out what he's preparing for this big soiree, find out how your prosthetic works? After all, you do have the capability."

"He . . ." Thomas mumbled, then trailed off. There he was, trying to protect the man, and he didn't even know why. Was it really to defend Jethro or to defend his own comforting illusions? "He just doesn't want to say. He wants to keep it a secret. I could steal his ideas or some such. It's perfectly understandable," he insisted again, weaker this time.

"Oh, sure. That's a perfectly reasonable explanation. You keep telling yourself that." Farfarello stood up, straightened his tattered green coat, and then spread his palms in the air. "But then again, aren't you even a little curious?"

*Touché.* The man really knew how to tap into Thomas's weak spots. Though "curious" was kind of the understatement of the year, wasn't it? He was dying to know how it all worked. His hand, the other prosthetics, and that thing on the table. Real or otherwise, it was the most unbelievable thing he'd ever seen in his life, and he would *maybe* even give back the hand for a chance to open it up and see how it worked.

"The prosthetic is attached to you now and will be for the rest of your life. Doesn't it bother you at all to think that it might not actually be Jethro's genius? That it might be the devil's magic making it function?" Farfarello asked, looking with sudden interest at Thomas's mechanical hand.

Thomas thought he could see a red light flashing in the devil's eyes, and a stabbing pain coursed through his wrist, making him wince. Instinctively, he held it protectively to his chest.

"What if it suddenly *stopped*?" Farfarello continued. "You wouldn't even have a clue how to fix it. And neither would Jethro. How irresponsible of him, to deceive you about something so important. You had a right to know what was being attached to your body before you made that decision. Don't you think?"

"I . . . I don't . . ." Thomas's tongue felt swollen, unable to move properly to form the words, and he wasn't quick enough to move before Farfarello stepped close to flash him one of his cold, snakelike grins.

"I think you'd better have a look around, toymaker. And fast," he whispered, that hateful curl never leaving his lips. "We wouldn't want there to be any foul play here, not when you have one of his inventions attached to your own body, not when the sand in the hourglass is so close to running out and you have no idea what will happen to your precious hand when it does."

Thomas closed his eyes briefly, shaking his head. It was so hard to piece together the clouds of thoughts floating through his head, to grasp what the hell Farfarello was saying. "The hourglass?" He could see the dark, shimmering sand in his mind, gleaming like bared fangs as it trickled down. "What does that have to do with—"

"Less than ten days to the end of the deal, toymaker," Farfarello interrupted, taking off his hat and waving it in an old-fashioned salute. It was so ragged that the pink feather fell right off, fluttering lazily to the floor. "So you'd better hurry."

And with that the devil vanished, leaving behind nothing but a cloud of sulfur-smelling dust and the faint tinkling of silver bells.

Thomas remained standing where he was, stunned. He wasn't even sure he could have moved even if he'd wanted to. His hand and feet were freezing, and he was alone in the silent dream laboratory, mouth dry and throat on fire, head pounding. Searing pain now shot through his right wrist, making it almost hard to breathe. His head was spinning madly, as if caught in the waves of a storm, and he stumbled to catch himself on the edge of the table, his eyes shifting from the swirling chaos all around him to the only thing that was still clear, at the heart of it all: the amazing and terrifying invention that had sparked the whole conversation.

And just before the world toppled over and everything went dark, he could have sworn he'd seen those porcelain lips curl up in a mocking smile.

# CHAPTER 10

The sand inside the hourglass was rushing down now, cascading, roaring in Thomas's ears like a raging fire. He was on the floor and could feel the flames getting closer, *closer*, but his legs seemed made of stone. He couldn't move, couldn't breathe, caught in nightmarish clouds of smoke.

His stomach clenched as he raised his gaze. Mechanical hands were crawling all over the walls, on the ceiling, inching steadily toward him, and then suddenly they were spiders, thin-legged with blinding-white bodies, staring at him with porcelain eyes. He saw the face of that creature, the automaton, the monster he'd seen in his dream. It was sitting by the window, resting its chin on its mechanical hand, looking at him with something like sadness in its eyes.

"Time is running out, Thomas," it said in the devil's voice, and the laboratory was filled with the stench of fire and sulfur, bells clinking as the automaton's eyes turned a clear aqua green. "What are you going to do?"

Thomas tried to speak, but nothing came out except a strangled groan. He was soaked in sweat, and he turned his head to try to see his arm, his hand—his mechanical hand. Was it still there?

"Thomas! Good Lord, Thomas, are you all right?"

A voice was calling to him through the fire roaring in his ears. But that was wrong, there had been nobody there. No hands reaching for him as they were doing now. He blinked against the burning sunlight. Wait, sunlight? No, it was fire. He couldn't move, trapped under the debris as his laboratory was consumed by the flames, and his arm—

He was catapulted back into reality by excruciating pain coursing through his arm, as if somebody were chopping it off with a goddamn ax. Thomas was awake in an instant, eyes wide open and body screaming. He thrashed wildly against the arms holding him, but he was too weak, too uncoordinated, and whoever it was managed to pin him down easily.

"Good grief, you're burning up. Calm down, Thomas. For God's sake, it's me. It's Jethro. Calm down. Everything's all right, I promise." The concerned yet soothing voice somehow managed to pierce the pain roaring in his head, and Thomas blinked as the world swam into focus. Yes, it *was* Jethro, with his now-familiar black curls messed up as usual, his beard scruffy and those olive eyes gleaming with anxiety.

"Jethro," Thomas said, or he wanted to say, but he couldn't quite speak. His throat was so dry. He was so thirsty, burning up, his head still full of too-loud jingling. The stranger, the devil and his words, the secret workshop and that monstrous invention lying there . . . It all came rushing back to him, and he turned his head, sagging toward the floor, and heaved. A single, blade-sharp thought sliced through his jumbled brain. His hand. *His hand* . . . He couldn't feel it, and for a moment, he was overwhelmed by panic. It was gone, it was gone again.

*Oh God* . . .

Jethro held Thomas as he fought to stop his stomach from contorting, and as soon as he could keep it under control, Thomas was frantically craning his head to check his mechanical hand. It was still there, thank God. He could finally breathe again, the relief so strong it made his head spin, made him even more light-headed. It was short-lived, though, fading as soon as he tore his gaze away and saw the frown on Jethro's face, his darkened eyes behind his spectacles. He prodded the skin of Thomas's wrist, under the flap of leather that hid where the implant was attached to his arm, looking closely.

"Damn, something's wrong," Jethro muttered.

Thomas tried to move, shifting his hand in Jethro's grasp. It didn't respond properly: the fingers jerking abruptly, clenching and releasing. All he could see was that the skin was reddened, and—

"Argh!" he screamed as Jethro's fingertips touched a sensitive spot, and a flash of brutal pain scorched a trail through his body. He tried to yank his arm away, but Jethro pinned Thomas down with his knee, keeping him in place.

Jethro hissed, his lips tight, his face dark. "Goddamn it. What the hell is going on? I need to fix this. Now. Thomas, can you move? Can you hear me?"

But Thomas was sinking, his head spinning, his stomach churning. The aftershocks of the pain felt as if someone had kicked him in the gut. He wanted to throw up, and he was afraid that if he stood, he would. But he nodded anyway, so Jethro bodily pulled him into a seated position and put Thomas's good arm around his shoulders. Jethro might not have been a big man, but he was all solid muscle, much stronger than he looked.

"Don't be afraid, all right?" Jethro said. "I don't want you to worry about a thing. I can fix this. I *will* fix this. Understand?"

Thomas nodded weakly. He desperately wanted to trust him, but a combination of anxiety and sheer terror was clogging his throat so brutally he couldn't even speak. He remembered the flash of sea-green eyes and the stabbing pain in his wrist. He hadn't felt this awful in a long time, not since . . . *since* . . . He just wanted it to stop. But he did what he could to help Jethro heave him upright, and then squeezed his eyes shut when the world rolled so violently it made him nauseated. He leaned more heavily on Jethro's shoulders, against his body. The whole world was rollicking and tumbling around him, and Jethro was the only steady thing in all that chaos. Thomas clung to him.

As they walked slowly toward the stairwell, Jethro gently rubbed Thomas's elbow with his thumb, holding him tight to prevent him from falling and, maybe, a fraction tighter to offer a measure of comfort. His voice was a low, soothing murmur in Thomas's ear as he repeated, over and over again, "It will all be fine. Don't worry, Thomas. I will fix it, I promise. I will fix you."

The next thing Thomas knew, he was lying on the narrow wooden table in the laboratory, his shirt soaked with sweat. He was boiling hot one moment, ice-cold the next, and he groaned as he blinked against the piercing sunlight. Through the haze of mist swirling in his brain, he could see a man sitting beside him, his face half-hidden by welding goggles, a small bottle and a cloth in his hand.

When Thomas tried to move, he found he couldn't. His hand—his mechanical hand—was strapped down, and it sent a surge of panic through him. In an instant he was back lying on another table, out of his mind from the pain and the laudanum, leather straps preventing him from moving as he bit down on a piece of fabric, the chirurgeon hovering over him in a blood-spattered apron.

*"Don't worry, it will be quick, boy. I'll be done before you know it,"* he'd said as he lifted the bone saw.

It roared in his ears, the horrifying noise of the saw as it had hacked through his bones, and Thomas wanted to scream, to throw himself off the table and escape what he knew was coming. But the sheer terror froze him in place, his breath fast and shallow. Not again. *Not again.*

"No, please," he choked out, powerless tears collecting at the corners of his eyes. He was too frightened to be ashamed. Another image flashed in his mind's eye—the wicked smile of the man with the spider—and for a moment, Thomas saw him right there once again, standing over him, those goggles obscuring his face. "Farfarello? Is that you? What are . . . what are you doing?"

He hadn't begged the chirurgeon. Back then, he couldn't have spoken even if he'd wanted to. He'd just screamed and screamed and ground down on the cloth so hard he had thought his teeth would shatter. He'd fought against the straps, but there had been no escape, and this time he was too tired to do anything but wait for the blinding pain. *Any moment now . . .*

"What did you call me?" The man stopped, his hand in midair. He nearly dropped the bottle, hastily pushing his goggles up, and familiar, concerned green eyes meet his. Thomas recognized Jethro with a start, a sliver of reality slicing through the confusion in his head. "It's me, Jethro. Where . . . where did you hear that name?"

Thomas's thoughts were too jumbled for him to manage an answer. Tears trickled down the side of his face as he whispered, barely audible, "It . . . it hurts. Please . . ."

Jethro looked torn for an instant, and then he awkwardly leaned over to press his dry, warm hand to Thomas's forehead. "Shh. It's all right, no need to talk now. I'm so sorry. I shouldn't have left you alone so soon after the operation. I didn't think anything would happen. It never has before . . . I'm so sorry."

Thomas felt the knot in his stomach melt, all the tension drain from his muscles. He slumped, boneless, on the table, his breath finally slowing, except for a few lingering hiccups. That simple touch seemed enough to calm him, and Jethro must have felt it, because he lingered a few seconds longer, bringing his hand to rest on Thomas's damp hair.

"Try to rest now," he murmured. "I'll sedate you and strap you down, just as I did before, and I'll take care of this. You won't feel a thing, I promise you. You'll be just fine."

Thomas turned his head to look Jethro in the eye, and before he could think better of it, lifted his good hand to brush Jethro's cheek, catching him by surprise. Jethro stiffened, his eyes widening, and for a moment—a mad, feverish moment—Thomas thought him the most beautiful man he'd ever seen, even with the dark smudges under his tired, green eyes, with the smear of grease on his forehead where he must have brushed back his tousled hair. In the chaotic debris floating in the murky waters of Thomas's mind, something bobbed to the surface: how long had it been since anyone had touched Jethro so affectionately? How long since he'd been the one to touch or kiss someone?

After a painfully long, tense moment, Jethro relaxed under Thomas's touch, eyes closing, pressing his cheek to Thomas's hand. His breath escaped him in a hiccup, and in that instant he looked so raw and vulnerable with his forehead creased and his lips trembling that Thomas convinced himself nobody must have done it in years.

A few seconds later, Jethro slowly pulled back, even though it looked like it hurt to do so, and he swallowed heavily. He opened his eyes yet avoided Thomas's gaze, fiddling with the cloth in his hand. His voice was rough when he spoke. "Don't worry, Thomas. It will all be better when you wake up."

Thomas just did his best to nod and obediently closed his eyes, waiting for the pungent-smelling cloth to be placed on his mouth and nose. His chest was clear now, and he could breathe, the tangle of fear and anxiety soothed at least for a time, as if a cluster of stones had been dislodged from his stomach. And really, emptiness had never felt so good.

# CHAPTER 11

Thomas hesitated, standing by a desk in the laboratory, trying not to stare at the large hourglass in the middle of the workshop. The sand was still steadily swirling down, those black and silver grains dancing as he watched. He couldn't help but remember the words that strange devil had spoken in his dream. What was the hourglass actually counting down to? It certainly couldn't be counting down to the end of a devilish deal. He shook his head. *Such nonsense.*

Physically, he was feeling better. A couple of days had gone by, and whatever had been wrong with his hand was now fixed, but Jethro still wasn't willing to reveal any details about it. Thomas had tried to insist, maybe a little too much, but nothing. And try as he might, he couldn't stop thinking about that dream, or hallucination, or whatever it was. Even if it was just a product of his imagination, his subconscious was right. He should know what was attached to his body.

His thoughts were still a blur overall, as if it were wrapped in cotton, and the memories of that night were particularly tangled, but a few things stood out quite clearly. The room behind the clock. The automaton, with its painted porcelain face. And the weird devil, telling him those strange things. Not to mention that moment afterward with Jethro. He wondered sometimes whether that too had been nothing but a dream. The softness of Jethro's skin, the vulnerability in his eyes . . .

He had to start working on something before he went out of his goddamn mind. Thomas wasn't made to sit around and wallow.

The previous afternoon, he'd seen Mina hover outside the kitchen window, staring at the ribbon with sad eyes, trying to touch it as it fluttered in the wind. It had broken his heart a little. Jethro had given him the go-ahead to start working in the laboratory, telling him to feel free to use whatever he needed. So, that morning, Thomas had gotten up at the crack of dawn and poked around, locating pretty much everything he would need in a couple of boxes of scrap pieces—small leftovers of wire and brass sheets, bits of wire, some mismatched bolts and nuts. He definitely knew how to work with scraps. That was how he'd started back in the city, after all. It was somehow fitting that he should start again the same way. "Buckle up, Thomas," he murmured to himself. "It's just you and me. If you screw up, well, at least nobody will know." Better than making a fool out of himself in front of Jethro, anyway.

He spread out the parts, and started looking through them. And slowly, slowly, it began to take shape. His brain worked intuitively, figuring out how to combine them, how to modify them. *Attach this wire to that one, fold that little plaque, weld those two bits together . . .* His mind drew up diagrams on its own. It was an instinct he'd always had; he didn't even need to think about it. He could picture it now, a little mechanical horse. That piece could be the head, and that would make its legs move, and . . .

He opened his eyes and looked at the instruments lined up by his elbow. They were so familiar, they might as well be an extension of his own body. In a way, now he had a new instrument that was literally such a thing. All he had to do was learn how to use it as best he could. He gave a deep sigh and reached out with his mechanical hand, very carefully picking up a miniature leg.

"I didn't expect to find you up already."

Jethro's voice jolted him out of his work, and he lost control of the mechanical hand, snapping a little knee joint in two.

"Fuck!" Thomas shouted, dropping the pieces on the table, his heart pounding—maybe from the surprise, maybe from the sudden frustration roaring in his head. For a few moments, he'd forgotten everything, and there it was again, the reality of his inability to work as he used to. To his utter shame, he felt tears escape from the corner of his eyes.

"Oh God, I'm sorry. I didn't mean to startle you. Here, let me . . ." Jethro reached out to help him.

"No!" Thomas snapped. His hand shot out, gesturing for Jethro to stop. Then he collected himself as Jethro gave him a stunned look. "I mean . . . let me do it. I have to do it."

"I . . . Of course. Go ahead." Jethro immediately stepped back, waiting in respectful silence as Thomas collected the pieces he'd broken.

When Thomas finally lifted his gaze from his work again, he found Jethro observing him intently, seeming quite impressed . . . and surprised. To tell the truth, many people were when they saw him—a rugged, strong, tough-looking street guy—doing such careful intricate work, and on toys, of all things.

He was actually having quite a bit of trouble focusing on such a small scale with the mechanical hand, but when he saw that he'd gotten it right, that the little knee was folding exactly the way he'd wanted it to, his chest swelled with pride. Thomas tried to calm the nervous fluttering in his stomach. He hadn't done anything wrong earlier; it had just been a minor accident. He'd been caught by surprise, so focused on his work. And now, he realized, he had no idea what time it was.

There was sunlight coming in through the windows, and when he put down the toy and emerged from the workflow, he also realized he was starving. Still, he felt . . . good. Accomplished. For the first time in months, the crippling anxiety was gone, and he felt a little like himself again.

"So I trust the hand is working well?"

Thomas opened and closed his hand into a fist. "Yes, it is. I . . . I don't know how to thank you, Jethro. It's perfect."

Jethro seemed chuffed. He looked down, tucking his hands in his pockets, but he couldn't quite hide the pleased smile on his lips. "Well not quite perfect, really, but I'm glad to hear it."

Thomas rolled his eyes and smiled as he leaned back in his chair, stretching his back and shoulders. He wasn't used to bending over a worktable anymore, but it was such a pleasant ache. "Just take the compliment, will you?"

Jethro harrumphed, taking off his spectacles to polish them with the hem of his shirt. "Why don't you start working on the tea maker? Try to fix it. It will be a good project to begin with. After all, if you destroy it, I won't lose much sleep over it. Unless you need to finish this first?"

"No. No, it's fine. I'm ready," Thomas said. "This is just a little side project. I'll work on it in my spare time." *If I have any*, he silently added to himself.

"What is it, by the way?" Jethro craned his head to take a closer look.

"Oh, it's just a little toy horse. For Mina, you know," Thomas replied, standing up.

"For Mina?" Jethro tilted his head to the side. With everything that had happened, Thomas had completely forgotten to ask Jethro about her.

"Yes. It's just that she's bored. You know, not being able to touch anything, no company, just stuck there. I thought it might cheer her up a bit."

Jethro nodded. "No. Yes, sure. I . . . I just didn't know you'd met her."

"Yes, out in the garden. I met her on my first day here." Thomas rolled his shoulders, easing the ache in his muscles. "She's really quite a lovely girl. Who is she? I mean, where does she come from? Do you know anything?"

Jethro seemed to be caught by surprise once again, as if he'd never given it much thought before. "No, not really. She was already here when I arrived. She's been here a long time, I guess."

"And you never asked her anything?" It was Thomas's turn to be surprised. If he had a ghost living in his garden, he would surely be curious about it, at the very least.

"I . . . No, I was busy." Jethro lowered his eyes and shuffled his feet, actually looking a little embarrassed at how pathetic that excuse sounded.

"Well, since we're talking about it," Thomas said, leaping at the chance. He wasn't sure he would catch Jethro off-balance like this again anytime soon. "You know, she really likes my hand. And she's been talking about the possibility of maybe having a body built for her . . ."

Jethro seemed distracted, though, tormenting the hem of his waistcoat between his fingers. "Sure. Sure. There was something I've been meaning to ask you, actually. When you were feverish, at some point you . . . you called me a strange name. Do you remember that?"

Thomas froze. He certainly remembered how, in his delirium, he'd thought he'd seen Farfarello standing over him, but he didn't think it was necessary to share that particular absurd dream with Jethro. Carefully choosing his words, he mumbled, "I . . . I can't say I remember, but you should pay no mind to it, you know. I was pretty out of it."

"I see."

Jethro's gaze was on him, and Thomas did his best to keep his expression as impenetrable as possible. Jethro appeared to be doing the exact same thing. A dark current was sizzling between them, a silent game of wills, until eventually, somewhat reluctantly, Jethro backed down. "Well, feel free to get started, then. I'll be over there if you need anything."

With that, he went to sit at a table on the opposite side of the lab, resolutely turning his back to Thomas.

It took him the better part of the morning to repair the broken valve on the tea maker's cistern and go over every single wire and connection, trying to figure out if anything was out of place, anything at all that might explain why it had suddenly gone haywire. Of course, he had to try to figure out how it worked first, because even though Jethro sat hunched a few meters away, Thomas was determined not to ask for help if he could avoid it. He wanted to show Jethro he could hold his own.

Around midday, Jethro told him to take an hour off and grab something to eat, but Thomas wasn't really hungry. He just quickly nibbled on a piece of cheese and decided to get back to work. When he returned to the workshop, though, Jethro was nowhere to be seen. Maybe he was taking an hour off too. Thomas hadn't seen him upstairs, though.

He tried to immerse himself in work, but he couldn't focus. His eyes kept lifting from his desk to peer at the big pendulum clock. It seemed heavy and impossible to move, ticking away loudly and regularly as always. It was antique dark wood, with a slow bronze pendulum. There was nothing odd about it whatsoever. It looked entirely normal, not like some secret door to a hidden laboratory as it had been in his dream or hallucination, or whatever it had been. And still, Thomas was almost magnetically attracted to it.

With a sigh, he dropped the pliers on the desk and stood. He was never too keen on doubt and mysteries, so he might as well get it off his mind once and for all. He scanned the room, making sure Jethro wasn't on his way back in, and walked to the clock. He examined it with folded arms, craning his head to slowly inspect every inch of it. Nothing seemed out of the ordinary. No obvious hinges on the side, no poorly hidden keyhole, no suspicious marks where it rested against the wall. With another glance at the door, Thomas actually braced his shoulder against the clock, flexed his muscles, and pushed with all his strength. It didn't move an inch. He even tried to look behind it, checking for a fissure between the wood and the stones, but it seemed fused to the wall.

He dropped his gaze with a sigh. He was being a gullible fool, and he should just go back to his desk and forget about—

Thomas froze.

He knelt down, reaching out with suddenly trembling fingers to brush against what was trapped between the pendulum clock and the wall. It was soft under his touch and utterly, undeniably real.

A long, pink feather.

# CHAPTER 12

The pendulum clock slowly opened, and Jethro slunk out into the laboratory, looking around.

Thomas emerged from the shadows. "I was waiting for you." He'd been patiently standing in a corner for the past half an hour, tucked as far back as he could go to make sure Jethro wouldn't be able to see him should he look out a peephole.

Clearly Jethro had sent him out of the workshop for the lunch hour so he could sneak off undetected. And for once since Thomas had received that goddamn letter, he'd actually listened to his gut—something he should've been doing all along—and decided to confront Jethro.

Jethro froze in place, not even stuttering an excuse. Thomas stepped forward. "What is really going on here, Jethro? I think it's time you told me the truth."

Jethro quickly turned to push the clock back into place, but Thomas moved faster, stopping it easily with his mechanical hand. They looked each other in the face, Jethro's eyes wide and shocked, and Thomas . . . Thomas was just sick of it all and trying his damnedest not to let the anger, or the disappointment, get the better of him.

"No. Enough with the secrets. You're going to show me what's behind this door."

Part of him was saying that this was none of his business, that he'd barely known Jethro a handful of days, that he was his assistant, nothing more, but to hell with that. He had one of Jethro's prosthetics attached to his body, and that sure as hell made it *his* business. It was his fault for plunging into this headlong, without stopping to think, too desperate to believe in something that was obviously too good to be true, but if Jethro had been lying to him, Thomas was damn well going to get the truth. Now.

Jethro's hands were shaking. "There's . . . there's nothing there."

"Don't lie to me. I already *know* what's behind there. I *know*, Jethro," Thomas said, staring him right in the eye. "Yes. I know about the automaton."

Thomas could see right away he'd hit the target from the way the blood drained from Jethro's face. He opened and closed his mouth, unable to speak, and Thomas was filled with a mix of terror and perverse satisfaction. That meant it was true, it hadn't been a dream, and it made his stomach knot.

Eventually, Jethro's shoulders slumped. The panic was gone from his face, and it looked like the tension and exhaustion had finally caught up with him. Or maybe, he'd finally deemed Thomas worthy of the truth.

"How . . . how do you know that?" Jethro asked.

Well at least he was no longer trying to deny it. Thomas half expected to have to go through a long, frustrating exchange of fake excuses and lies. He was glad to be spared. It would just waste both their times and, maybe, cause his respect for Jethro to drop even more.

"Just like I knew about your prosthetics and about your big event. Your *friend* showed me," Thomas said with more bite than he meant to, feeling a twisted pang of satisfaction when Jethro flinched. It made him want to continue, as though he'd smelled blood and now felt compelled to go for the kill. No more half-truths. Time to get to the bottom of this. "Funny, how a devil can be more honest than you."

"You've met Farfarello?"

"Yes, I did. In fact, he seems to have lured me here. I'll be damned if I know why, but I'll find that out too." A stab of anger shot through Thomas's rib cage. So it *was* true. All of it. Who knows why the devil had been so determined to manipulate Thomas, but he'd fallen for it like a complete fool. "Now let me through."

Jethro hesitated, clenching his hands, but he finally moved aside and let Thomas stride through the door. He stomped along the corridor, barely glancing at the mechanical organs neatly lined on the tables as he entered the secret lab. Yes, it was the one from his dream, narrow and poorly lit. It even had the same discolored tapestries hanging from the walls.

He heard Jethro's quick footsteps behind him. "Wait, Thomas, just wait," he said, sounding kind of panicked.

There it was.

Thomas stopped, frozen in his tracks. Jethro stopped too, a few steps behind him, and from the corner of his eye, Thomas saw him lower his head. But his attention was captivated by the automaton, just like the first time he'd seen it. It was lying on the table, all gleaming brass and coiled wires, a lot more complete than the last time he'd seen it. Its chest was closed now, and its legs seemed finished. Only the head was still open, the metal flap spread like a strange, mechanical flower, revealing the intricate network inside—the wires, plates, and delicate, perfect connections. Despite everything, he was still as amazed as he had been the first time. And he was an inventor . . . Imagine how a crowd of amateurs, how the general public, would react upon laying their eyes on something like this.

They might be amazed and worship Jethro as a genius. Though, if he knew anything about people, it was just as likely that they would burn him at the stake and chase the automaton off with batons and spades. And judging from the devil's involvement, perhaps it might just be the right response.

It didn't feel right to yell in a place like this. When he spoke, his voice was barely more than a hiss, as if it could somehow disturb the sleep of the creature lying on the table. "What did you attach to my body, Jethro? Is it really working because . . . because of a goddamn devil? Is that how all your prosthetics work? What about your other inventions?"

Jethro's silence was damning, as big an admission of guilt as any verbal affirmation.

A small voice in his head seemed almost cruelly satisfied to hear it. *See, he isn't such an amazing inventor after all. No wonder you couldn't understand how they worked . . .*

Jethro had been cheating all along. But it didn't even matter now because the prosthetic was already part of Thomas. Fuck, it was literally attached to his body, a hunk of metal and wires and devilish magic. He felt dirty, like darkness was coursing through his veins, like he was an accomplice in something awful.

"Why didn't you tell me? It's part of my body now, for God's sake! Don't you think I had a right to know?"

He'd been betrayed. He'd trusted Jethro, and the man had implanted something in him that ran on black magic, and Thomas couldn't trust *that*. Technology he had no problem having as a part of him. In a way, it had always been part of him, even though not in such a literal way. But something supernatural? That was frightening. His first instinct was to snatch some instruments and rip the thing off his body.

Legs shaking, Thomas grabbed a stool and sat down heavily, trying to calm his pounding heart. His voice was rough when he spoke. "You have to tell them."

Jethro looked at him, perplexed. Thomas realized his thoughts had run ahead of the conversation. "All the folks down at the village. You have to tell them the truth. You've implanted these things in their bodies too. They deserve to know."

"And tell them what exactly?" Jethro was almost deathly pale. "Hello, did I happen to mention that the mechanical lung that's keeping you alive is the devil's work? How the hell am I supposed to tell them something like that?"

"From what I gather you've had *years* to come up with a way to explain. But you weren't planning on telling them ever, were you, Jethro?" Thomas gritted his teeth, trying to keep his anger from flaring out of control. "You must at least warn them of the risk they're running. What's going to happen when the deal is up? In a year, in five, in ten? Is the devil going to keep their—*our*—prosthetics running once you're in Hell, or will we all find ourselves with dead lumps of metal attached to our bodies?" Thomas was shaking. Damn it. He had allowed himself to *believe* in this miraculous fix for his problems, even though he'd known it had been too good to be true, and now everything had come crashing down again. He should never have deluded himself.

"No! No, they will keep working. I just won't be around to do maintenance, but—"

"And how do you know that?" Thomas snapped. "Your friend Farfarello told you that?"

"It's part of the deal!" Jethro was shaking. "It was part of the deal from the very beginning. He won't . . . he won't take that back."

Thomas snorted, barely stopping himself from slamming his mechanical hand on the table. God knew what damage he would have caused. "That's wonderful. A devil promised you, so we can all rest easy, right? How can you trust him?" He shook his head, trying to gather his scattered thoughts. "How can you trust one of his kind? And how do you know what this thing will do once it comes to life?" He gestured at the automaton. "I mean, it must be stronger than . . . Hell, I don't even know. What could we do to stop it if it decided to rebel against us, to harm someone? If the devil wanted to use it for, for . . ." He trailed off as he tried to come up with something appropriately nefarious.

Jethro cringed. "I . . . There would be nothing I could do." His voice dropped so low Thomas could barely hear it. "You're right. You should know about this. You should know *everything*. Because . . . because if something goes wrong . . ." He swallowed. "If something goes wrong, I . . . I won't be around to stop it."

Thomas's eyes went wide, and he turned to look at Jethro in disbelief. "What's that supposed to mean? You're just going to leave? This is your creature, Jethro, and your responsibility."

"I'm . . . I'm going . . ." Whatever it was, Jethro couldn't seem to say it. He took a deep sigh and slumped, running a hand through his hair. "I'll be dead."

Thomas's mouth fell open. "*Excuse me*? You'll be what? Why?"

"Dead," Jethro repeated. "Listen. It's the deal, you know?" He was wringing his hands, looking like an animal caught in a bear trap, watching the hunter come closer and knowing there was absolutely nothing he could do to save himself. Except in this case, Jethro had been the one to willingly shove his leg into the damn thing. "The devil gives me something, and I give something to the devil in exchange. That's how it works."

"Your life?" Thomas was trying to wrap his mind around it, but the shock was making it hard to think. How could Jethro have made such a stupid deal? How could he value his life so little?

Then Farfarello's voice came into his mind. *"Would you ever have made a deal with the devil, selling your soul to have your hand restored to you?"*

So that's why he had asked . . .

"You sold your soul?" Thomas asked quietly, the impossibility of it all overwhelming him. All his anger had suddenly drained from him, replaced by horror and fear.

"My life, my soul, same thing." Jethro walked to a stool near the table and flopped down onto it. He looked at the automaton, resting his hand on its metallic, lifeless arm. "So I won't be around to take care of things. Afterward."

Thomas swallowed. "How . . . how long do you have?"

Jethro's lips twisted into a bitter smile. "You know the hourglass?"

Thomas nodded, still a little stunned, his brain spinning too slowly to keep up with the flood of information. He vaguely remembered Farfarello mentioned something about the hourglass too.

"It marks the time to the end of the deal. And to the soiree . . . It will all happen that night. At the stroke of midnight. That's when the devil will come. The automaton will come to life, and that's when I— When Farfarello will take his due."

"This is madness!" Thomas got up and started pacing. "How do you know your automaton won't go berserk and murder everyone around it as soon as you drop dead? What the hell were you thinking?"

"I wasn't! Do you really need me to say it out loud? I bloody wasn't thinking at all!" Jethro finally snapped. "I was out of my mind with grief, and I just needed . . . I needed . . . something to live for. All I felt I had left was my work, to be a legend in death, if my life wasn't worth anything in the here and now."

"Grief? You're going to blame your *grief*? For fuck's sake," Thomas interrupted, being much harsher than he'd intended to be. "You were an arrogant fool who just wanted to build something nobody had ever done before, no matter the cost and no matter the fact that it isn't even your glory to take! So what, all your work is just pretense? The devil is actually doing it for you?"

"No. No! I'm the one who builds the machines, I make them functional. They can move, he just . . . Farfarello just . . . gives them life, and—" Jethro stopped, shaking his head. Thomas shuddered. Surely a devil shouldn't be able to have that kind of power. "Yes, you're right. I was an arrogant fool. What do you want me to do about it? I'll be paying with my life. Is that enough of a punishment?"

Thomas was shaking. With anger, with fear, with . . . Damn it. He wanted to hit Jethro, and at the same time wanted to hold him, to kiss him until he ran out of breath, and then longer. "And what about *my* punishment? You're leaving me to clean up your mess and deal with anything that might possibly go wrong. I never agreed to any of this. I never agreed to have the devil's work attached to my body. This is your deal. Why did you drag me into it?"

Jethro cringed. All the fight seemed to have drained out of him. "I . . . I know. God, Thomas, I'm so sorry. I . . ."

"And what were you planning to do with this thing? Let it run amok on its own, not telling anyone about it? Did you even *bother* to think about it?" Thomas's voice was rough, and it sounded like a shout in the suffocating room. "In fact, what if I hadn't confronted you? Were you even planning on telling me at all? Maybe the night of the soiree, right before you got dragged down to Hell, so you could leave me with a nice surprise?"

Jethro buried his face in his hands. "I was . . . I would have maybe told Dragana, or . . ."

"Oh, dear Lord. As if she doesn't have enough problems!" Thomas snarled. "What did you expect her to *possibly* do?"

Jethro remained silent. His shoulders were shaking. "I messed up, all right? I've messed up all these years, and apparently I keep making a mess of it. I can't even *die* right, for fuck's sake." His voice was broken, and still, Jethro sounded so angry. At himself. "So what now? What do you . . . what do you plan to do? Are you going to leave? Are you going to . . ."

Thomas was furious, and part of the reason was because he *couldn't* leave. He could never, even if he'd wanted to. "Leave? And make poor Dragana sort out this mess? You know I can't do that. I'm stuck here now. Thanks to you and the nice little trap you laid out for me."

Jethro flinched as if he'd been slapped. "I didn't mean—"

"Oh, I'm sure you didn't mean *any* of this. Maybe perhaps you should have thought about it more before making a deal with a fucking devil!" Without thinking himself, he grabbed Jethro's collar and yanked him closer. Sheer anger roared through his veins, and part of him wanted to hit him; the other part, a mad, irrational part, just wanted to— Jethro was so close, flushed, those green eyes impossibly captivating, his lips parted as he took ragged breaths. Thomas just wanted to—

With a bang and a crash, a brass gleam shot into the room, banging against the wall, then the roof, before landing in a tangled heap on the table. Thomas's head snapped to the side. He was so tense he very nearly jumped out of his skin. But it was just the goddamned mechanical pigeon, which was now screeching as loudly as possible.

"What now?" he groaned, letting Jethro go as the inventor staggered toward the table.

Jethro collected the confused-looking machine and unhooked the small capsule tied to its leg. He unrolled a strip of paper, and his face darkened as he read the message.

"What?" Thomas snapped.

Jethro swallowed. "It's from Herman. More prosthetics are failing. Luka, he has a . . . a set of lungs—mechanical lungs and rib cage. After he got silicosis working in the mines. He's having trouble breathing. Herman says he could be dying. Goddamn it . . ." He crumpled the note, and for a moment, he looked nothing short of furious. "That damn bastard. If he's sabotaging the prosthetics on purpose . . ."

Thomas felt the color drain from his cheeks. "You think he could be doing this intentionally? Farfarello?"

"I don't know. I don't know what to expect from him," Jethro said. The hand holding the note was shaking.

Thomas snorted. "Yeah, well. You should have known it would be ridiculous to put your trust in a devil."

That hit right on target. Jethro's face crumpled, the rest of his body tensing as if he'd just been punched. "I . . . I have to go. I have to save him."

"I'm coming with you," Thomas said, heading to the door.

Jethro hurried after him, seeming unsteady on his legs. "No, Thomas, that's really not necess—"

"I'm coming with you," Thomas interrupted. He'd never been more certain of anything in his entire life. "And that's final. Let's go."

# CHAPTER 13

They quickly shoved instruments and replacement parts into a pair of thick leather bags, and by the time they were done, the hansom cab was waiting for them.

They spent the ride in tense silence. Thomas's mind was spinning loudly enough as it was, deafening him with swirling thoughts and questions. Goddamn it. A deal with a devil? How was he supposed to wrap his mind around that? He could barely even look at his mechanical hand. It now seemed nothing short of terrifying, far from the miracle he'd thought it was. Part of him wanted to demand to have it taken off as soon as they got back.

But then he glanced up at Jethro's face. His lips were pressed in a thin line, his knuckles white where he was clenching the handle of one of the leather bags. Thomas wanted nothing more than to be angry with him for lying, for getting Thomas into this situation, but maybe he should have been angry at himself more than anything. He'd been a fool, wanting to believe in magic and miracles. He'd known better than that.

Not a word was spoken the entire ride, and eventually they arrived at the ramshackle pub deep in the bowels of the village where Herman was waiting for them.

"Come on in," he said, his face drawn, ushering them past the creaking entrance door. "Thank you for coming so quickly. Luka is over there."

A couple of tables had been pushed together in a corner, and a man was lying on them, wheezing loudly. Thomas winced. It was painful even to listen to those ragged breaths. They sounded more like the hissing of a faulty mechanism than actual breathing, like air leaking out of a pipe. Luka's thin face and hollow cheeks were frightfully pale, and his chest was exposed under his open coat. It seemed to be covered by some kind of metallic exoskeleton applied to his skin, or maybe replacing his skin altogether.

"There are a few other people here to see you," Herman added, keeping his voice low. "Some hands and legs malfunctioning again. Minor stuff. If you'd like, I can ask them to come back another time."

"No, that's fine," Jethro said, his eyes never leaving the figure lying on the tables. "Thomas, you take care of them, please."

Thomas's gaze snapped to him. He glanced at the small, colorful queue of people waiting. There were maybe a dozen of them, mostly men around his age. He could see mechanical legs and hands similar to his own, but they looked like earlier models. A couple of men sported mechanical eyes, and one had a large brass plaque replacing the most part of his skull.

"But Jethro," he said, carefully choosing his words, mindful of Herman's presence. "I have never . . . I might not *know* how to fix them."

"Don't worry. The last time I came here, right after your operation, the malfunctioning prosthetics were just clogged with dirt and grit." Jethro put down his leather bag and got rid of his jacket, then rolled up his shirtsleeves. "Chances are all they need is a good cleanup. If there's anything you don't know how to handle, just ask them to wait for me."

"Yeah . . . yeah, all right," Thomas replied.

Jethro acknowledged him with a nod, then strode to the corner where Luka was waiting, followed by Herman. As the two bent their heads to examine the man's chest, talking in hushed tones, Thomas looked around and picked an empty table where he could lay out his instruments, gesturing for the first man in line to come forward.

He started off inspecting the hand and wrist of a rusty-bearded man named Andrej, who seemed pretty nervous. From the way he kept doubtfully glancing to the side, it was obvious he would have preferred Jethro to check his prosthetic. As soon as he spotted Thomas's mechanical hand, however, he instantly relaxed. In fact, he even offered a small smile of camaraderie. After all, they were part of the same exclusive, albeit unfortunate, club.

"This looks like it's still functioning. It's not a mechanical problem," Thomas said, his spectacles perched on the tip of his nose, as he examined the juncture of the wrist, which was not moving properly. *No wonder*, he thought. It really was encrusted with dirt, oil, and God knew what else the guy had picked up on the street. No sign of any devilish foul play, as far as he could tell. Thank goodness.

"Andrej, is it?" Thomas asked. "You just need to be more careful about keeping it clean. I'll give you some solvent and some clean cloths. Do you think you can do that?"

"I'll do my best, sir. Gets kind of busy on the street, you know." The man's voice was rough. Thomas figured he was a veteran from the war—most of them probably were. Judging by the bulging shoulders under their jackets, most of them must be miners now. Almost all of them looked like they were leading pretty hard lives. Truth be told, Thomas felt quite at home; these were the kind of people he was used to hanging around.

"You're going to have to try," Thomas added. "Or it might break down for good. All right?"

Andrej shrugged. He glanced down at Thomas's mechanical hand, and smiled. "Yours is a nice one. New, is it?"

"I . . . Yeah. Just got it a few days ago." Right on cue, the hand jerked midmovement, and he dropped the screwdriver. "Damn. Sorry. I'm still getting used to it."

The man nodded wisely. "Takes some time, but it'll be fine, you'll see. Jethro's a damn good one."

"Er . . . sure." Thomas wanted to bite his tongue to make sure nothing unkind escaped him. He wondered how well these people knew Jethro and how they would react if they knew the truth. "If you don't mind me asking, uh . . ." He glanced to the side as he carefully scraped off a few more particles of grit. Jethro was bent over the table, completely focused as he slowly twisted a long, thin screwdriver. Thomas wasn't sure how much Jethro charged for his prosthetics, but they couldn't possibly be cheap. If he'd implanted all these people . . . Hell, he must have made a fortune.

Thomas lowered his voice. "How much does this cost?"

Andrej scratched at his rust-colored beard. "Don't know. Couldn't have afforded it for sure. We can't all earn a scientist's wage, you know?"

Thomas flushed hard. He realized how his words must have sounded. "Oh, I couldn't, either. I'm working for Jethro. To repay him."

"I see. Neither could I; neither could any of us, I'd wager." He gestured vaguely toward the others with their mismatched clothes and their shoes held together by strips of fabric. "But we didn't have to. Jethro just gave them to us."

Thomas's hands stilled, and he looked up, a little stunned. For some reason, he hadn't even entertained that thought. Sure, with his house close to falling apart and his kitchen stocked with nothing but stale bread, cheese, and salted meat, Jethro seemed to be perennially penniless, but he'd figured Jethro probably spent everything he was earning on equipment for his laboratory.

Andrej carried on, oblivious. "That was back then, you know, right after we came back from the war. Before he got too busy with his fancy inventions or whatever it is that he's been doing. We hardly ever see him anymore."

Not for the first time, Thomas wondered about who Jethro used to be. Dragana's words echoed in Thomas's mind, and he tried to imagine what he must have been like if all these men used to be his friends. Despite their faces, prematurely wrinkled and worn because of the hard lives they were leading, they seemed more or less the same age, and it was a small village. Hell, some of them looked even younger than Thomas. The blue-eyed man with the trumpets implanted on the sides of his head, for example, must have been just a boy when he'd headed off to the front. Maybe his eardrums had been shattered by an explosion, Thomas figured as he loosened some bolts and removed the dirt accumulated inside.

What had happened to Jethro to make him seclude himself in his empty mansion? Why had he even considered striking such a dreadful deal? Thomas couldn't help but think about that one comment Dragana had let slip, about this Stefan who'd died. Why had it affected Jethro so much?

Thomas shook his head. These musings wouldn't get him anywhere, and he needed to focus on his work. Fortunately, all the malfunctions seemed to be caused by lack of proper maintenance, and grease and dirt clogging the mechanisms. After he was done with the last veteran, cleaning up the miniature hinges that would allow the lens of a pair of artificial eyes to shift, he turned back to Luka's makeshift cot. The man was now sitting up, nodding and muttering something while Jethro prodded a corner of his metallic exoskeleton. Thomas was glad to hear that the wheezing sound was gone, replaced by the steady, regular hiss of a well-functioning air pump.

"So how did you do?" Herman said, appearing at Thomas's side carrying a chipped plate laden with dark bread and a strong-smelling piece of goat cheese.

Thomas gratefully accepted it. He'd been so busy and so concerned, he hadn't realized he was absolutely starving. "It looks like you didn't have anything to worry about. They all seem to be working fine. Just neglected is all."

Herman harrumphed. He seemed a little embarrassed. "I should have been able to fix 'em myself. Bit rusty, I'm afraid. Too long in the market, too little in the workshop, you know."

They were joined by Jethro then, whose frown had disappeared, his eyes nearly shimmering behind his spectacles. "Just a faulty valve in the mechanism, thank God," he said, his relief almost palpable. "I've replaced it with a new one, and he should be just fine."

"Thank you, Jethro. And as for the rest, I'll make sure everyone will be more careful with maintenance," Herman said. Thomas took the chance to shove half the goat cheese in his mouth. "I promise we won't waste any more of your time."

"No waste at all," Jethro said, firmly shaking Herman's hand. "But that's an excellent idea, Herman. After all, I won't be here to keep them clean for th—" Jethro's mouth snapped shut. Clearly he realized what he'd just said.

Herman tilted his head to the side, looking curiously at him. "Oh? Are you going somewhere?"

Jethro's eyes had grown wide behind his glasses. "Uh, no. I mean, yes, I . . . I . . ."

Thomas hurried to swallow the mouthful of cheese, nearly choking himself in the process. "Oh, you know, he's got this big event planned in five days or so. To officially present his prosthetics. Chances are, they'll whisk him away on a world tour or something afterward."

"About time, I'd say! A hotshot like you, what are you still doing in this shitty little town?" From the corner of his eye, Thomas could see Jethro nearly sag with relief when Herman laughed and patted him on the arm. "Now, how about joining us for a bite to eat, eh?"

Deaf to Jethro's protests, Herman all but shoved them to the table where the veterans were sitting, Luka among them, a big pot of steaming soup placed in the middle. Thomas didn't waste time digging in as the others laughed raucously and competed for who had the fanciest prosthetic, showing off how well they were working now, how shiny and polished. Luka loudly called for a toast, and a loud chorus of, "To Jethro!" followed as everyone joined in, clanking their tankards together.

Andrej found an out-of-tune accordion somewhere and started playing—or attempting to, at any rate—drawing more laughter from the group.

"You sound like a choir of skinned cats." Herman groaned. "Maybe you should let Jethro fix that too, eh?"

"Yeah, before I unscrew my ears," the man with the ear trumpets murmured.

The good humor filling the room was contagious, and, for a moment, Thomas was content to forget the goddamn devil and his cursed hourglass and just watch Jethro enjoy that brief moment of glory. He deserved it. And Thomas had a feeling this was worth much more than the cold accolades of the scientific community could ever be. Thomas had certainly never seen Jethro smile like that. Mugs of beer kept being shoved at him, hands slapped him on the shoulder, barely allowing him to take a sip without spilling it all over himself. He seemed to be trying to make himself small, quite clearly shy and unused to so much attention, but the little smile on his lips was so bright it warmed Thomas's heart.

He sighed. With what they had waiting for them, he was in no hurry to leave.

# CHAPTER 14

When they finally emerged from the pub, the sky was dark, a thin drizzle making the uneven cobblestones gleam, even though the rain was light enough to only make their clothes uncomfortably damp. They walked away slowly, shoulders slumped, Thomas carrying the two heavy leather bags in his mechanical hand, and once they were far enough for the chatter from inside the tavern to be nothing but a distant buzz, Jethro turned to look at Thomas.

"You . . . you didn't tell them?" Jethro asked, his voice low.

Thomas sighed. He'd be lying if he said he hadn't thought about it, but he shook his head. "No, I didn't. For one, it's not my place. If you ever decide to confess what you did, you have to be the one to do it. But mostly . . ." He paused, racking his brain to find the right words. "Well a deal's a deal, and if the prosthetics will really keep working, why frighten them for nothing?" He swallowed, tightening the fingers of his mechanical hand around the leather handles. "Maybe for them it can remain the miracle they think it is."

Jethro just nodded slowly. "I . . . Yes. Just . . . thank you."

Thomas was opening his mouth to reply when he stopped in his tracks. The street they were walking down seemed familiar. Somewhere around there should be Dragana's shop. If his memory served him right, it was just around a corner a few yards ahead. He thought about it for a moment. The day was already gone; they would barely manage to get any work done when they returned to the lab, especially after all the beer they'd ended up drinking. He might as well try to fit in one more quick visit. After all, he had promised Dragana.

"So Dragana's shop is nearby, isn't it?"

Jethro stiffened and didn't say a word. He merely started to walk faster.

"You should go see her. Look, I don't pretend to know what the history is between the two of you, but . . . but she seems to care," Thomas insisted, hurrying after Jethro. "Don't you think you should at least say good-bye to her? Hey, stop! You've been lying to everyone all along. Maybe this is your chance to tell the truth at least to one person."

"I . . . No, thanks. It's already late."

That reaction only encouraged Thomas to insist more strongly. "Exactly. What's a few more minutes? Look, she said she wanted to meet you before she closes the shop."

That was *definitely* a flash of fear he'd seen in Jethro's eyes. The inventor seemed stunned, and not in a good way. "What do you mean closing the shop? Did she say why?" He looked like he wanted to grab Thomas's lapels and shake the answer out of him.

"She didn't say. Just another reason we should go in. Then you could ask her yourself."

Jethro's eyes darted to the corner ahead of them. He fussed with his coat, clearing his throat. "I haven't seen her in . . . God. It's been years." He swallowed. "I . . . Fine. Fine, then. Let's go."

By the time they reached the door to the shop, Jethro was so visibly tense that Thomas was surprised not to see sparks sizzling all around his body. He was bristling, like a stray cat ready to bolt. When Jethro opened his mouth to speak, Thomas knew, he just *knew*, the man was about to come out with some half-baked excuse not to go in.

Before Jethro could utter a word, Thomas leaped ahead, reaching the door in two strides, yanked it open, and called out, "Dragana! You've got visitors!"

*Too late, mate.*

He tried to keep his face straight as he held the door open for Jethro, who stepped inside, dragging his feet. Thomas quickly shut the door behind them. Oh, he wasn't afraid to play dirty when necessary.

The shop was dark as usual, perfectly silent except for the quiet, regular clicking of the spiders' metallic legs, and Thomas was worried that nobody was there. A moment later, however, the beaded curtain leading to the back room shifted as Dragana stepped forward. "Yes, how may I—"

She stopped dead in her tracks, hand midair as she fixed a shawl around her shoulders, her golden earrings gleaming. She sniffed the air cautiously. Thomas wondered if she could even find their scent beneath the strong aroma of beer and stew.

"Good evening, Dragana. It's . . ." Thomas started, but she wasn't listening. She was turned toward them, her blind eyes staring directly at Jethro.

When she spoke, her tone and expression were unreadable. "It's you."

Jethro swallowed loudly and murmured, "Yes. I—"

She moved so fast that, for a second, Thomas thought she was going to attack Jethro. But she threw herself in his arms instead, holding on to him fiercely. After a brief hesitation, Jethro hugged her back just as tight, and Thomas, discreetly taking a few steps back, couldn't help but smile.

Thomas was sitting cross-legged among the pillows scattered on the carpet, watching as Dragana, perched on her stool, painted one of her spiders a warm plum color, carefully measuring the spider's body with her fingers before delicately dabbing at it with the brush. Jethro was standing by the wall, adjusting his spectacles on his nose as he peered closely at the spiders. He grabbed one, snatching it away from its web, and folded one of its legs this way and that.

"Fascinating," he murmured as the spider clicked its legs together in what Thomas thought sounded like annoyance.

"Jethro, would you stop bothering my spiders, please?" Dragana asked.

Looking sheepish, Jethro put the creature back and shuffled to the desk, awkwardly taking a seat on the stool in front of Dragana. He watched her paint for a moment, then cleared his throat. All the tension was back in his shoulders, and then some.

"You should really let me fix your eyes, you know."

Dragana sighed deeply. "Will you ever drop it? I don't know how to say no to you any more."

Jethro drummed his fingers on the desk. "I just don't understand why you keep resisting. You know my prosthetics work."

"Yeah, well," she muttered under her breath, "that's not what I hear lately. And I don't want anything like that attached to my body, since Heaven only knows how you're making them work. Though, from what people say, 'Heaven' might be the wrong word."

Jethro flushed, and Thomas had the sudden urge to go invisible. *Uh-oh.*

"I'm just saying," Jethro snapped, defensive, "I can fix you, and you're too stubborn to accept my help."

"I don't need to be *fixed*," she snapped right back. Then she sighed again and put down the paintbrush. They'd clearly had this discussion before, and they were both exasperated. "Listen, it's kind of you to offer your help, but you know what? My life is my own, and you should accept my decision and stop yapping about it. What's it to you? At the end of the day, what I do is none of your business. Why are you so obsessed with forcing your inventions on people, forcing them to accept help they didn't ask for and don't want?"

Jethro's cheeks looked like they were burning. "I'm not forcing anything on anyone! I'm just trying to make you understand that I can . . . I can help. I can fix you—"

"I said I don't *need* to be fixed! There is nothing broken about me."

Dragana's words fell like stones in the room, and Thomas felt like a couple might have hit him right in the face. He lowered his eyes, self-consciously brushing his mechanical hand. She was right. Of course she was. He could see it clear as day, and her conviction was the only proof he needed. And in some twisted way, unlike Jethro, who truly and deeply didn't get where she was coming from, Thomas understood. Maybe Jethro simply couldn't understand, through no fault of his own. He simply had never been through what they— Thomas and Dragana—had been forced to face and learn to deal with.

But a little voice whispered in his mind: *Then how come you can't believe the same thing about yourself?* Why was he so deeply convinced that he was broken? Even if he tried rationally to tell himself he wasn't, his gut just replied, *Nonsense, of course you are.* His fear and his shame would scream at him, telling him how irreparably shattered and messed up he was, and being fixed, finding someone who could fix him, was the only thing that could make it any better.

So the voice continued, and it sounded suspiciously similar to a devil's voice whispering in his ear. *You've come all the way here to get the great Jethro Hastings to fix you, and he has given you a brand-new hand. You don't have any more excuses now; you are fixed, as you wanted. Was it enough? Did it work? Do you feel whole now? Did it magically fix all your problems, erase your fears, the terror, the shame? Was it the miraculous solution you were looking for?*

Thomas's heart began to race. No, it wasn't. It had been a nice illusion to think it would be; he'd clung to it so desperately. *If only I get this fixed*, he'd kept repeating to himself, refusing to think any more about it, refusing to investigate his thoughts any further, to delve deep in the shadows where the truth lay. *If only I get this fixed, then everything will be all right. Everything will be back to what it was. It will be as if nothing ever happened. I will be fine.*

It had been such a comforting illusion, and now . . .

Damn. The tension between Jethro and Dragana was sizzling through the entire shop, and Thomas really felt as though he shouldn't be there.

"You're unbelievable. You've been gone for years, and now you show up and want to tell me how I should live my life." Dragana paused, looking like a predator readying herself for an attack. "And what about Stefan? Did you even bother to visit him at all?"

Jethro jumped up from the stool, nearly knocking it down. Thomas's breath caught in his throat, and he wished he could melt into the tapestry. "I'm not going to have this conversation now."

"Like hell you aren't. Feel free to ignore me if you'd like, but at the very least you should honor his memory."

"I do." Jethro went to rest his fingers on one of the framed pictures, a mechanical spider dangling placidly from a corner. He frowned as he looked intently at the faded photograph. Just like the others, it must have been there for a while, and for some reason, Dragana had chosen not to take it down even though she obviously couldn't see it any longer.

Thomas paused, staring. The photo portrayed the same handsome young man as the others, with wavy hair and slanted eyes, and that thin, hooked nose and strong chin. In the black-and-white photograph, his pale skin looked like a porcelain—

Thomas's breath caught, suddenly remembering the face of the automaton. That's why it had seemed so familiar . . . It was the face of *this* man.

*Oh God.* Whoever this Stefan was, Jethro was honoring his memory all right. In his own twisted way, maybe, but . . .

"And how do you do that, Jethro? You can't even find a moment to go place some flowers on the tomb of the man you used to call a brother?" Dragana bit, and Jethro flinched. Thomas breathed in sharply through his nose. A . . . a brother? So that was what Jethro had meant when he said he used to have a family.

"Listen, the way I mourn him . . . It's none of your business, all right?" Jethro's voice was strained.

"Fine. Suit yourself." Dragana threw down her paintbrush, smearing plum paint all over her desk. When Thomas looked at her, he saw she was nearly shaking with anger. But she pulled herself together quickly, wrapping the shawl more tightly around her shoulders. "Anyway, it doesn't matter. I'm going to close the shop soon, so you don't have to concern yourself with me or anything to do with me anymore. Not that you care."

Jethro turned away from the picture, and his face grew dark. "So it's true. Dragana, you can't be serious. You can't close the shop."

"Why not? It's mine. I can do what I please."

"But . . . but you can't! How are you going to support yourself then?" Jethro was nearly pleading, and he sounded almost frightened.

Thomas was surprised. For once, Jethro didn't sound like the detached and indifferent Jethro he'd come to know. He truly cared about this shop, but why? Thomas wanted to know more. He watched, fascinated, as the two kept talking, as though they'd forgotten he was in the room, which was just fine by him because he had no place here. In fact, he considered—for about a second—going outside and minding his own business. But he decided not to move. He didn't want to distract them and interrupt anything. But mostly, he had to admit, he really wanted to hear their conversation.

"Is that really why it bothers you so much?" Dragana's voice was biting. There was a moment of silence where Jethro looked pained, torn.

He took a deep breath. "Because I . . . Because this place is . . . Look, Dragana, you just *can't* close it."

At that, she very nearly snarled. "Why? You haven't been here in years. Hell, I was beginning to wonder if you were dead. And now, all of a sudden, you show up and you have the gall to tell me what to do with my shop, with my home, with my life?"

Jethro seemed to shrink under the weight of her fury. Yet, he managed to murmur, "It's . . . it's *my* home too."

Thomas's throat went dry.

"You sure don't act like it," Dragana said. "I'm not going to keep it open just so you can hang on to your childhood memories. My purpose in life is not to be a nice, comforting memory so you can feel all warm and fuzzy inside." She folded her arms and raised her chin, defiant. "You want the shop, you take it if it's so important to you."

Silence.

Dragana's smile was sour. "I knew it. So is there anything else?"

Jethro fingered the hem of his jacket, but didn't look away from her. "How . . . how are you going to support yourself once the shop is closed? At least let me give you some money to . . ."

"No, thank you. I really don't need your money," she said, shooting him down without hesitation. "I don't need anything from you."

Jethro flinched at her words, looking hurt and ashamed. "I'm . . . sorry. I know you're angry at me, and you have every right to be, but—"

"You *know*? Really? Somehow I doubt it, considering the nerve you have showing up here like nothing happened," Dragana snapped. "When Stefan died, I lost *two* brothers, not just one. You weren't the only one suffering, Jethro. *I was too*. I needed you, and you just left me alone to deal with it. You just *left*." Her face was a grimace between anger and pain, so raw Thomas had to look away. "You abandoned me. And *you* did it deliberately. Stefan didn't die on purpose."

And to that, Jethro obviously didn't know how to reply. As for Thomas, he just swallowed, feeling an acute pang of nostalgia for the light, relaxed atmosphere of the pub. He'd known this conversation wasn't going to be easy, and he'd been looking forward to discovering more about Jethro's past, but he hadn't meant to bring out more pain.

Although maybe, just maybe, it was something Jethro would need to deal with before he—before the end of the deal.

"Now if you're done trying to tell me how to live my life, I think this conversation is over." She waited for a moment, then smiled bitterly. "And one last thing . . . I don't know what the hell you're doing, but do you know what people are saying about you? Do you have any idea how frightened they are? What the hell are you playing at, Jethro?"

But Jethro didn't reply to that, either. He just got up, moving stiffly, and walked over to grasp her hands and kiss her on the cheek. "Then it is good-bye, I guess. Take care of yourself, Dragana." With that, he turned on his heel and walked out, leaving Thomas behind.

This wasn't how he'd hoped the conversation would go at all. Thomas hesitated, standing in the corner of the room, eyes darting to the open door. Part of him thought he should go after Jethro, but he also felt he should say something to Dragana. She was standing with her arms crossed, shaking her head.

"Go, toymaker," she said. She didn't sound sad so much as resigned and kind of discouraged. "I don't know what's going on with that boy, but he needs someone to keep an eye on him, and obviously, that can't be me. So please, if you can, don't let him do anything too stupid."

Thomas wasn't sure how to reply. He suspected they both knew there was no stopping Jethro once he set his mind to something. So he just said, "I'll do my best," and left, disconsolately shaking his head.

# CHAPTER 15

"**A**re you *sure* you want another one?" Thomas stared, wide-eyed, as Jethro just grumbled something unintelligible and dug into the fresh beer tankard that had been placed in front of him.

Thomas was still somewhat in disbelief, so stunned that he was neglecting the plate of roasted chestnuts in front of him. It was as though he'd been plunged into some alternate reality without noticing. After they'd left Dragana's workshop, Jethro had all but dragged him down a rather dodgy side street, and they'd ended up tucked in a corner of a small, crammed inn, smoke hovering in the air like clouds.

Thomas popped a chestnut in his mouth and wiped his fingers on his trousers. Jethro hadn't even touched the food, and was instead steadily working through drink after drink—not counting the ones he'd had back at the tavern. He was resting both elbows on the scraped wood of their little table, his jacket hanging on the chair, tie undone, hair a mess. His eyes were glassy as he rubbed his nose on his sleeve, muttering something under his breath.

Thomas swallowed. "'Scuse me, what?"

Jethro seemed sad and lost when he said, "Do you think . . . she'll really sell the shop?"

He sounded like he wanted anything but an honest answer, like he just wanted Thomas to give him the answer he needed to hear, to reassure him it wasn't going to happen. But Thomas had no idea. He had no reassurances to offer.

"I don't know, Jethro," he said carefully. "I . . . I think she might."

Jethro groaned and buried his face in his folded arms. Thomas distractedly picked a slice of bread from the plate and nibbled on it.

It was almost unbelievable what he was seeing. Jethro didn't even look like the same man. He was truly hammered.

"But she can't," Jethro protested petulantly, his voice muffled. Thomas waited for him to continue, and when he didn't, he gave Jethro a little nudge.

"But I mean, it's . . . it's her shop, so why shouldn't she?" he asked.

Jethro sighed, heaving himself up and waving his hand around like he was making a point. "'Cause it's home, that's why. You understand?"

Thomas's usual policy with Jethro would be not to pry, but it seemed like he might actually *want* to talk this time. "Home," he drawled. "Your home?"

"Yeah, of course." Jethro stared at him like it was the most obvious thing in the world. "It's where I grew up. Where *we* grew up. Me and Dragana and . . . and . . ." His face crumpled. He couldn't bring himself to say the name, but Thomas had a pretty good idea who he was talking about. "And Mr. Kovac, he . . . he wouldn't let her. He would never want to sell the shop, never."

Thomas swallowed his food and rested his chin on his hand. "Mr. Kovac?"

"Their grandfather," Jethro answered. His eyes glistened with unshed tears. He took off his spectacles and tried to wipe the glass with his shirt, then just dropped them on the table. "Best inventor I ever knew, Mr. Kovac. Taught me everything I know."

Thomas folded his arms and tilted his head. "Their grandfather? But I thought they were your siblings." He didn't want to specifically mention Stefan being Jethro's brother, even though that's what Dragana had said.

"No. Not . . . not really." Jethro shrugged lopsidedly. "Can't even remember my fam-family. Just Mr. Kovac. He took me in, taught me a job. Gave me a home. A family, everything." He paused, and his gaze turned somewhat darker as he repeated in a whisper, "Everything."

Thomas pushed the plate away. He hadn't expected that, and he didn't quite know how to reply to it. These kinds of conversations were not exactly his forte. But from what little he knew, he could assume they weren't Jethro's forte, either, and he was having a hard time, so the least Thomas could do was make an effort.

"I'm . . . sorry to hear that."

Jethro rubbed the bridge of his nose. "When he died . . . he made us promise we would take care of the shop. Dragana and me. But then she . . . then she went blind and Stefan . . ."

The pained grimace on Jethro's face every time that name was mentioned made Thomas's heart ache. He wished he could understand better, say the right things, do something, anything, to ease that pain. Hell, he would give his hand back to make that expression go away and never, ever return. He seemed to have a surprisingly low tolerance when it came to Jethro's pain.

"Did he also work in the lab? Was it the three of you?"

"No, no. Stefan never wanted anything to do with inventions and science." Jethro's bittersweet smile broke what little of Thomas's heart was still intact. So much tender affection . . . "It was never his thing. Hated to spend time stuck in the lab. He didn't trust tech-technology. He always wanted to be outside. To *do* stuff." Jethro swallowed. "He became a . . . a soldier. And when the war came, he went to fight."

*Ah.* There it was, the story slowly coming together.

Jethro seemed to be in so much pain talking about Stefan that Thomas tried to slightly divert the conversation away from him specifically. "So you grew up there with them in the shop?"

"Yeah. Only home I ever had, that place. Used to spend so much time in the laboratory, and—" Jethro blinked "—she was like a sister to me, and Stefan like my brother. He was my best friend."

"I understand." Thomas rubbed a tired hand over his face. God, he'd been such an idiot, jumping to conclusions about who Stefan might have been. "I thought . . ."

He fell silent, and Jethro raised his eyebrows, looking at him. "What?"

"I just thought he might be . . . That you two . . ." Thomas's cheeks heated up. "Never mind."

Jethro's interrogative gaze suddenly turned to one of surprise. "Oh. *Oh.*" He actually chuckled. "No. Not him. There were a few others, but . . . in Montrale? 'S a village, you know. It's difficult."

Thomas's mouth dropped open. He'd been wondering, but to hear him say it out loud was surprising.

Jethro rubbed his face with his sleeve, looking sleepy. "She just *can't* sell it," he finally said, sounding utterly miserable. And with that, he fell into a sulky silence, resting his cheek on his arm, eyes shining from the sadness. Thomas figured Jethro must've been wiped. It had been an intense day, between all the prosthetics they'd examined, then Dragana bringing up all those memories.

Thomas thought of Stefan. It was obviously him in all those pictures in Dragana's shop, and all of a sudden, the image of the automaton wearing Stefan's face was at once heartbreaking and blood-chilling. He wondered what she would think if she knew. Or even worse, what *he* would think. Thomas, for one, sure as hell wouldn't want anyone honoring him by putting a replica of his face on a devilish machine. The mere thought made his skin crawl.

It was an unexpected development, that much was certain. Within a few hours, he'd learned more about Jethro and his past than since he'd arrived, maybe more than was his right to know at all.

He glanced at the ancient clock on the wall. It was way too late to go back to the house, and in Jethro's current state, he didn't want to load him into a wobbling carriage. Chances were he would throw up all over the place. And then he would fall asleep and Thomas would have to carry him to his room and who knew what else. Jethro would probably be embarrassed enough in the morning, with a slew of things he would want to pretend had never happened, without adding that, too.

So Thomas took the situation in hand and made a decision. "All right. It's time to get you to bed. Let's see if they have any available rooms upstairs, yeah? You wait here. I'll be right back."

Instinctively, Jethro tried to protest. "No, no. 'M perfec-perfectly fine. Got to go home, got work to do and . . . and . . ."

"Oh no you don't." Thomas caught Jethro as he almost toppled off the stool trying to get up. "You're not getting within ten feet of your instruments in this state. If you destroy everything you touch, who's going to hear about it tomorrow? Just let me handle this and you can sleep it off."

He held Jethro up, trying not to think about how close they were, about Jethro's unusually vulnerable green eyes staring right at him. There was turmoil hiding there at the bottom of his gaze, sadness and pain, and it was almost as if he was begging Thomas to take them away.

"All right," he slurred eventually, and Thomas left him half napping on the table as Thomas went to check with the innkeeper about a room.

"Come on, let's get you into bed now." Thomas stood with his hands on his hips, watching as Jethro wobbled across the room and fussed with something on the old, scraped dresser rather than heading toward the bed.

*The one queen-size bed*, Thomas thought as he side-eyed it. It was the only room left, and he figured it would work just fine. If Jethro managed not to puke all over him, at least, which judging by the way he was swaying and groaning, was not guaranteed. It was actually not entirely unpleasant to see him like this. His movements were a lot smoother, more relaxed than usual, and almost sensual now that he wasn't so stiff and uptight. It might even be attractive. Well maybe a few beers earlier it would have been, but this was a bit too much, and Thomas was too sober.

He looked around for a basin and placed it on the nightstand. "Look, I'm going to put this here just in case you feel sick." Jethro was still swaying lightly, and Thomas wondered whether he would fall asleep right there, standing at the desk, or throw up. "You won't need me to undress you, right? You can do that by yourself?" Thomas wasn't too keen on getting his hands on Jethro and *stripping* him, for Heaven's sake.

No, actually the problem was that part of him was way too keen on it. That olive skin created a mouthwatering contrast where it disappeared under his pale shirt. His full lips, his mesmerizing eyes, and the smooth way he was moving . . . God.

Thomas shook his head. Maybe he'd had a bit too much to drink after all. Because this was the most inappropriate moment ever to be having such thoughts. Jethro was drunk and upset. Thomas wouldn't feel comfortable doing anything now, even if Jethro had been more sober, given what Jethro was going through emotionally. Not that Jethro wasn't interested, of course . . .

*Oh man.* He shook his head again and ran his hand through his hair. He had to stop that line of thought right there. He most definitely had imbibed too much.

He tried to collect himself and took a step forward. He needed to get some sleep. He was just a bit drunk and confused, and that's all there was to it. By morning, everything would be back to normal. Whatever *normal* was supposed to be.

"Jethro, maybe we should . . ."

"He never came back."

Thomas stopped in his tracks. Jethro wasn't slurring. His voice was rough but steady, sounding so dark and pained it caused an unpleasant knot to tighten in Thomas's stomach. Jethro had his back turned to him, but even from the way he was standing—his shoulders hunched, every muscle tense—Thomas could clearly see the pain that was still there, still burning after all that time.

Thomas went silent, not sure what to say. It seemed like Jethro hadn't talked about this with anyone ever. Not even with Dragana. It must have been eating him up inside for a long time, maybe for years. Maybe ever since it had happened. But if he needed to finally let it out . . . Well, Thomas was willing to help.

He just hoped he could *be* of help somehow.

He tucked his hands in his pockets and looked at Jethro's back, trying to gather what little bits of information he'd acquired so far. "Did you ever find out what happened?"

There was a moment of silence. "No, we didn't. We never even knew where or how he died . . . Or if he'd died at all, at first. He just . . . he just vanished on one of those battlefields." Jethro turned around and leaned back against the dresser, hugging himself weakly.

"When the soldiers started trickling back after the war, with missing limbs, their faces disfigured by bombs, their bodies shredded and ruined by explosions, by infections, Dragana and I would be at the station waiting, scanning the faces, waiting to see his." He paused with a trembling breath, his face tense. "We went every time a train came into the village bringing another load of them. So many times we waited there . . ."

Thomas didn't quite know what to do with himself as he listened. He shuffled his weight from one foot to the other, unable to look

Jethro in the eye. He remembered what it had been like then. So many of the street kids had joined the army. They had no other prospects, and at least the army promised food and some pay. If they survived. He remembered when they'd come to pick him up and put him to work in that weapons factory. He'd hated every minute of it to the point that he'd even considered running off to join the front, but he hadn't. Truth be told, he'd been too scared. And with good reason as it turned out. He wasn't ashamed to admit it.

Jethro had gone silent. Hesitantly, Thomas finished for him. "But he never came?"

It wasn't a real question—not one that needed a reply, anyway. He doubted he needed to say anything at all, but maybe Jethro needed a little prod to continue speaking. If he was going to get it out, he might as well get everything out. Thomas knew that after the accident, once he'd brought himself to finally start talking about it, for some time he couldn't *stop* talking about it. He'd spoken to anyone who would listened, even complete strangers, often ones slumped in the corner of a pub after one too many drinks, as Jethro had been tonight. And it had helped somewhat. As if telling the tale over and over again had somehow helped him come to terms with it, somehow wrapped his mind around what had happened, the fact that it had *really* happened. Somehow saying it out loud had made it more real, and talking it through was sometimes all that had gotten him to hang on for another day.

He didn't know whether it worked the same way for everyone, but if Jethro had never done it, maybe it would help him too.

Jethro nodded tightly. "Eventually I stopped going. I just couldn't bear the disappointment any longer. But she kept going. Even after the soldiers stopped coming, she still went to the station and waited. Until they sent the . . . they sent the coffin."

"But I thought they didn't tell you what happened?"

"They didn't. They didn't know. To be honest, we're not sure if it was really even him in there. They said it had been so long that the body couldn't be identified properly. Something about his clothes, though." Jethro rubbed his hands over his face. "Not that it matters. There was nothing I could do to help Stefan then, anyway. So I helped them, instead."

Thomas opened his mouth to ask who he meant, then thought about that afternoon and suddenly understood. "The soldiers who came back."

"Yeah. At least there was something I could do, you know?" Jethro finally looked at him, and surprisingly, the pain didn't look as raw as it had earlier. He just looked very, very tired. "I had the house—my parents had left it to me when they died—so I moved in there. I just couldn't stay here any longer. And I worked. I gave them arms, legs. Gave myself something else to think about. Maybe I got a little . . . obsessed." He gave a small, sad smile. "At least I didn't have time to miss him. Too much to do, you know."

The funny thing was, Thomas understood perfectly. Whenever he was upset, that was what he liked to do too: bury himself in work so he wouldn't have time to think about things. That was why this was so hard. Now that his one source of solace, his go-to thing when he needed relief, was what had hurt him, he was too scared to go anywhere near it. It was all wrong. He was too lost, and he didn't know what to do with himself. And listening to Jethro talk, he felt a small pang—of envy, maybe? He wanted it back too. He wanted it all back: his work, his purpose in life, the one thing he was good at.

He flicked a glance at Jethro. While Thomas had been distracted by his musings, it seemed like Jethro had also carried on with his own train of thought.

"She's right, you know," he said, burying his face in his hands. "I haven't even visited his tomb in . . . It's been years. I'm a horrible, horrible person. What right do I have to—"

"You're not, Jethro," Thomas interrupted. "You're not. It's not easy. I understand. I haven't visited my folks at the cemetery in . . ." He didn't really want to think about the specifics. "Well, in way too long."

After a long groan, Jethro lifted his head, a sudden, determined expression on his face. "I have to. Have to go." He sprang forward without any warning and almost toppled over as he tried and failed to put his jacket on. He'd gotten an arm in the wrong sleeve, but still that look of stubborn determination remained on his face. "I have to go see him, I—"

Thomas gaped at him. "What? Now?"

He had his answer when Jethro wobbled toward the door, tripped on the carpet, and almost fell facedown on the floor.

"Whoa! Easy there." Thomas caught him and held him up, trying to restrain him. "Don't even think about it. We'll go tomorrow, all right? Now you've got to sleep."

"No!" He shook his head, stubborn as only Jethro could be and surprisingly strong, too. Thomas had to really work to hold him back, even as he threatened to plop down on the floor at any moment. "I have to go. I have to."

"And you will. I promise! But there's no way— Stop struggling! Jethro, we're *not* going to a cemetery in the middle of the night when you're too drunk to stand up straight. Hey!" He shook Jethro by the arms and looked him in the eye, but the burning pain in there was enough to make him soften his tone. "Look. We will go tomorrow, first thing in the morning. The cemetery is probably closed now, anyway."

That bit of logic seemed to break through Jethro's drunken haze. He blinked slowly. "It's . . . closed?"

"Yes. Yes, it's definitely closed." Thomas nodded emphatically, even though he had no idea, while simultaneously maneuvering Jethro to sit on the bed and tugging off the jacket he'd half slipped on. "Tomorrow, all right?"

"Tomorrow morning?" Jethro looked at him like a child waiting for him to promise that everything would be okay. Thomas wanted to hug him, but he just ruffled his hair instead, more sweetly than he'd intended to.

"First thing. I promise."

He managed to get Jethro to disrobe down to his undershirt and trousers, placed his folded glasses on the nightstand, and made him lie down on the bed. Jethro groaned. Oh, Thomas was ready to bet Jethro was going to have a mother of a migraine tomorrow, and likely be in a foul mood, as well. And Thomas was going to have the pleasure of dealing with it. Lucky him . . .

With a sigh, he lay down beside Jethro, who was curled on his side. His back was relaxing, definitely not as tense as before. Thomas was just thinking he'd probably fallen asleep as soon as he'd touched the mattress when Jethro turned toward him. Jethro's face was suddenly so close, and he looked at Thomas so intently, that those eyes, so vulnerable and warm, took Thomas's breath away. He hadn't expected that, and he definitely hadn't expected Jethro to murmur, "Thank you," his voice barely more than a sigh, then raise his hand and place it on Thomas's cheek. Jethro looked at his mouth and, excruciatingly slowly, traced Thomas's bottom lip with his thumb.

Then, before Thomas could react, Jethro leaned forward to close the distance between them with a gentle kiss, intimate and unexpected. Thomas remained stunned in place. His brain spun madly, overwhelmed by Jethro's scent, his warm body so close, and those soft lips pressed against his, tasting of rich, dark beer. He couldn't even find anything to say when Jethro pulled back and smiled at him—a sweet, sensual smile, just a little wicked. Thomas had never seen such a look on Jethro's face, but it made him want to kiss Jethro again and again. But before he could follow that impulse, Jethro rolled over with a sigh, and that was it.

By the time Thomas recovered from the shock, Jethro's breathing was deep and regular. He was fast asleep, peaceful and blissfully unaware of the turmoil he'd unleashed. Thomas rolled onto his back and stared at the ceiling, wide-awake, feeling like he wouldn't be able to so much as close his eyes for the rest of the night. He brushed his lips with his hand, still tasting the ghost of that kiss.

# CHAPTER 16

The following morning, predictably enough, Jethro was in a bad mood and all too keen on backtracking and pretending the whole conversation had never happened. He busied himself by rummaging in his bag, even though there was nothing he needed to retrieve, trying to sound stern. As for the kiss, he didn't say a word about it, and Thomas didn't have the courage to bring up the topic. He wasn't sure if Jethro remembered it at all. And besides, what would he say? It would be much safer for all concerned to focus on the topic at hand.

"We shall head back right away, and that's final. We've wasted enough days already. It's not the time for a picnic at the cemetery," Jethro said, voice clipped, and then he winced as if the sound of his own voice was enough to make his head hurt. Which, if Thomas's experience with hangovers was anything to go by, was probably the case.

"Nice try," Thomas said, arms folded over his chest. "We'll waste much less time if we just go there than if we keep arguing about it. Let's just get it over with, all right?"

Jethro scowled, snapping his bag shut. "I don't even *want* to go. Look, it was nonsense. You know, I was out of it. Just forget about it."

Thomas chased after him as Jethro strode down the stairs, making a beeline for the exit. "Oh no you don't. Yesterday I had to bodily restrain you to prevent you from wandering through the town, drunk, in the middle of the night, that's how much you wanted to go. And now you expect me to believe—"

"I expect you to mind your own business," Jethro interrupted brusquely.

"Well, that's too damn bad. I'm not good at that, in case you haven't noticed." Thomas stood in front of him, blocking the doorway. He swallowed. He knew it was really none of his business, but Jethro had been such a mess the night before, and . . . Maybe Jethro wouldn't be able to fix things with Dragana anytime soon, but this was something he could do. And, if it would help Jethro, Thomas was willing to go to bat for it, maybe even take a punch to the face if need be. After all, he really *wasn't* that good at minding his own business.

"Look, the way I see it, you have two choices: you go to the cemetery on your own two legs to pay your respects to your brother, or I throw you over my shoulder and drag you there by force. Take your pick." He meaningfully flexed the fingers of his mechanical hand. "But I have to tell you, your reputation in this village is bad enough without you making a spectacle out of yourself."

"Technically *you'd* be making a spectacle out of me," Jethro mumbled petulantly.

"And we don't want that to happen, now do we?" Thomas asked, staring Jethro right in the eye. It was a battle of wills he was determined to win. "So what will it be?"

Jethro shuffled from one foot to the other, then eventually relented, deflated. And maybe a little bit scared too. "Fine. Fine. Let's go, then."

By the time they reached the cemetery, Jethro *definitely* looked scared and nervous. He kept fidgeting, minute movements that Thomas noticed nonetheless—pulling at his cuffs, constantly straightening his glasses, mussing up his hair.

"Must you follow me every step of the way?" Jethro was clearly trying to sound grumpy, but his voice had no bite to it. It was just shaky.

"I wouldn't want you to accidentally take a wrong turn and end up elsewhere, say, holed up in a bar somewhere with another bottle," Thomas replied, keeping his tone light. Jethro was upset enough; he didn't need Thomas to give him a hard time too.

The truth was, he was there mostly out of moral support. Jethro was so pale and shaky that a gust of wind might just knock him over, and yes, the hangover probably wasn't really helping. So Thomas shadowed him, trying to keep his concern hidden behind a carefree banter. At least one of them had to be in good spirits—or pretend to be, at any rate—and hopefully it would be of some comfort to Jethro.

They stood silently in front of the cemetery's gate. The day was early, and the two men were alone under the gray dawn sky. They had only passed a few people as they'd scuttled along the streets—a hansom cab driver napping on his post, a delivery boy from the bakery, a girl with a basket full of lavender sprigs.

Jethro just stood there, staring at the rusty gate with something like dread in his eyes. He swallowed heavily, shoving his fingers through his hair once again. Thomas hesitated for a moment, then gently placed a light hand at the small of Jethro's back in a silent gesture of support. After the previous night, he figured he was allowed at least that small touch.

"Take all the time you need," he said. "I'll be waiting here."

Jethro nodded, yet he still didn't move. It seemed as if his feet were nailed to the spot. Then he closed his eyes, pushed up his glasses, and brushed Thomas's elbow, as though seeking comfort. It seemed he found a little, at least, because he looked back with a weak smile and just replied, "All right."

He stepped inside, slowly making his way straight between the tombs. He stopped every now and then to look around, trying to orient himself. It was obvious he wasn't sure where the tomb was located, but still he walked until he was nothing but a small shape in the distance, among the unkempt bushes and trees that littered the graveyard.

Thomas just waited, staring at Jethro's back as he stood still in front of one of the tombs. It must have been Stefan's. When Jethro's shoulders hunched, Thomas averted his gaze, wanting to give him some privacy. He turned on his heel and strolled aimlessly by the gate, hand in his pocket, kicking a stray stone into the gutter. He waited, listening to the noises of the town as it woke up to begin another day, then a movement around his feet caught his eye. It was a spider—a small ceramic one, tiptoeing on thin brass legs just outside the cemetery. It quickly climbed up the stone pillar by the gate and stopped just about eye level with Thomas.

"Hey." He nodded to it, not even feeling too ridiculous talking to a spider. It was one of Dragana's inventions, obviously—maybe a companion she'd left behind to guard her brother's tomb in her absence. He was wondering if he should try to touch it, see if it would crawl on his hand, but just when he started moving, he was distracted by the sound of approaching footsteps. The spider vanished in an instant before Jethro reappeared.

Thomas looked at him. Jethro's face was torn between raw pain and some kind of relief, Thomas was fairly sure. Despite Jethro's obvious sadness, he walked as if a weight had finally, *finally* lifted off his shoulders, and Thomas was certain that was indeed the case.

Jethro stopped outside the gate and opened his mouth to speak a couple of times. Nothing came out. Thomas thought about taking him in his arms, telling himself it was just to offer comfort and not because the sight of Jethro in pain was knotting heavy strings around his heart, but stopped himself before he did so. Eventually, Jethro pushed his glasses up his nose, lifted his gaze, and straightened his shoulders. He seemed exhausted but at peace somehow.

"I'm sorry he never came back," Thomas blurted before he could think better of it. He had no idea what it was like to lose a brother. He'd never had anyone besides his grandmother. But he remembered that disorienting, devastating feeling when she'd passed away, and blood or not, Stefan had been Jethro's family. That was all that mattered.

"Thank you," Jethro replied. His hand twitched as he reached out to briefly hold Thomas's real one, his touch light and warm. Then he said, "Let's go home."

As they walked off, their fingers loosely entwined, Thomas cast a last glance toward the tomb, and at that moment, he caught a glimpse of the spider, quickly zigzagging through the graveyard to get back to its silent post.

# CHAPTER 17

As their hansom cab got closer to the house, Thomas's stomach grew steadily tighter. Getting back to the whole mess—the devil; the cursed hourglass with that black sand swirling down, marking the time to Jethro's death; and the automaton, waiting for them on its table—was tearing him up inside. But there was much to be done anyway. If the deal couldn't be stopped, Thomas wouldn't let it end in vain.

Without even needing to discuss it, they headed to the secret workshop and stood beside the automaton. A chill ran down Thomas's back when he looked at that expressionless porcelain mask, and his attempt to be logical slipped. It was pure madness. The automaton would come to life while Jethro lost his? What a sickening trade-off. The machine seemed utterly horrible to him now—a monster, a vampire that would suck Jethro's life. Neither of them seemed willing to start speaking, and Thomas certainly didn't feel like picking back up the fight they were having before they'd left for the village.

With a sigh, he finally broke the silence. "Jethro, why . . . why didn't you tell me what was going on?" Thomas raked his hand through his hair, distractedly rubbing at the scarred skin on the side of his head. "When you decided to take me in, I mean. You knew then that I would be the one who would have to deal with this. So why didn't you tell me the truth?"

"At first, I just didn't want to risk word getting out about it. Not before the soiree. I want—wanted—for it to be a big reveal. Maximize the effect, you know? Surprise and amaze them so much that they would make me . . . a legend." Jethro's eyes were distant, shimmering with desire for glory and recognition. Thomas had never been enthralled with such things. He'd actually gone in the opposite direction, shying away from all recognition and fame because it made him uncomfortable. And maybe, just maybe, he'd never believed what he did was good enough to deserve it. Still, he could recognize its pull. He figured any inventor, or perhaps any man, had a spark of it somewhere inside. He knew for sure he was feeling something tugging at him now, just as it had that night he'd spoken to Farfarello, the first time he'd seen the automaton. *Damn it.*

Thomas shook his head, refocusing on their conversation. Jethro had said *at first*. "And then?"

Jethro looked at him with a sad, defeated smile on his face. "I just didn't want to . . . disappoint you." He was almost whispering. He shrugged apologetically. "I wanted to tell you. But you believed in me so much, you were so happy about your prosthetic, and I . . . How could I tell you the truth about it and still look you in the eye?" He cringed. "And I just made it worse. I didn't even have the guts to be honest and come clean about it all. And now you despise me, and . . ."

Thomas remained silent. He didn't despise Jethro. He hadn't even lost true respect for him. What was happening between them had been unexpected to say the least. Sudden. Uncertain. Hell, Thomas wasn't even sure if there *was* something happening between them at all, or what their odd friendship or attraction meant. And despite what his wounded pride was telling him, there was actually no reason why Jethro should have felt obligated to confess his secrets and his failures to him, a mere stranger.

"So you can . . . you can have it all," Jethro said. "You can take my laboratory. I will show you how my prosthetics work, I will tell you all about the automaton, and . . . and you can take my place. If you want. It will all be yours. The house, the workshop, all of it." He looked at Thomas, a mixture of hope and despair in his eyes. "You're good, Thomas. You're the only one who can do it."

Thomas was absolutely stunned. Of all the things that could have been said, he had *not* seen that coming. "Me? I can't do this. I'm not capable enough."

"Yes, you are. And you're very good, with only your God-given abilities. You're not cheating using a devil to help you." Jethro grimaced.

Thomas just stared at him. He couldn't even fathom taking over. Jethro's house and laboratory, becoming his? What the hell was he supposed to say to that?

Jethro swallowed. "So?"

"I . . ." Thomas started, and then his voice faded into silence. He raised his hands somewhat helplessly. "I had a nice, self-righteous rant all prepared, and now I don't even know what to say." He shook his head and glanced at the sleeping automaton. God, that thing looked so strong and powerful, Thomas was actually frightened at the idea of it coming to life. Frightened and fascinated, he had to admit. On the one hand, he couldn't wait to see it in action. The first thing of its kind to ever grace the Earth. But on the other hand, he wished he could be on the other side of the globe when it happened.

Thomas's gaze darted to the instruments laid out on the table, then to the automaton. It would be so much simpler to just take a hammer to it and smash it into a thousand pieces.

And yet . . .

They were— No. *Jethro* was so close. To creating something that had never been created before, devil or no devil. And he had given his life for this. It would be so wasteful to destroy it now. Thomas could feel that pull again, the same temptation he'd felt when he'd spoken with Farfarello. After all, maybe it wouldn't go rogue. There was no reason why it should, was there?

Jethro swallowed, his Adam's apple bobbing in his throat. He stared at his creature and rubbed his thumb over its arm with something like affection, but also like hatred, in his eyes. "I gave my life for this. Do you think we should . . . destroy it?"

Thomas looked at it. There was no question about it. "We . . . Yes. We should. But . . ." He stood behind Jethro, inspecting every inch of the automaton. It was monstrous, and yet . . . "I am angry at you. For the position you've put me in. For your lies. For so many things. But . . ." He swallowed with some difficulty. "But it's so close to being finished."

"So you'll help me?" Jethro turned around, so near to him that Thomas could feel his warm breath on his skin. He closed his eyes.

"I . . . I will," he breathed. He was shaking, he was terrified, but he felt drawn to Jethro. He was going to lose him soon, and he wanted him. He wanted him, so much. Their lips brushed, sending an electric shock down his spine, and they grabbed each other, holding on for dear life. "God help me, I will . . ." he whispered before their mouths fused in another kiss.

A loud crash came from somewhere in the nearby rooms, followed by the sound of glass shattering. They looked at each other, still for a moment, and the next instant they ran out of the lab.

*Goddamn it. The damn tea machine must have gone crazy again . . .*

Hell, it might destroy half the laboratory before they got to it.

They burst into the main laboratory. It wasn't the tea maker but the knitting machine. It had grabbed a prosthetic leg in one of its many arms and was using the prosthetic like a hammer, striking blindly at the surrounding tables. A bunch of prosthetics were scattered on the ground, and under their horrified gazes, one of the tables shattered under the blows, spilling instruments all over the floor.

"How the hell do you stop this?" Even as Thomas yelled, he sprung forward, instinctively tackling the thing to the ground. It had thin arms and a weak body, and he was a big man . . . He hit the thing with a thud and brought it down, toppling another table and rolling on the floor under a rain of nuts and bolts. But the machine was fast, too fast, and before he knew it his back slammed against the floor as the thing turned on him.

He had a split second to realize he might have just done something really, really stupid before Jethro yelled, "Thomas, watch out!" The machine raised the prosthetic once again, aiming it right at his goddamn face, ready to bash his skull in.

He saw it come down and reacted on instinct. His right hand shot up and the two metal prosthetics met with a bang. The shock reverberated all the way through his forearm and elbow, and for a moment he wondered if he'd broken any bones. But his arm was still working, and so was his mechanical hand. He clamped down on the leg and held it steady midair as the knitting machine kept pushing down, trying to break his resistance. He barely had time to silently thank Jethro for his excellent craftsmanship—it had just saved his life!—but unfortunately, the rest of his arm was still flesh and bone, and he was not strong enough to keep this up.

"Jethro!" Thomas yelled. "Shut it off! I can't hold it much long—"

He couldn't even finish the sentence before Jethro was on the machine, brandishing a large screwdriver. He jammed it into a juncture on the machine's body with surgical precision, and the thing stopped, turning to dead weight. It collapsed atop Thomas, knocking the breath out of him. Luckily it wasn't too heavy or it would have shattered his rib cage.

Jethro helped him push it off and then rolled it away. Thomas lay on his back, sore and panting, heart still racing, adrenaline pumping through his veins. The next instant, Jethro was on his knees by his side. "God, Thomas, are you all right?"

Thomas raised his mechanical hand. "I'm fine . . . I think. God, my ribs." He grimaced as he turned onto his side, but there was no sharp pain, just a dull soreness. He knew pain—he'd had his fair share of brawls back in the city, and growing up on the street meant he'd gotten his ribs broken a few times by somebody kicking the ever-loving shit out of him—and he knew he hadn't broken anything. He was going to have the mother of all bruises for a while but should be fine.

"Thanks to your contraption here. Without it that thing would have smashed my head in," he said, lifting his prosthetic to look at it. The hand didn't hurt at all, only his elbow, which was still ringing with pain that shot down through the bone. The hand looked good, just a bit dented on the palm but not a crack, not a single finger malfunctioning. He really was impressed with the quality of Jethro's work. And the fact that he was still in one piece to appreciate it was a testament to it.

"Yeah, well, maybe next time you'll think before tackling a raging hunk of metal. This makes it twice now, you know." Jethro's voice was shaking even as he tried to crack that joke, helping Thomas up with a huff. "Good Lord, Thomas. For a moment I thought I would need to scoop you up like jam from the floor. Don't you ever do something that stupid again, all right? What if the hand had failed? What if—"

"Got it. Now stop worrying. I'm fine. Will just be sore for a while, that's all," Thomas interrupted.

Jethro was motionless as Thomas stood more or less upright, then his arm hooked over Jethro's shoulders. They were so close, their mouths mere inches apart. A sizzling tension suddenly rose between them as they looked at each other. It was kind of cute how Jethro had been ranting at him, reprimanding him, and now Thomas's eyes dropped from Jethro's green ones to his plump parted lips. All he wanted was to—

*Oh, to hell with it.*

Thomas grabbed Jethro's face and kissed him.

"Let's go upstairs," he murmured, and Jethro just nodded, shakily, holding him a little tighter.

# CHAPTER 18

They didn't talk about it. Mostly, they tried to not even *think* about it, or at least, that was what Thomas did, throwing himself headlong in the pile of work still left to be done before the soiree. There were still invitations to send, and dozens of chairs to rent and set out in the big hall on the ground floor, and food to order for the refreshments. Plus, Jethro still had mechanical parts for him to work on. A metallic plate to be fashioned into a breastbone. A knot of pipes that would allow the automaton to utter sounds. A piston to be inserted in a calf.

Thomas surprised himself with how quickly he picked up new skills under Jethro's guidance. Jethro was trying to pass along as much of his knowledge as possible—sometimes too much, leaving Thomas's head spinning as he tried to process the sheer amount of information. It seemed Jethro had well and truly appointed him as his successor, but Thomas still couldn't think about that. He just tried to shift gears and focus on learning. It was all he could do.

At night, though, he couldn't quite prevent his thoughts from wandering. He had dark bags under his eyes because he couldn't sleep, tossing and turning, cataloging in gruesome details every worst-case scenario he could picture, every horrible way the devil could choose to kill Jethro and drag him down to Hell. Thomas had dim memories of bedtime horror stories he'd shared with his friends as a child, stories about hellish black dogs with eyes of burning coal and sharp, gleaming teeth ready to tear damned souls to shreds. He vaguely recalled mental pictures of tortured, broken bodies and, most of all, blood. Too much blood.

He tried his best to shut down those thoughts, squeezing his eyes closed, tearing the blankets as he clutched them too hard in his mechanical hand, but the anxiety never faded. It was always there, a wild animal prowling around in his head, making it difficult to eat and impossible to fall asleep. Judging from the matching dark circles under Jethro's eyes, he didn't seem to be faring much better. Except he wasn't even bothering to try to sleep anymore.

One night when he was being tormented by those horrible visions, Thomas jumped out of bed and set out to Jethro's room, unable to bear the images for one minute longer. He had this irrational, panicky feeling that even just touching Jethro, just feeling him under his hand—alive, and warm, and *still there*—would soothe him enough to finally allow him to sleep. But nobody answered his knock, and when he silently pushed the door ajar, he saw that the room was empty, the bed untouched. It was no mystery where Jethro might be, though—where he'd been spending every waking moment.

With that goddamn automaton.

Thomas sighed and headed downstairs. His footsteps were muffled by the worn-out carpets as he made his way through the dark, quiet house to the laboratory. As he walked to the pendulum clock, which was now always open, he forced himself not to look up at the hourglass, even though he could almost *feel* it pressing down on him. In the silence, he thought he could hear the soft hissing of what little sand was left, still steadily trickling down. He hated that hourglass. He doubted he would ever be able to stand being around one ever again.

In the no-longer-secret laboratory, he found Jethro fast asleep, his head on his folded arms, right next to his creation, that *thing*—along with his prosthetics—that he'd sold his soul for. Thomas looked at the strange picture of the condemned inventor asleep by the shoulder of the creature he'd damned himself for, and for the first time, he found himself thinking about the connection that existed between those two.

As irrational as it was, he couldn't help being somewhat jealous of that machine. It was so important to Jethro, to the point that he'd given it his brother's face. Important enough for him to give up his life, his soul, and even though it made no sense, no sense *whatsoever*, he wished it were him. He wished *he* was important enough for Jethro to not die, but to *live*. To live for him, to have a chance to live all the moments they would otherwise be denied if Jethro died. And he had to die because of that damn automaton, and Thomas and Jethro would be robbed of everything they could have had together,

For a moment, Thomas was so pissed—at Jethro, at his stupidity and stubbornness, at Farfarello and his blasted deal, and at the automaton. In that moment he wanted to destroy it, to hammer its pretty porcelain face into pieces because *that thing* would keep on living, and that was too unfair. And for an instant, nothing more than a heartbeat, he felt angry at Stefan, too, who had gone and gotten himself killed, sending Jethro into the downward spiral that was going to cost him his life.

Thomas was immediately ashamed of those thoughts, stamping out those embers of anger, knowing he was just lashing out, so desperate to find someone, anyone, to blame. The poor guy had done nothing but die, and none of what had happened afterward was his fault. He knew that the blame fell squarely on Jethro's shoulder. And yet, he was the only one Thomas couldn't bring himself to hate, no matter how much he wanted to.

Deflated, Thomas sat down next to Jethro. His hair was a mess, and his glasses were askew on his nose. Thomas carefully took them off him and folded them neatly on the table. Jethro seemed thinner too, and even more tired. He was working himself to the bone for this. After all, he truly had nothing left to lose. Thomas slowly inched his hand closer to Jethro's until their pinkies were brushing, the contact almost too light to even be felt. Jethro didn't stir. It was odd how such a little thing made Thomas feel somehow relieved, how it managed to loosen the heavy knot lodged in his stomach. He closed his eyes to enjoy that moment of peace and tried really hard not to think about what would happen once Jethro was gone. It made his heart hurt.

# CHAPTER 19

I t was a lovely sunny day when they finally left the lab and stepped out into the garden, although Thomas could hear the wind howling against the glass panels, seeping in through the broken ones. He was holding a bundle wrapped in a cloth and cast a glance at Jethro beside him, who was holding a large hammer.

"Go ahead," Jethro said with an encouraging nod.

Thomas smiled. "Mina! Where are you? I've got a present for you!"

He hadn't thought he would have the time to get it done, but despite the imminent soiree—only two days to go—Jethro had actually insisted Thomas take the time to finish Mina's toy. In fact, he'd insisted that he help Thomas too. "I owe her, the poor girl. I've been ignoring her for years," he'd said. "This might not be enough to earn her forgiveness, but before I— Well, it's something I can do."

Between the two of them, it had only taken a few hours to complete from where Thomas had left off. And he had to admit, it had been really pleasant working side by side with Jethro on something so simple, something that didn't involve devil magic or anything of the like.

Within the blink of an eye, Mina was standing before him, head tilted to the side, her long translucent braid dangling. "A present, Thomas? Oh, Jethro. Hi . . ." She turned suddenly shy, taking a step back and awkwardly twisting her hands in the skirt of her dress, looking up at the two of them from beneath her lashes.

Jethro smiled warmly at her. "Hello, Mina. I'm so sorry I haven't been out to visit you in such a long time," he said, then prodded Thomas with his shoulder. "Thomas has prepared something for you. I just have to take care of a little something while he shows you . . ."

He stepped around her and headed to the glass panels enclosing the garden, weighing the hammer in his hand. Meanwhile, Thomas kneeled on the grass and started unwrapping the bundle.

Mina tiptoed closer, leaning down to take a peek. "What is it?"

"Well," Thomas said, carefully pulling down the cloth, "you said you were bored, and so I thought I would build you a little something. But since you can't touch it, I found a way for it to work on its own."

He was interrupted by the loud sound of shattering glass. He smiled to himself while Mina turned around, covering her mouth with her hands. Jethro was hammering the glass, the panels exploding into shards, littering the grass at his feet.

"What is he doing?" Mina exclaimed.

Thomas just chuckled. He hadn't believed it himself when Jethro had offered to do it. And judging by the energy with which he was swinging the hammer, he seemed to be rather enjoying it.

"Don't worry," Thomas replied. "Just something we need for your present to work. And here it is!" He let the last piece of fabric drop to reveal a mechanical horse that came up to about knee height. It was mounted on large wheels, the cogs and wires connected to a large sail made of waxed cotton. The polished plaques making up its body captured the sunlight, gleaming a warm bronze color.

Not as bright as Mina's smile, though.

She clasped her hands, delighted. "Oh my goodness! It's beautiful! Thank you, Thomas!"

He smiled. "That's not all. Look at this . . ." Thomas unrolled the sail and secured it to the thin metallic shaft sticking out of the horse's back. He already felt the wind coming in through the broken glass to ruffle his hair, to bite through his clothes. As soon as he had secured the sail and stepped back, the waxed cloth flexed, then caught a gust of wind and puffed out, pushing the horse forward. As it rolled, the cogs turned, making its legs bend and straighten again, mimicking a gallop. The horse started rolling onto the grass, picking up speed as the sail flapped and filled. It was encircled with a paper-thin, flexible metal band, and when it bumped into a tree, it easily bounced away and kept rolling onto the grass.

Mina clapped her hands and chased after it, laughing. Thomas could barely contain his own satisfaction at seeing the first invention he'd built with his new prosthetic hand at work. And of course, at Mina's reaction. This was why he loved being a toymaker. It might not bring the fame and glory that Jethro's work did, but to Thomas, this reward was much more valuable.

"See? This way, you don't need to touch it in order to play with it," he called after her.

Jethro came to join Thomas watching her, holding the hammer over his shoulder, a decidedly satisfied smile on his face. "So, it seems to be working well," he commented. "Nicely done, Thomas. You're really good at this."

A pleasant heat rushed to Thomas's cheeks, and he had just opened his mouth to brush it off—compliments made him a bit uncomfortable—when Mina ran back to them, her braid bouncing.

"Thank you so much! This is wonderful. And when I have my body, maybe I can ride it too!"

The smile froze on Thomas's lips as Jethro stiffened beside him.

Oh, heavens. Thomas had hoped maybe she'd stopped wishing for that. He was still trying to come up with a suitable reply when Mina continued, wringing her hands.

"Do you know . . . do you know how it's going?" she asked, looking at Thomas. Then to Jethro, "I heard that maybe you're working on something like that . . . Right?"

Now *that* caught Thomas's attention. He looked at her intently, suddenly suspicious. "I— Where did you hear that, darling?"

Mina's eyes darted to the side. She was most definitely not a good liar. It was obvious she didn't want to answer. "Maybe," she muttered eventually, "*maybe* someone told me."

"I see." Thomas carefully thought about how to prod for more information. He could practically feel Jethro's silent gaze burning on his skin. Thomas certainly hadn't said anything of the like to Mina, and there weren't many sources she could have heard it from, were there? "And who told you that? Do you have other friends around here?"

Mina still seemed unsure, then apparently decided she trusted them, for she looked around conspiratorially, then put her hand to her mouth and leaned in close to whisper, "He said I shouldn't tell anyone."

Thomas leaned forward too, getting in on the secret. "Who?"

"The man. You know, the man with the spider."

Thomas stiffened. He and Jethro exchanged glances, Jethro's green eyes growing wide behind his glasses.

"The man with the spider?" Jethro crouched to look Mina in the eye, his voice gentle. "My dear, do you remember what he said, exactly?"

She shrugged, turning kind of cagey once again. "I don't know. That maybe you were working on it, and maybe there would be a body for me very soon. Is that true?"

Her eyes were shimmering, so full of hope, and Thomas felt a wave of anger heat the blood in his veins. *That bastard.* He was getting off giving this poor girl false hopes like that? It was just cruel.

Jethro harrumphed, adjusting his spectacles on his nose. "Mina, I-I'm afraid I'm quite busy on another project at the moment. I'm really sorry, but—"

Mina's brow furrowed. "Oh." She stood somewhat awkwardly, shuffling from one foot to the other. "But . . . but maybe when you're done?"

Thomas cringed. It was actually painful to watch Jethro squirm under her hopeful gaze, struggling to find a kind way to let her down. Maybe Farfarello just enjoyed watching them struggle.

*Fucking devil and his goddamn games . . .*

"I might leave for a while . . . after I am done. But maybe we could talk about it more later?" Jethro suggested. His lips twisted in a grimace, as if he'd just been forced to swallow a frog. "But in the meantime, you have your new toy to keep you company. That's nice, yes?"

Mina straightened up, seeming to remember the horse, which was still rolling around the lawn. "Yes! Thank you, Jethro. Thank you, Thomas! I will play with it all the time." With that, she ran off, chasing after the toy and dancing around it as the horse's legs moved slowly.

Thomas and Jethro exchanged a glance. Jethro's shoulders had slumped, and he looked utterly dejected. Instinctively, Thomas reached out to grasp his hand and gave it a comforting squeeze before gently tugging him along as they stepped back inside. Thomas supposed they had handled it as best as they could.

He stared at Jethro. "What do you think that devil's up to?" he whispered.

Jethro shook his head, his eyes dark. "Hell if I know. But I think we'd better keep our eyes open."

# CHAPTER 20

Thomas sat alone at the large worktable in the middle of the main laboratory late that night, elbows resting on the ancient wood, eyes unfocused on the little bolts and gears scattered in front of him. Truth be told, even though he was trying to work, he just wanted to drop his head on the table and spend some time groaning and feeling sorry for himself. He was fairly sure he'd earned that right. Plus, getting the gears and bolts embedded in his forehead, then having to remove them and stitch the wounds would certainly give him something else to think about, at least for a little while.

He didn't know how to wrap his mind around it all. A deal with the devil, good Lord. It would be crazy if it wasn't the most believable explanation—in a curious and wild way—for all the impossible things Jethro had been building. That damn automaton really existed, and it would *work*. And then . . . then, Jethro would die. Leaving behind a fatherless creation, something entirely new that was ready to wreak havoc on the world.

Thomas rubbed the bridge of his nose. There must be something wrong with him, because he still couldn't bring himself to blame Jethro completely. No matter the inventor's intentions, this was wrong, it *had* to be wrong, and yet, it was also so amazing, and Jethro's determination was so strong that Thomas couldn't help but admire him a little. That was not to say he would have done the same thing. Even if he'd known, and most importantly *believed*, that something like this was possible, he wouldn't have done it. Not with that price to pay.

It astonished him how Jethro could care so little about his own life. Surely it had to be all part of a grand plan or something. He just couldn't see the bigger picture or comprehend how he figured into all this.

If he could just clear his mind and focus for a while, surely his natural knack for circuits and logic would kick in and he would know what to do. But his thoughts seemed to be leaking out of his head like heavy smoke from an exhausted machine. Every little noise and movement was amplified in the quiet laboratory, echoing in the semidarkness. A little teacup with delicate mechanical legs was tiptoeing around like a spider. A marble on a rusty spring kept bouncing against a wall with a repetitive squeak.

And of course, there was the heavy ticking of the big pendulum clock, the soft whirring and clacking of its perfectly oiled mechanism as its various quadrants turned, mapping a journey of stars and planets that Thomas didn't comprehend. If he looked at it hard enough, he could almost *feel* the gaping void behind, almost hear the noises of those devilish mechanical organs at work—beating, pumping, *breathing*. He could almost see the monstrous creation lying in wait on the table with its expressionless porcelain mask.

Not for the first time that night, he lifted his gaze and watched the shimmering black sand seeping into the bottom half of the hourglass, minute sparkles dancing among the dark grains as they fell, as if the night sky had been ground up and poured in.

A loud, cracking explosion nearly sent him toppling off his chair.

"What in the name of *Hell* are you doing!?" Farfarello burst into view in a sudden flurry of feathers and fabric, puffed out like an angry rooster. "You are screwing everything up! I swear, in *centuries* I have never had so much trouble. Time is running out! Why won't you two just do what you're *supposed* to?"

Thomas sneezed as the bitter cloud of sulfur enveloped him, making his nose burn and his eyes water, speechless in the face of that outburst.

There he was again, the strange devil, with his ramblings that made no damn sense. The one thing that remained painfully clear, however, was that whatever he was up to, he was the one who would take Jethro away, the one toying with Jethro's life—heck, with both of their lives—and before he could think better of it, Thomas's temper flared.

"Well, maybe if you *told me* what it is you want me to do, it would be a hell of a lot easier for everyone involved!" he snapped.

The devil froze, his mouth dropping open. He probably expected to intimidate everyone with his power. And yes, he probably could crush Thomas like a baby bird with a flick of his fingers, but who gave a damn?

Farfarello recovered swiftly from the surprise. "You were supposed to *say* something! Scold him, reprimand him, I don't know, be the righteous inventor or something, and make him see the error of his ways."

Thomas shook his head. "What . . . what on earth are you talking about?"

Farfarello threw his hands in the air. "Do I need to draw you a picture? You've seen what excellent work he was doing, building his prosthetics for the poor. He was a decent inventor then. I was actually kind of happy to help out. And then, then he goes and gets his head full of crap about glory and his name going down in history, and ugh! It's gotten to the point that it's clouding his talent, and that's a damn shame. Somebody needs to give him a little push to help him."

"And that someone is you, I suppose?"

Farfarello shot him a meaningful glance. "Maybe. But *maybe* I need some help with that. Someone to show him how *wrong* what he's doing is. And *maybe* that's *your* job, because somehow I doubt he would take a lesson in morality from a devil all that seriously."

"Look, Farfarello, why do you even care?" Thomas asked. "What difference does it make if you'll be dragging him to Hell in a couple of days anyway?"

"Yeah, sure. That's all I do. Every time. Of course." Farfarello snorted. "It's about wasted potential, don't you see? I hate it, and I'm in the position to do something about it, so that's what I do."

Thomas just stared at him. He figured waiting might be more effective than asking more questions.

Farfarello held his gaze for a few more seconds, then dropped his head again, chuckling. He'd never seemed as human to Thomas as he did in that moment. "Let's just say maybe that's a mistake I made when I was alive. A long time ago . . . I never had a chance to fix it, never got to give to the world what I could have, and . . . I don't really have anyone else to blame except myself."

For the first time, Thomas found himself wondering about who Farfarello truly was. Had he been human, then, before becoming a devil? Thomas had never thought about how devils were born. Had Farfarello also made a deal once? How long ago? What did he want, that he never got to achieve?

But it looked like those questions would have to remain unanswered because Farfarello straightened up, pulled himself together, and spoke in the tone of someone wrapping up a conversation. After all, he must have had decades, possibly centuries, to mull over his poor choices. Surely he didn't feel like explaining himself to a stranger, and besides, Thomas had to admit that it was really none of his business.

"It was a rather unfortunate affair, let's just say, and it ended in disaster. A big waste all around. And I hate waste. That's why I do this." Farfarello tucked his hands in his pockets. "You, however, have thrown a wrench in my plans. That's what I get for underestimating you humans once again. I suppose it was a little lazy on my part, really, to simply bring you here and wash my hands of things, expecting you to do the work for me. I'm getting complacent in my old age."

He shook his head, silver bells jingling, and patted down his jacket. A small cloud of dust rose in the air, spreading a faint scent of sulfur.

"You two . . . I swear, you'll be the death of me. Or something."

And with that, he was gone, once again leaving Thomas gaping and not quite sure what the hell was going to happen next.

# CHAPTER 21

There were people *everywhere*. Carriages filled the driveway, some parking in all sorts of precarious places just a few inches from tumbling down the mountain. Doors were slamming, vomiting an endless stream of guests in oversized gowns and equally oversized top hats, who milled about the garden and trickled into the large ballroom of the mansion. Thomas and Jethro had managed to make the space almost presentable for the occasion with dozens of mismatched chairs lined up before a makeshift stage hidden by moth-eaten velvet curtains.

Thomas's head was spinning. He hadn't expected so many people to show up. Jethro must have sent out a lot more invitations than Thomas himself had handled. It looked like scientists had come from all over the country—probably from some neighboring countries too—as if everyone even remotely involved in mechanics had answered Jethro's invitation. It seemed he was a lot more famous than Thomas had given him credit for.

Thomas nervously tugged at his collar, standing on the doorway to welcome the guests. He'd worn his best shirt and trousers, which wasn't saying much, and the dusty jacket he'd borrowed from Jethro didn't quite fit properly. There was a button missing, the sleeves were too short, and the cravat was kind of strangling him.

"Excuse me, young man. Where may I be seated?" An elderly lady in a mechanical wheelchair materialized before him, wearing a ruffled black gown, the plumes on her hat long enough to tickle Thomas's nose.

"Um, right this way, madam. Allow me to accompany you," he offered. He was beginning to feel more like a butler than an inventor.

"Mighty generous of you, dear. Do lead the way," she chirped, adjusting her tiny silver binoculars. The chair wheezed, huffed, and puffed as she sped off, and Thomas scrambled to get ahead of her into the crowded main hall.

They'd programmed some of Jethro's inventions to help them, and the machines were bustling among the guests, squeaking as they moved, and leaving trails of steam puffs behind them. The tea maker, for example, had been adorned with ribbons and a rosette and was wandering around with a tray laden with mismatched teacups. They'd hastily mounted another tray onto the knitting machine that held an array of canapés that Thomas had prepared, including some cheeses and a minced-meat recipe he'd learned from his grandmother. After he guided the older woman to the front row, he caught himself actually standing on his tiptoes, nervously looking to see people's expressions when they tasted his food, then promptly felt a little ridiculous for it. Of all the things he should have been worrying about . . .

The big soiree had come all too soon. They'd been keeping busy, caught in a swirl of activity to get everything ready, and with last-minute invitations, the constant anxiety over sudden mechanical malfunctions, and the fact that between the two of them they had no idea how to host members of high society, well, it had somehow snuck up on them.

Of course, it wasn't the only thing to have come too soon. The sand in the hourglass was reduced to a trickle now, and there was just the smallest bit left in the upper half. For the last couple of days, Thomas had tried really hard not to stare at it, yet as he worked in the laboratory, he'd often found himself distracted, his eyes lifting up almost on their own from whatever he was working on to stare at the hourglass, nervously assessing the steadily decreasing amount of sand at the top. As though by sheer willpower he might somehow make it slow down, make it stop.

He hadn't agreed with Jethro's idea to move the damn thing into the hall, ominously hanging above the entrance where it was impossible to ignore during the event. But they had to make sure things were timed just right since the automaton would come to life precisely at midnight, the moment the deal would end. The moment . . .

The moment Jethro would die.

A dash of color in the entryway caught his eye as someone stepped in wrapped in a bright-red knitted shawl. It was Dragana, feeling her way along the wall beside the entrance.

Thomas hurried through the crowd to reach her. "Dragana, hi," he said, his voice wavering slightly.

Why was she here? He and Jethro had debated it at length and had decided not to send her an invitation. She shouldn't be here to witness Jethro's death, even if she wouldn't be able to physically see it. They'd known she would be offended, of course, and that she'd probably think Jethro had gone out of his way to exclude her while inviting every other scientist under the sun. But it was better than the alternative . . .

"Oh, Thomas, hello." She shot him a mischievous smile. "Would you be so kind as to escort me to a seat?"

"I, um, sure." He took her arm and led her to one of the few seats still available, one close to the back . . . and to the exit. She wouldn't be able to see anyway, and he wanted her out of the way should something go awry. "So what, um, are you doing here?"

Dragana sat down, her back ramrod straight. "Ha! As if I was going to miss this, invitation or no invitation. You don't know me very well, toymaker."

He took a deep breath, trying to figure out how to handle this. Jethro was going to die tonight, and it would be yet another shock for her. He and Thomas had both been hoping to spare her. Should he take her to their makeshift backstage so she could at least say good-bye to him since she was already here? But Jethro was a bundle of nerves as it was, and this was just going to rattle him more. But . . . Oh God. Thomas was going to be the one left with the task of telling her what had happened, of explaining Jethro's horrifying deal with Farfarello. Yet another burden Jethro was leaving on his shoulders. Thomas cursed silently, but very colorfully. Jethro's recklessness was going to hurt people. And Thomas, while busy keeping it together himself, was going to have to take care of it. *Damn it . . .*

"Would you . . . would you like a canapé?" Thomas asked, desperate to avoid the topic of Jethro at the moment. "I made them myself." He felt like such a hypocrite, like the vilest liar in the world, but what was he going to say?

Dragana shook her head. "No, thank you. Maybe a cup of tea? I'm just interested in finding out what all the brouhaha is about. Maybe afterward you could take me backstage, let me touch this fabulous invention of his? I won't be able to see very well, you know."

"I, um..." Thomas wanted to climb to the top floor of the villa and throw himself out a window. He couldn't lie to her face so shamelessly, but as he struggled to decide what to say, how to explain—how to warn her—the gaslights in the room dimmed and the crowd's murmuring suddenly dropped in volume.

Dragana waved him off, whispering, "Go do your thing. We'll have time to talk later."

*Oh yes, we will.* At length, he imagined. And Thomas was most certainly not looking forward to that.

"All right." He grasped her shoulder a little harder than necessary. He was going to have to find a kind way to break the news to her. Later, when they could be alone. She was going to have questions too, and it wasn't the kind of explanation one rushed. How could he explain, though, when he barely understood it himself? *If* he understood it at all. "I'll come back for you later. Be safe."

She frowned, but Thomas walked away before she could get a word in. God, how was he going to justify that he'd chosen to help Jethro in his madness instead of trying to stop him . . . even though there was nothing he could do? Maybe she would understand. She was an inventor herself . . . But something told him she was going to chew him out for it.

And the thing was, he was going to deserve it.

Actually, Jethro was the one in need of a good chewing-out, but he wasn't going to be around to get that, either. As he hurried backstage to help Jethro, Thomas cursed the man once more. Profusely.

Jethro was waiting backstage, wearing his best suit—it looked almost as old and frumpy as Thomas's own outfit—and combing his fingers through his hair, which was even more of a mess than usual.

Not for the first time, Thomas wished they had some help for the event. Actually, he wished *he* had some help for the event. And to sort things out in the aftermath . . .

When he would be alone.

"How are you holding up? Ready for the big moment?" Thomas asked. He tried to sound calm, but his heart was pounding in his chest. He didn't want to look at the prosthetics lined up on a large, wheeled table, didn't even want to *glance* at the red drape covering a slate cot, outlining the shape of the automaton underneath. It wasn't working yet, but that devil would show up and bring it to life soon.

The fear, the utter terror, had congealed into a lead weight at the bottom of his stomach. Even though he hadn't had a bite to eat in hours, hadn't even managed to nibble on some bread, he was about to keel over and vomit. The time had come, and there was nothing he could do to stop it.

All he wanted to do was grab on to Jethro and hold him. Hold him and beg the devil to please, *please* not take him away. If only there was a way, if only they could have had a little more time, just one more week, one more day . . .

"I'm . . . well, as ready as I will ever be," Jethro said, shooting him an unsteady smile. How he could manage not to be a screaming ball of fear, considering what was in store for him, Thomas had no idea.

"Jethro," Thomas started. The words died in his throat, as if he were choking, and he didn't know what to say. There should be something meaningful he could say, a . . . a *thank you*, a *fuck you, you selfish son of a bitch*, a . . . *something* appropriate for a good-bye to someone who had completely changed his life in just ten days. "Jethro, I . . . I just . . ."

Jethro reached out, hesitating for a second before cupping Thomas's cheek with a shaky hand. Thomas closed his eyes, feeling the tears burning behind his eyelids, and leaned into the touch.

"You know . . . you know how to handle it, right? You'll be all right?" Jethro murmured.

Yes, Thomas knew. They'd talked about every possibility over the previous few days, coming up with contingency plans for all scenarios, trying to ensure Thomas would know how to manage the automaton after the soiree.

"I won't unstrap it from the table," Jethro went on. "If it doesn't . . . if it doesn't obey you, then just—"

"Yes, Jethro. I'll destroy it." They had lined up hammers and tools on a smaller wheeled table just behind the curtains. And Jethro had carefully showed Thomas all the creature's weak spots. Besides, if all else failed, his prosthetic would be able to do quite a lot of damage.

"And should it function properly instead—"

"Don't worry, Jethro. I know. I will make sure it doesn't fall into the wrong hands."

Thomas clutched Jethro's wrist, looking him in the eye, trying to sound confident. He needed to somehow reassure Jethro that everything would be all right, even though Thomas wasn't so sure of it himself. If he couldn't save Jethro from dying, at least he could make sure Jethro went as peacefully as possible.

Jethro tried to smile at him, a small, pained smile. "Thank you for all your help. For . . . everything." He looked as if he was about to add something else, but he didn't. Maybe he couldn't find the words, either. Maybe there were no words.

So Thomas closed his eyes as Jethro leaned closer and kissed him. It was a long, chaste kiss, their warm lips pressing together. They breathed each other's breath when they parted, resting their foreheads against each other, and for a moment, Thomas couldn't even think. He just wanted to hold Jethro as tightly as possible and weep and scream and beg him not to go.

But Thomas stepped back instead, even though the loss of that contact was worse than when he'd had his right hand hacked off, and straightened his shoulders.

"Then let's get this party started, shall we?" His voice shook, his turmoil so transparent that there was no chance Jethro could believe his fake upbeat tone. But Jethro just swallowed and smiled back, then turned to grab the edge of the table laden with prosthetics.

"Let's do it."

"And as you can see, following a simple impulse, the fingers of the hand will bend, allowing the owner to securely grasp any object."

Thomas was standing in the back of the room, arms folded over his chest, watching as Jethro demonstrated the functions of his mechanical hands and legs, as an introduction of sorts before he brought out the automaton. He'd asked Thomas to be onstage and give an actual demonstration, but Thomas had adamantly refused. There was no way he could hold it together *and* stand on that stage being showcased like a circus freak in front of all those people. No fucking way.

The crowd responded positively for the most part, *ooh*ing and *aah*ing appropriately. There were a couple of muted gasps and screams, though, when Jethro showcased the pair of prosthetic lungs, their thin leather sacs inflating and deflating rhythmically. Thomas looked over the audience. Dragana was leaning forward, resting her chin on her hands, listening with rapt attention. Then he caught a couple of people making the sign of the cross, looking absolutely scandalized.

A crooked smile twisted his lips. Oh, they had no idea how appropriate that was . . .

Every now and then, Jethro would shoot a glance above Thomas's head—at that damned hourglass. He could practically hear the grains shifting, but he steadfastly refused to look. He couldn't. Jethro was nearing the end of the presentation, and Thomas didn't want it to be real.

"And now, ladies and gentlemen, the real reason why I called you here tonight . . ." Jethro straightened his jacket. His hands were shaking a little. "You are about to witness the unveiling of one of the greatest inventions ever created by humankind, something that will revolutionize the whole scientific world and, indeed, life as we know it."

Some people muttered and chuckled sarcastically while Jethro disappeared from sight to roll in the automaton. Panic surged inside Thomas's chest, constricting his lungs, making it hard to breathe. Maybe, he thought desperately, if he could stop the devil once he arrived and talk to him, maybe he could convince him to let Jethro out of the deal. Thomas didn't know what he would say, but surely he would find the right words. If he could just talk to Farfarello for a few moments. But the damn devil was nowhere to be seen.

Thomas's attention was drawn back to the stage when a collective gasp rose from the audience. There it was. Jethro's creation. The one he'd given his soul for. And no matter how often Thomas saw it, he was still awestruck. Devil or no devil, it was incredible what Jethro had achieved. The automaton looked truly amazing—polished brass plaques, tubing, pipes, wires, not an unnecessary piece on it. It was a flawless mechanical creation. And that porcelain face, so delicate and beautiful with Stefan's features.

The crowd began to stir even more. A few people screamed, some got up as they shook their heads, other people pulling them back down. Thomas was trying to figure out if they were impressed or if they were simply horrified.

Jethro was standing very still onstage, waiting for the crowd to quiet down, his eyes fixed on the automaton and an unreadable expression on his face.

"I . . . was going to demonstrate how a man-made machine could function just as a real human body would. Such an invention could change the world as we know it. I imagined a series of these robots helping men in the fields, working tirelessly in factories, day and night. And I imagined how if an army had even just one of these machines, it could save so many lives. It would have saved so many lives if we'd had them at our disposal during the war, if our young men hadn't needed to go to the front and sacrifice their lives." Jethro's voice had turned somber. He took a deep breath, then raised his head, his jaw set.

"I was going to demonstrate it, but I am not. Instead, I have a confession to make to you all. I wanted this invention to bring glory to my name, but the truth is, there is no glory here. Because what I was about to show you is not a product of my skills alone, and I deserve no credit for it whatsoever. Neither do I deserve all the credit for the prosthetics I have shown you. So I want to take this occasion to apologize to you all for misleading you, as well as the scientific community at large."

The crowd was now silent. Thomas gaped at him, even while his heart tumbled inside his chest with a mixture of surprise and a rush of pride.

Jethro turned to pick up something from one of the trays—a large, thick scalpel and a hammer. "There is a dark power at work in this machine. A power I should never have sought out and brought into the world. I apologize to everyone I deceived, to everyone I dragged into this blasphemous affair. While it is too late to undo what I set in motion, there is one way I can try to make amends, at least in part.

"So what you will see now, ladies and gentlemen, is this . . . creature, this automaton, being destroyed. It should never have been built in the first place, since the only way it could ever function is through the intervention of evil, destructive forces that should have nothing to do with technology and progress. When you leave here, that is what you should tell the world: that this kind of technology cannot exist. And from today, it will no longer exist."

Thomas looked on, astonished. He'd had no idea Jethro was going to do that. The anxiety tightening his chest like a vise finally snapped loose, letting him breathe again, and he knew Jethro had made the right choice. He glanced at the hourglass. It was time, only a handful of shimmering sand left to fall . . .

Dragana craned her head around, maybe searching for Thomas. She'd grabbed the arm of the man sitting beside her, and he was obviously quite agitated if the way he was waving his arms around was any indicator. Was he describing the automaton to her?

Thomas glanced around, searching for that familiar plumed hat, listening for the sound of silver bells. Was the devil going to show up? What would he think of Jethro's sudden change of heart? Would he make an appearance or—

He froze. Mina was at the back of the hall, her eyes fixed on the stage, something like wonder on her face.

"There it is," she murmured, staring straight ahead. Then she turned to look intently at something by her side, something Thomas couldn't see. She nodded, as if responding to some inaudible voice. Then she straightened her shoulders, collected herself, and walked forward, seamlessly cutting through chairs and guests alike while Jethro, onstage, had stepped toward the automaton and was placing the scalpel under the edge of one of the plaques covering its chest.

Nobody turned around. Nobody even glanced her way. Thomas pushed through the audience to try to intercept her, but it was difficult to move quickly. Several people were standing, a few were trying to leave, and they were all getting in Thomas's way.

"Mina," he called out, as loud as he dared, trying not to attract too much attention. "What are you doing?"

She ignored him completely. Her eyes were fixed on the stage, on Jethro. No, not on Jethro, Thomas realized. She was staring at the automaton, her face transfixed. She glanced back quickly, as if seeking reassurance from someone who wasn't there, then nodded and kept going. Thomas couldn't see anyone who might be encouraging her, but he had a nagging feeling he knew who it might be.

*"Maybe there would be a body for me very soon."* Her voice echoed in Thomas's ears, making his blood run cold, a shudder shooting down his spine.

*Oh no . . .*

"Finally. I have waited so long," she muttered.

"No, Mina!" he yelled, not caring that everyone was now looking at him as if he were a madman. Even Jethro was stunned.

But Mina continued to ignore Thomas as she reached the stage and effortlessly fluttered onto it. She was headed straight for the automaton.

He yelled at Jethro, "Stop her, Jethro! Stop her," even though he didn't know how. They couldn't even touch her, goddamn it. He should have seen it coming. That fucking devil, fucking Farfarello . . .

Then mayhem erupted.

In an instant Mina was gone, merged with the automaton, and she started moving at once. She ripped off the leather straps as if they were cobwebs, and then tumbled forward as people screamed and jumped to their feet, trying to rush to the exit. Jethro was frozen in place, looking utterly horrified, as Mina took a few awkward steps and jumped off the stage, landing with a loud *thump*, and threw herself toward the door. She careered through the chairs, and the panic exploded even more—people running, falling, bringing down chairs, crushing and trampling one another. They were clogging the exit, and she was running in the same direction, mechanical limbs jerking awkwardly, destroying everything in her wake.

In the chaos, it took Thomas a few seconds to realize the other prosthetics were going mad too. An arm had leaped off the table and was punching a man in the face, a hand had stolen the wig from a bejeweled lady and was waving it in the air, the knitting machine was flinging canapés like grenades all around the room.

*Why are they alive, too?*

He saw him then: Farfarello, hanging upside down from the rafters, moving his hands like a music conductor, grinning and looking like he was having the time of his life guiding the prosthetics in their crazed dance. God, this had been his plan all along, hadn't it?

Their gazes met for an instant, Thomas's wide eyes and Farfarello's amused, aqua-green ones. The devil winked and disappeared from sight.

"Thomas! Thomas!" A woman was calling his name—Dragana.

He threw himself into the crowd, looking for the bright-red flash of her shawl. When he found it, he saw that she couldn't orient herself in the mess and was standing, surrounded by fallen chairs, trying to find her way to a corner while people bumped into her, frantic to get to the door, and Mina . . . Mina was plowing right toward Dragana, single-mindedly focused on the very same thing, leaving a trail of crushed wooden chairs in her wake.

"Dragana, watch out!" Thomas shouted, shoving the tea maker out of the way and leaping toward her. They fell among the debris, rolling out of the way just as Mina rushed past, obviously deciding to skip the crowded door and smashing a hole right in the wall, exploding into the garden outside.

"Stop! Don't do it! Stop!" It was Jethro, running after her through the upturned chairs, his instruments still in hand as he dodged his wild prosthetics as he tried to keep up with Mina.

Despite the rush of adrenaline, Thomas was stunned for a moment at how incredibly powerful the mechanical body Jethro had built was. Mina had torn the stone wall apart as if it had been made of butter. A sharp crack came from outside, like glass shattering. She must have finally broken out of the glass prison where she'd been locked for such a long time, finally free to go out into the world.

He turned to make sure Dragana was all right. She was shaking her head, trying to get up, muttering, "What the hell just happened?"

He didn't even know where to start. The automaton was gone, the devil was gone, and—

Thomas's gaze flew up to the hourglass—the *empty* hourglass.

*Oh God. Jethro* . . . He could be dropping dead in the garden this very second.

Thomas helped Dragana up, his heart hammering in his chest, as he kept looking toward the ragged hole in the wall, barely able to stop himself from screaming Jethro's name. He didn't want to frighten Dragana further, and he didn't want to take her outside, didn't want her to be there when . . . *if* he found Jethro's dead body. But he couldn't leave her in the ballroom, not with the prosthetics still crawling on the walls, dangling from the curtains.

"Come—let's get outside," he told her, carefully guiding her through the debris and past the collapsed stones around the opening. He led her to one of the wrought iron benches, where he was certain she was far enough from the prosthetics to be safe. "Just wait here, just for a moment."

She was already nodding, grasping the armrest and sitting down. "I'll be fine. Go find Jethro."

Thomas darted off, frantically looking around the garden. All the guests had left, leaving behind trampled grass and the occasional fallen hat. "Jethro!" he called out, his throat so tight he could barely get the word out. He spotted him then, a lone figure standing by the wall of shattered glass, the shards scattered all around him, reflecting the lights of the dozen hansom cabs still maneuvering around one another to hurry down the too-narrow path. He looked dejected, his clothes askew and his hair sticking in every direction, the useless hammer still in his hand, but he was still standing. He was still alive.

Thomas's heart leaped in his throat as he sprinted forward. "Oh God, Jethro, are you—" He hadn't even finished the sentence when Jethro turned to face him—*he's alive, he's alive*—and Thomas nearly crashed into him, pulling him into a fierce hug.

"Where is he? Did you see him?" Jethro rasped when they managed to pull apart, and for an instant Thomas had no idea who Jethro was talking about, too overwhelmed with relief, too busy pressing his fingers to Jethro's face, his cheeks, his chin, making sure he was still there, still breathing. Then he shook himself out of it. There were more pressing matters now. For one, Dragana was waiting for them. There would be time for this. At least, he hoped so.

"I don't know," he said, shaking his head. "I saw him inside, but . . . he's gone. I think he left."

Jethro's hands were unsteady as he pushed his hair back from his forehead. "But . . . but why? The time is up; he should . . . he should have . . ."

"I don't know." Thomas swallowed. He had no idea, and he didn't want to think about it right now. "Come, Jethro. Dragana is waiting. We're going to have to explain everything to her. And Mina . . . Mina's gone. There's nothing more we can do for now."

Jethro cast another glance at the jagged edges of the broken glass, hesitating, but Thomas resolutely grabbed his hand and dragged him away. "Come on. Let's go."

# CHAPTER 22

There was significantly less yelling on Dragana's part than Thomas had thought there would be.

They tried to explain about the deal with the devil, the prosthetics, and the automaton as best as they could—careful to leave out the detail of the porcelain mask bearing Stefan's features, at least for the moment. Dragana had heard the rumors, of course, and she'd had her suspicions, so Thomas supposed maybe it wasn't too surprising to her. Or maybe she was just really good at masking it, sitting wrapped in her shawl, her face devoid of expression as they talked.

Though, it was Jethro who did most of the talking, as it should be. The wild prosthetics had mostly escaped into the garden, where they were crawling like oversized, gleaming insects up the trees and all over the glass enclosure. But it was too dark to chase after them now, so the three inventors had retreated to the kitchen and huddled around the stove, where Thomas was warming some water for tea. Maybe he could have retrieved some canapés from the ballroom floor, where the knitting machine had tossed them, but he wasn't hungry in the least, and he doubted the others were, either.

Once Jethro had finished his explanation, Dragana sighed and shook her head. "Heavens, Jethro. I'd heard what the people were saying down in the village, but I cannot believe you were *actually* so stupid."

Jethro hung his head, keeping his eyes low.

"Then again, maybe I can. I . . . I should have tried harder to keep in touch when you secluded yourself up here. I'm sorry, I—"

"Dragana, please. Don't apologize," Jethro reached across the table to place a hand on her arm. "I'm the only one to blame. I'm the one who shut you out. You were suffering too. I should have stayed close to you. We could have helped each other through this instead of . . . instead of me going and making a gigantic mess of things."

After a few, excruciating seconds where Thomas held his breath, Dragana's lips curled into a small smile. "Well at least now you'll finally have to admit I was right in not wanting one of your prosthetics."

That actually startled a chuckle out of Jethro. He raised his arms, as if about to say something, then just shook his head and buried his face in his hands, still laughing, an irregular, hiccupping laugh somewhere between exhaustion and relief.

Thomas looked down to his own prosthetic hand, which was obediently holding the handle of the kettle. For some reason, it hadn't gone berserk along with the others. Hopefully all the villagers' prosthetics were still working too. They'd have to send a messenger pigeon to Herman immediately to make sure.

"So I guess you were the only wise one among us, Dragana," he said, now chuckling too. He felt light-headed with relief. The night had been an unmitigated disaster, but Jethro was alive, sitting right there in front of him. And even though he had no idea why the devil hadn't taken Jethro away, Thomas was too grateful to think about it too hard at the moment.

"Indeed. Did you have any doubts?" She tightened the red shawl around her shoulders and took a deep breath. "All right. So hopefully we'll be able to round up a hansom cab to take us down to the village. Send a pigeon, grab some clothes, and we'll go."

Thomas and Jethro turned to look at her. "What? Why?" Jethro asked.

"Well, you can't stay here. The house is half-destroyed." She shrugged. "You'll come to my place. You know there's plenty of space."

"But . . ." Jethro swallowed. "But the prosthetics . . ."

"Oh for Heaven's sake. They might clobber you in your sleep for all you know," she replied. "You can come back to round them up in daylight. It will be much safer."

Jethro fidgeted, pulling at his cuffs. "Yes, but . . ."

She tilted her head to the side. "What's really bugging you?"

Jethro shot Thomas a helpless glance, and Thomas just lifted his shoulders, silently joining in Dragana's question. What was he up to?

"The . . . the devil. I mean, he might still come. I don't want to draw him to your home."

Thomas's stomach dropped. He didn't even want to consider that a real possibility.

"Well, let him come, then. I have a few choice words for him myself," Dragana replied. "Come on, get your stuff. We'll figure something out after a good night's sleep."

"Another one?" Dragana muttered as a mechanical pigeon swooshed in through the open window, landing with a clank on the table, where five other pigeons were clucking about.

Thomas groaned, still wrestling with the oversized pigeon in his arms, trying to still it. "Jethro, what am I supposed to do with this one? It's pretty insistent."

"Just send it back with the others," Jethro deadpanned. He was slumped in an armchair, resting his forehead on his hand and sternly refusing to lift his gaze. He had dark shadows under his eyes, looking rumpled and haggard. He hadn't slept a wink that night. Thomas had snoozed a little bit, uncomfortably leaning forward on the table, but he hadn't been able to relax, constantly waking up with a startle, wondering if the devil had come.

Thomas managed to shove the pigeon out the window. The clockwork creature squeaked and flew off in a flutter of metallic feathers. He sighed and glanced at the others still crowding on the table. They had been arriving in a steady stream since sunrise. It wasn't even midday.

Jethro scowled. "How the heck do they know where to find me?"

"I'll bet that hansom driver didn't keep his mouth shut like we asked him to," Thomas replied. "Look, shouldn't you at least check what the messages say? They might be important."

"What for? I already know what they say. My reputation is ruined, as it should be. I'm not interested in trying to salvage the wreckage. It was what I wanted . . . what I deserve."

Thomas stepped closer to him and silently rested his hand on Jethro's shoulder, squeezing it, trying to comfort him as best as he could. He wasn't quite sure what to say. He didn't think *At least you're not dead* would be very helpful.

"All right, so you're a pariah now, congratulations. Let's talk about the important stuff," Dragana said. "I think you two should move in with me."

Jethro and Thomas both turned to stare at her.

Jethro's brow furrowed. "I . . . Why would we do that?"

"For one, your house is half-destroyed. But mostly I think it would do you good. I don't want you holed up there ruminating on the error of your ways. Not again. I let you do it once already, and look how that turned out." She shook her head, drumming her fingers on the table. "Besides, you're adamant I shouldn't close the shop, and I don't want to run it anymore. So I could use someone taking care of it."

"Dragana, be serious," Jethro said with a sigh. "I can't do that. After what happened, people won't even come close to the shop if they know I'm here."

Dragana raised an eyebrow. "Good point, indeed. But don't be so self-centered. I wasn't talking about you."

A moment of silence followed her words. *She can't mean . . .* Then Jethro turned to look at Thomas and tilted his head.

Thomas dropped the pigeon he was holding and raised his hands. "Me? Oh no. I couldn't possibly do that."

"Why not? You had a toy shop, didn't you? And now you're here. You'll need a workshop, and I need someone to keep this place open." Dragana shrugged, a smug look on her face. "Seems pretty darn perfect."

Thomas opened his mouth to protest, but he didn't find any suitable objections. She was right. But . . . "Do you think . . . people would even be interested in my toys, here? I mean—"

She waved him off. "Unlike Jethro here, I still have quite a few good contacts. So give it a try. If it doesn't work, well, at least you won't have any regrets."

Thomas shot a quick glance at Jethro, trying to gauge what he might have been thinking, but his expression was unreadable.

"How—" He cleared his throat. "How would we arrange things?" Thomas thought it would be quite complicated to negotiate the cohabitation of three inventors in one single laboratory. They all had their peculiar quirks and interests, and they would be invading Dragana's home, after all. There was a reason why inventors were usually viewed as loner lunatics.

"Don't forget there were once several people living here. As a family. My rooms are on the first floor. You two can have the attic. And three inventors can share the workshop. It's big enough. I could take the mezzanine. Could use some peace and quiet to paint my spiders, anyway. And you two can share the lower floor."

Jethro shook his head. "I won't be working anymore. It's all over."

"Well, if the villagers come asking for help with their prosthetics, you'll have to help them," Dragana replied matter-of-factly.

Thomas worried his lip. He wanted to say yes, but it wasn't really his decision to make. He needed to talk about it with Jethro. In private.

"We don't have to decide right now," Thomas said, stalling. "Why don't we go up to the house to sort out the prosthetics and grab some stuff, and then . . . Maybe while we're there, we should try looking for Mina. Do you reckon she might have come back? It's her home too, after all. . ."

Jethro sighed heavily. "Another thing I have no idea about."

"Do you think—" Thomas stopped. "Well, another question with no answer, I suppose. I just hope she's, you know, happy."

"I hope so too. Somehow." Dragana huffed, shaking her head. "At least the damn automaton will be good for something. But back to my question . . ."

Thomas cast another glance at Jethro, feeling completely at a loss. "I . . . We'll think about it, Dragana, I promise. We'll have an answer for you soon. Thank you for the generous offer."

"All right. You do that," she said, shooing them toward the door. "At this hour, you might still be able to persuade a cab driver to take you up there. If you're willing to pay enough, of course." She winked and closed the door behind them.

As it turned out, the drivers were actually stomping over one another to be the one to drive them back to the house. They all wanted some juicy gossip to report at the tavern that night. But Jethro and Thomas rode in silence, not giving the driver anything.

Once they entered the house and reached the hall where the soiree had been held, Thomas surveyed the wreckage, his hands on his hips. The prosthetics were thankfully back to being inanimate lumps of metal and wires, scattered on the floor of the room and out in the garden, past the ragged hole in the wall. One mechanical leg was even dangling from the chandelier. The knitting machine was moving about, though, fiddling with a shredded curtain over and over.

Jethro completely ignored the messy room and made a beeline for his laboratory, Thomas on his heels. He opened the pendulum clock and stepped inside, and after a moment's hesitation, Thomas followed him in there too. The secret lab was untouched, the only glaring change the absence of the automaton.

Jethro stood beside the empty table, placed his hand on the wood, and lowered his head. "Why didn't he take me?" he whispered.

Thomas didn't need to ask. He knew perfectly well who Jethro was talking about.

"Why?" he asked again. "The deal was clear. He would get my soul. That was his reward, and now he doesn't want it?" He turned around and leaned against the table, shaking his head. "I don't understand. Is it just another cruel trick? Let us relax for a couple of days and, just as soon as we feel safe, he'll come?"

Thomas sighed. He looked around, located a chair, and dragged it over to sit down, resting his elbows on his knees. "I don't know. I've been thinking about it all night, and—" He paused. "I should probably tell you that I talked to him again."

Jethro's gaze snapped up, his eyes wide. "What? When?"

"A couple of days ago. He came to see me."

Jethro blinked slowly. "All right. What . . . what did he say? What did he want?"

"He said a lot of things. I wasn't quite sure what they all meant. I think he wanted . . ." Thomas huffed, rubbing his hand over his face. He'd spent a lot of time trying to make sense of the ramblings of that devil. "Look, I know it doesn't make much sense, but I think he wanted to teach you a lesson."

"A lesson? What kind of . . . ? Why?"

"I won't pretend to know what's going on in that head of his, but he said some things about how he wasted his potential when he was alive, and how he hates seeing people . . ." Thomas shook his head. "Anyway, I think it might be why he hasn't taken you. Because maybe he thinks you have learned something." He paused. "Do you think . . .? Have you? I mean, what you said at the soiree . . ."

Jethro tightened his lips. "I don't know about a lesson. But I guess I have . . . changed. Everything has changed since . . ." He lowered his head, sheepishly. "Well, since you arrived. I guess I always had some doubts, but then you came along, and I couldn't stop thinking about it. I couldn't remember why it all had ever seemed like a good idea. Why I was so hell-bent on doing it. I just . . ." He paused, and Thomas waited in silence for him to continue.

"I just couldn't go through with it," he said. "Everyone would have thought I was such a genius, I would have been immortalized, dead at the very apex of my genius. The scientific community would have talked about me for decades to come. And it would have all been a lie."

He shook his head, frowning. "And with Stefan's face, on top of everything else . . . I thought it would be a way to honor him? Right. Being the face of the lie of the century. The face of a monster brought to life by the devil himself." Jethro hid his face in his hands. "I don't know what the hell I'd been thinking. How I could ever think he would have wanted something like that . . ."

Thomas opened his mouth, then paused. He didn't want to interrupt Jethro. So he just muttered, "I think you're right."

"And then I thought I finally understood, but it was too late, you know? I was going to die. There was nothing I could do to fix things except tell the truth for once. I was ready to die. And instead . . ." He raised his gaze to look at Thomas. His eyes were wide, and he looked so vulnerable. And lost.

"I'm alive. I never planned for that. My work, the automaton, it consumed my entire life for years. There was nothing else for me, and there would be nothing else afterward. And now it's over, and I'm still here, and I don't know what to do." He rubbed his hands together nervously, looking at Thomas as if he might somehow have all the answers. "Where do I go from here? What do I do now?"

Thomas listened, his lips parted. All he wanted to do was stand up and hold Jethro close, hug him and somehow reassure him that it would be all right. But he cleared his throat instead, absentmindedly brushing his thumb on the polished brass of his prosthetic. "You take it one day at a time. That's all you can do." Jethro tilted his head questioningly, and Thomas straightened his shoulders and continued. "I had a life and a plan too. And then the accident happened, and I lost my hand *and* my plan. All of a sudden, it was all just . . . gone. And so I . . ." He trailed off.

Slowly, Jethro nodded. "You took one day at a time."

"Yes. And somehow, along the way, I created another life. It wasn't my plan—I don't have a plan anymore—it just . . . happened. And I would like to let it continue. See how it goes. One day at a time."

"Without any plans."

"Yeah. No. I mean, maybe a little plan." Thomas swallowed. "What do you think about Dragana's idea?"

Jethro waited so long to reply, Thomas thought he wouldn't. Finally, he sighed deeply. "I don't know. I don't know about anything right now. My laboratory is here, all my equipment is here, but I guess . . . I guess I could bring down what I'll need. If, you know, if the villagers need help with their prosthetics." He turned and leaned against the table, folding his arms. "What about you? You would like it, right?"

Thomas could think of a hundred reasons why it wouldn't be a good idea. His plan all along had been to get his hand, then get back to Lunaris and resume his old life. And now, somehow, he'd ended up starting to build a life in Montrale. But . . .

"Yes. I would like that. I would like to stay. I . . ." He stood. He wanted to reach out and touch Jethro's hand, but he didn't. "I would like to stay. With you. If . . . if you . . ."

Jethro raised his head and looked Thomas in the eye, and for the first time in what felt like years rather than days, Jethro smiled. "I would like that." He closed the distance between them, gently placing his hand on Thomas's and twining their fingers together. "I would like that very much."

Thomas smiled back, feeling a lump lodge in his throat, his heart tumbling in his chest. "Then let's clean up and get packed."

Bright and early the next morning, they sent Frida down to the village to fetch a cab. When the pigeon returned, the hansom was rattling along behind her. They loaded a few pieces of luggage into the car and headed straight back down the mountain.

They would send for the rest of their things later. They had time. Finally, the damn hourglass was empty; it was gone. Finally, they had *time*.

Thomas squeezed Jethro's hand as the cab arrived at the shop. They paid the driver and stood in front of the shop's door for a moment, luggage in tow. They exchanged a glance. Without a word, they twined their fingers together again.

Thomas took a deep breath and knocked. Dragana opened the door, an orange scarf wrapped around her head. She didn't say anything, just rested her hand on the doorframe.

Thomas smiled, even though she couldn't see him. "So . . . you still want us to live with you?"

Thomas was sitting in Dragana's workshop—he guessed it was his workshop too, now—in the wee hours, trying to finish a birthday present. A clockwork toy for a boy down at the village that he had to finish by morning, actually. He smiled as he worked. As promised, Dragana had been spreading the news that there was a new inventor in town, and thanks to her good words about him, people were slowly warming up to his presence. In fact, more than a few villagers had even popped in to inquire about his work and expressed interest in his toys.

He attached a miniature trumpet to the toy's little hands. As he moved to connect another piece, though, a jingling of silver bells attracted his attention. Even before he lifted his eyes, Thomas knew what he was going to see—or who, rather.

And sure enough, there he was. Farfarello sat on the back of an armchair, his booted feet resting on the cushion. He was still outrageously dressed but without his hat, and he somehow lacked that theatrical air he'd had in every one of their encounters. He was just sitting there with a small smile on his lips, the empty hourglass sitting between his feet. Thomas's stomach clenched at the sight.

The anxiety sunk its icy claws into him, as if it had never left. He knew they had been living on borrowed time, even if they wanted to believe Jethro would be spared for good, and now it was over. Thomas fought back the tears, even though the knot in his stomach made him want to double over and throw up.

He straightened his shoulders, swallowed the lump in his throat, and pushed away the fluttering, panicky feeling in his chest. He was determined to go down fighting, and this was a chance to talk to Farfarello, to try to reason with him somehow. He had nothing to lose. And in fact, he might well lose everything if he didn't.

"Hello," Thomas said as calmly as he could. They stared at each other in silence for a moment. "This is a rather subdued entrance for you. How unusual."

Farfarello just lowered his head, almost sheepishly hiding behind his messy blond hair. After another few seconds of silence that seemed to trickle slow and sticky like molasses, the devil took a deep breath. "I'm not here to take him away," he said, looking Thomas right in the face. "So you can relax. That is not what this visit is about."

"Oh." Thomas wanted to ask why, but really, why should he push it? It was what he wanted to hear, after all. Everything in him was screaming at him to just drop it and move on. But on the other hand, he didn't want to carry that anxiety with him in the future, so he'd better get to the bottom of this now. "Then *why*, Farfarello? Why all these machinations on your part, all this . . . planning, and working, and . . . What's in it for you?" He shook his head. "What do you want, if you're not even taking him? I mean, that was the whole point of the deal as far as you're concerned, wasn't it?"

Farfarello smiled. "I guess I should record this conversation. I've had to give this explanation more times than I can count." He took a deep breath, and it really sounded like he was reciting something he'd repeated plenty of times before. "Let's just say that Jethro needed a little . . . reminder. Of why he got into this business to begin with. Of what it was supposed to be about. People like him sometimes lose sight of it somewhere along the way."

Thomas looked down at the toy he was fiddling with.

"And as for why I'm not taking him . . . Well, I will. Just not now." Farfarello paused. "It would be kind of a waste of all my hard work if I took him away now that he can get back to work properly. Now I want to see what he gets done in the years he has left. I have time, anyway. A few decades will pass in the blink of an eye for me. No sweat. I can wait."

Thomas swallowed, uneasy. "So when he dies, he'll still have to . . ."

"Go to Hell? Yes. Yes, of course. There's nothing to be done about that. A deal is a deal, after all." Farfarello nodded. "But if it makes you feel any better, I'm pretty sure that's where you're headed too. I know what you were doing, back when you were living on the streets. Stealing, cheating . . . I mean, did you really think you were Heaven material?"

Thomas actually laughed at that. He'd never given it much thought.

"But you shouldn't concern yourself about it too much. Everyone always does, but really, I swear, we just get a lot of bad press." The devil shrugged. "It's not as bad down there as everyone thinks. A lot of interesting people, that's for sure."

Strangely, Thomas did feel kind of reassured. Besides, if that was how it was going to go, there was no point in panicking about it. He'd just deal with it when the time came.

"So . . . so why me, Farfarello?" he asked. "How did I end up in all of this? If Jethro was your target. You're the one who brought me here. At first I thought I was just a tool for you to . . . manipulate Jethro. Help him see the error of his ways, or whatever it was you wanted."

He could see things clearly in these terms, as if the world were a laboratory and people were tools influencing one another, complementing one another to build more complex machines than themselves. It was kind of safer to see it that way.

"And then . . . I don't know. I get the feeling that somewhere along the way, it became more than that."

Farfarello rubbed his chin with a bejeweled hand. The spider was peacefully strolling along his arm and shoulder. "What can I say, toymaker? You turned out to be quite interesting in your own right. I figured it wouldn't hurt to take on a little side project while I was at it. You know, to keep things from being too easy. Gets boring after a while, you know. Maybe I needed an extra challenge to spice things up."

Thomas raised an eyebrow. The devil's characteristic tone was there again—that flippant, carefree one that made Thomas think he was lying. Or at least not telling the complete truth. Thomas rested his chin on his hand and just stared. They looked at each other for a long moment, and he had the feeling that they understood each other, that there was some kind of mutual agreement. He knew Farfarello was full of shit, and Farfarello knew that he knew but wasn't going to say anything about it.

Farfarello shook his head, then gave in. "Jethro could use a lot less arrogance, but you, my friend, you could really use a little bit more. Your work has worth." He nodded toward the unfinished toy still lying on the table in front of Thomas. "You're not doing yourself justice, for one, but more importantly, you're doing a great disservice to your work if you keep ignoring its value and refusing to share it with the world. So I just thought you might learn a little lesson along the way too."

Thomas didn't reply. He wasn't sure if he'd learned that lesson, but . . . maybe. Maybe he had, a little, at least.

"And Mina? Did you take a special interest in her too? Do you know where she is? Is she all right?"

"Yes. Yes, she is. A little homesick, I should say." Farfarello turned his hand over, and the spider ran along it. Thomas couldn't help but notice that he'd carefully avoided answering the first question but decided not to push it. "I'm pretty sure she's scared. That you two will be angry with her and that she can't come home anymore. Actually, I was meaning to bring that up, so thank you for anticipating me."

"Oh," was all he could say for a moment. He wasn't angry with her, that was certain, though he wasn't entirely sure about Jethro.

But he was pretty confident Jethro wasn't angry, either. If anything, he seemed mildly ashamed of not having paid her more attention. "If you are in touch with her at all, maybe you could tell her— Just tell her to come home. We'll figure something out."

Farfarello nodded, seeming almost proud. "That's exactly what I was hoping to hear. I will surely do that." He stood. "So if there's nothing else, I will get on my way. I trust your curiosity is satisfied."

Thomas stood up too. Suddenly he felt a little awkward about saying good-bye because it truly *was* good-bye. And at the end of the day, he owed the man—the devil, whatever. Whether Thomas liked it or not, it was thanks to Farfarello that his life had changed so much.

He cleared his throat. "So . . . good-bye then, I guess. And . . . well, thank you." Thomas stepped around the table, getting closer to the devil, and instinctively extended his hand.

Farfarello gave a sideways grin, then shook it firmly. "See you in a few decades, toymaker. Keep out of trouble, yeah? Don't make me come back before it's time." He bent down to grab the empty hourglass, weighing it in his hand before putting it under his arm. "I'll be taking this with me. You don't need it anymore, after all."

Thomas glanced at the shimmering black sand that now rested at the bottom of the hourglass. He wasn't sure how he felt about that. "So you need it for some other deal, then?" He forced a smile, trying to crack a joke, even though it sounded false even to his own ears.

Farfarello seemed to read right through him, but he smiled in return anyway. "Maybe. Who knows? I do like to keep busy."

"Yeah, I've noticed that." Thomas lowered his eyes, shaking his head, a faint smile still hovering on his lips. "Hey, listen, Farfarello," he added. But when he looked up, the devil was gone—him and his hourglass—and all that was left was a mechanical spider already busy knitting a cobweb on the velvet armchair.

# EPILOGUE

*Three months later . . .*

"All right, so remember to just wind it up like this when it stops moving, and it will all work fine," Thomas said to a little girl with black pigtails. "Got it?"

"Yes, sir. Thank you, sir!" She clutched the clockwork mouse to her chest and happily bounced out of the shop, followed by her beaming grandfather. They had to squeeze past the small queue of people lined up outside while Thomas straightened his collar and turned to the next one.

"Yes, how may I— Oh, hello, Herman! Long time no see."

The dwarf waved at him with his prosthetic hand and smiled. "Keeping pretty busy, aren't you, toymaker."

"Can't complain, Herman, can't complain."

"Is Hastings around?"

"Yes, let me just get him for you." Then he called over his shoulder, "Mina, will you handle the customers for a moment?"

She scurried past him, carrying an armful of envelopes. More orders, it looked like, to add to the ones stacked in his workshop. They already occupied half a table.

He smiled at her as she set them down in the back. She now inhabited the body of a much smaller automaton, more suitable for a young girl, with delicate silk hair and filigree trimmings. It had been the first project Jethro had dived into once she'd returned, chagrined and so worried that they were mad at her.

Strangely enough, that body had taken much less time to ready than the original automaton, as if the pieces were coming together by magic. Sometimes, after going down to the workshop in the morning, Thomas and Jethro could almost swear some bits had slotted into place by themselves since the previous night. And when Mina's new body had been ready, she had been able to shift from one to the other seamlessly. Despite Farfarello's promise that he would stay away from their lives from then on, Thomas suspected the devil might actually have something to do with both those things, but for once, he didn't really mind.

As for the previous automaton, they had destroyed it. The only part they had kept was the porcelain mask of Stefan's face, which was safely locked away in a velvet-lined box.

"Yes, Thomas, don't worry!" Mina's tinny voice sounded cheerful as she came by him again, her mechanical feet clicking on the floor. She loved working in the shop, and she was never tired. She was always sweeping, arranging the shop window, putting up decorations, and making sure everything looked tidy and pretty. One of Stefan's pictures had been put in a brand-new frame, and Mina made sure it was polished, and placed fresh flowers on the table with it every day. But her favorite part was working behind the counter, dealing with the customers. By now, everyone knew Mina, and the kids absolutely adored her. She even had all the ribbons she could wear, ever since the boy from the haberdasher's had started coming around every morning, bringing her little trinkets and staring at her with cow eyes. And who could blame him? Her delicate porcelain had been carefully painted by Dragana, who had given her rosy cheeks and smiling lips.

Thomas walked into the backroom where Jethro had built his workshop. It was much smaller than his laboratory up at the house, but since they had moved into Dragana's building, they had been using the house mostly to store the bigger pieces of equipment that they hadn't had time to bring down yet. "Jethro? Herman is here to see you."

Jethro was sitting at his desk in the corner, the warm sunlight streaming in from the window beside him. He took off a pair of small, brass binoculars affixed on his nose and looked up with a smile that was just as warm. "Sure. I'll be right there."

He put down his screwdriver and headed into the shop, pausing to give Thomas a quick peck on the lips, brushing his arm before stepping out. Thomas followed him and leaned against the doorframe, watching.

"Why, Herman, nice to see you. The arm giving you any more trouble?" he asked, fixing his spectacles on his nose.

Herman waved him off. "Oh, nothing like that, Hastings. Just thought I'd pop by to say hello, if you're not too busy. Will you come by the market later this week?"

"Yes, absolutely. Thank you for stopping by. I actually needed to ask if you could order a couple of lenses for me. I might need to replace them on a pair of mechanical eyes and . . ."

Thomas couldn't help but smile. It was wonderful to see how much Jethro had changed since the soiree that should have marked the end of his time on Earth a few months earlier. He preferred to work in the laboratory, of course, but he came to hang out in the shop sometimes, actually smiling and chatting with the old friends that came to visit.

He was still kind of shy, and his smile was occasionally a little uncertain, as if he didn't quite remember how to be that person, but he was healing. And for the first time since Thomas had met him, Jethro actually seemed serene, happy even. As if the weight of the world had been lifted off his shoulders. Thomas wondered if this was what Jethro had been like before, but he didn't let himself think about it too much. If this whole ordeal had taught him anything, it was that who one was *before* really and truly didn't matter.

Thomas looked out at the shop, immense pride filling his chest. The place was practically Thomas's now, since his reputation had been steadily growing and the orders for his toys had multiplied within weeks. It had been frightening at the beginning, but he was getting important commissions now, which was just what they needed since Dragana didn't make any money, working solely for her pleasure, and Jethro was working for free, helping the local veterans and dispatching his prosthetics all over the country, wherever they were required. They were more basic, now that the devil's magic was gone, but they were still far more advanced than any others available.

Thomas had been worried about him, but surprisingly enough, Jethro really didn't seem to care about his reputation being destroyed in front of the whole scientific community. On the contrary, he seemed to find it almost a relief. Now he could just focus on what he loved. The villagers wearing his prosthetics often popped by the shop, a constant, colorful bustle of people coming to say hello and to get checkups. And despite Jethro's fears, all the machines were still working perfectly.

Thomas wasn't used to handling such a fast-growing business, but Mina was proving to be an excellent assistant and was learning quickly. She had a real knack for numbers and was already giving him excellent tips on dealing with the salesmen. In a couple of years, Thomas could see her running the shop. By then she would be much better at it than the three scatterbrained inventors were combined.

Indulging himself for a moment, Thomas watched Jethro talk to Herman while Mina presented a clockwork bluebird to a gaggle of delighted children, and heard Dragana's soft humming coming from up in the mezzanine. All he could do was smile. And while he still wasn't sure exactly who the new Thomas would turn out to be, he carried Jethro's fingerprints all over him, and it seemed that, at the very least, he would be happy.

He tapped his mechanical hand against the doorframe and smiled even wider. He had always thought his accident was the worst thing that had ever happened to him, yet he couldn't imagine *not* being here now, not having come to Montrale. This reality, with these people— Jethro, and Mina, and Dragana, and the villagers and even that crazy devil—this was where he belonged. He didn't want to be anywhere else. Even with all the pain, the anguish, the despair that had come before. If this was his reward, it had been worth it. It had all been worth it.

Explore more of the *Deal with a Devil* series:
riptidepublishing.com/titles/universe/deal-devil

Dear Reader,

Thank you for reading Cornelia Grey's *The Empty Hourglass*!

We know your time is precious and you have many, many entertainment options, so it means a lot that you've chosen to spend your time reading. We really hope you enjoyed it.

We'd be honored if you'd consider posting a review—good or bad—on sites like **Amazon, Barnes & Noble, Kobo, Goodreads, Twitter, Facebook, Tumblr,** and your blog or website. We'd also be honored if you told your friends and family about this book. Word of mouth is a book's lifeblood!

For more information on upcoming releases, author interviews, blog tours, contests, giveaways, and more, please sign up for our weekly, spam-free newsletter and visit us around the web:

**Newsletter**: tinyurl.com/RiptideSignup
**Twitter**: twitter.com/RiptideBooks
**Facebook**: facebook.com/RiptidePublishing
**Goodreads**: tinyurl.com/RiptideOnGoodreads
**Tumblr**: riptidepublishing.tumblr.com

Thank you so much for Reading the Rainbow!

AnglerFishPress.com

AN IMPRINT OF RIPTIDE PUBLISHING.

# ACKNOWLEDGMENTS

All my thanks and love to the people who supported me through a most difficult time, worked with me, and let me ramble at will: Adam, Seraf, Nidhi, Stefania, Francesca, Sophie, Raquel, and many others.

Thank you to all the wonderful people I met during my travels, who made those experiences unforgettable.

Thank you to my grandmother Annita and to my mother, Linda, for being my port in every storm.

And thank you, as always, to my wonderful editor Danielle for all her hard work.

*Deal with a Devil series:*
Devil at the Crossroads
The Circus of the Damned

Benjamin Pepperwhistle and the Fantabulous Circus of Wonders
The Ronin and the Fox
The Mercenary
Bounty Hunter
The Tea Demon
Apples and Regret and Wasted Time
City of Foxes

*Anthologies:*
Weight of a Gun
Weight of a Gun II
Wild Passions
Cross Bones
Elementary Erotica
Making Contact
A Brush of Wings

# ABOUT THE AUTHOR

Cornelia Grey is a creative writing PhD student, with a penchant for steampunk and classic rock. Born and raised in the hills of Northern Italy, where she collected her share of poetry and narrative prizes, Cornelia has since lived and worked in London, Japan, Spain, and Germany. She also works as a freelance translator.

She likes cats, knitting, performing in theater, going to museums, collecting mugs, and hanging out with her grandma. When writing, she favors curious, surreal stories, steampunk, and mixed-genre fiction. Her heroes are always underdogs, and she loves them for it.

Connect with Cornelia:
Website: corneliagrey.com
Blog: corneliagrey.blogspot.com
LiveJournal: corneliagrey.livejournal.com
Twitter: @corneliagrey
Facebook: facebook.com/corneliagrey
Goodreads: goodreads.com/Cornelia_Grey

# Enjoy more stories like
## *The Empty Hourglass*
## at AnglerFishPress.com!

*Prosperity*
ISBN: 978-1-62649-177-9

*Precious Metals*
ISBN: 978-1-62649-175-5

## Earn Bonus Bucks!

Earn 1 Bonus Buck for each dollar you spend. Find out how at
RiptidePublishing.com/news/bonus-bucks.

## Win Free Ebooks for a Year!

Pre-order coming soon titles directly through our site and you'll
receive one entry into a drawing for a chance to win free books for
a year! Get the details at RiptidePublishing.com/contests.